Hopefully, Eventually

A Novel

Chelsea Roe Hooper

ISBN 978-1-7355787-0-05
e-ISBN (ePUB) 978-1-7355787-1-2

Cover design by www.cocanour.com

To my mother,

*For always believing in me and showing me who
I want to be when I grow up.*

PART ONE

STEPH

"I'll be right there! Just one more sec!" I yelled to Mark, who was waiting in the driveway, as I fumbled through typing in the nine-digit code that unlocked our front door. I left my keys to the minivan in the house. We were already running late, and I knew Mark was rolling his eyes in the car. I imagined him saying out loud, "Typical Steph." But I had a reason for leaving my keys. I had switched out my daily purse for my elegant clutch for the evening, and while I was pulling up the directions on my phone, panicking that our estimated arrival time was twenty-seven minutes later than the beginning of the event, I forgot to grab the keys. Mark would tell you that I always have an excuse when I'm forgetful. And he's right. But I have a lot going on.

As I ran to the van in my heels, I kissed Mark and said, "Only twenty-nine minutes late now. Would be twenty-eight if you'd made our door code easier to remember." He winked at me and we finally backed out the driveway.

We were headed downtown to watch Ziah receive another

Women in Business award. I usually avoid downtown when possible. The lights, noise, and crowds create the perfect storm for my anxiety. But I always support Ziah, and my support has felt like a part-time job lately. Every time I turn around, she's won another award, or she's had something named after her, or she's appeared in another magazine. I am proud of her. She really does do so much. As everyone says, "If we could just clone her and put one of her in every community, this world would be in better shape." Sometimes I feel a little inadequate around Ziah. She would never do or say anything intentionally to make me feel that way. But she receives constant recognition for making this world a better place, while I work my ass off at home to keep the house tidy, do all the laundry, and put dinner on the table every night. We can't all afford a maid.

To prepare for the evening, I took one of my anxiety pills. I don't take them every day. I only take them if I feel an attack coming, or if I think I'll be in a situation that prompts an attack. This particular night was definitely one of those nights.

When I caught sight of Ziah, she looked breathtaking. Her tangerine silk gown offered the perfect contrast to her dark skin. She'd styled her hair short on the sides and curly on top. It was ultra-chic, and she looked every bit as sexy as sophisticated. She reminded me of Halle Berry.

Though we were late for the event, she hadn't received her award yet, which was a relief. Attendees still crowded the bars, ordering exquisite cocktails, and tuxedoed servers sailed through the crowd, doling out hors d'oeuvres from fancy platters. Mark gave my hand a reassuring squeeze as we grabbed a fruity aperitif off one of the platters and looked for our seats. He knew the city made me nervous, and he knew his presence always calmed me.

We found our names written in calligraphy, and I was ecstatic to see we were placed at a table with Chloe and Brett, Nora and Kyle, and Alexis. Ziah, Chloe, Nora, and Alexis are the closest things I have to sisters. We are a super tight group of best friends, and we've always said that no matter what, we will be there for each other. We have an ongoing joke from when we were younger that we still bring up regularly. The famous quote came from an evening when we had all been drinking wine in my apartment, binge-watching Sex and the City. After the episode where Carrie says that maybe women can be each other's soulmates, Nora said, "You know, I saw something in a silly email chain recently that said something along the lines of what I'm about to say. And it is so fitting for us. Ready? Here goes … you girls are all like the best bra ever. You're comfortable, supportive, you always lift me up, and you make me seem better than I am." We all laughed. Ziah said something about it being one of the silliest things that Nora has ever said, and we all giggled even more. Then Alexis added, "And also the most poetic." From that moment forward, it's been a common reference for us. We are like good bras to each other. It's always been that way, and it always will be.

As we approached the table, Chloe and Brett were laughing with each other. Nora and Alexis were visiting quietly, while Kyle looked at his phone.

"Hey! Hey! Hey!" Alexis said as we approached. "Now the party can start!"

"Shhh!" I said to her. Her loudness made me feel uncomfortable. I love Alexis, but she lacks a filter and laughs and talks at a higher volume than most. She stood up and gave me a hug and a kiss. Her newly plumped lips felt odd on my cheek. But as always, she looked great. A real-life Barbie doll is what we called her. She had long blonde hair, big blue doe eyes, amazingly long eyelashes, and a rocking body. Much of Alexis's exterior was fake—cosmetically enhanced—but she's one of the realest people I've ever met. She was the only one in the group still single. She constantly met different men on dating apps, but she hadn't met anybody who had made her feel a genuine spark in an awfully long time.

As she pulled away from me, she complimented my makeup. She always has a way of making people feel legitimately good about themselves. She zeros in on something particular to compliment, as opposed to sticking with an easy "You look great!" Her compliments have always been genuine. I could smell on her breath that she was already ahead of us in the drink department, which came as no surprise. Alexis has always known how to throw a few back.

Mark and I sat down, and Nora reached across to kiss my hand. "I'm so glad y'all made it," she said. "You know how much our presence means to Ziah at these things."

"Oh, of course. Wouldn't miss it," I replied, though I could think of a million things I needed to do in that moment instead of clinking glasses in formalwear on a school night. But Nora was right. Ziah really did appreciate us. This was a big moment for her, and just because she already had a lot of big moments, doesn't mean any one of them are less important.

The room began to quiet, and everyone who was still lingering quickly found their seats. It was time for the awards.

I glanced at my phone to check the time. There was one text message from Mark's mom—a cute photograph of the kids in a bubble bath. I estimated that we might be able to get out of there within the hour. We could watch the awards, find Ziah afterwards, give her a hug, and then slink out while she was visiting with everyone else.

The announcement of Ziah's name jerked me from my daydream. She walked on stage, gliding with such grace to the podium. She gave an endearing acceptance speech, all the while looking like a million bucks. She used her moment at the microphone to speak on behalf of children in foster care. Ziah is a huge foster care advocate. In fact, a lot of her recognition in the city has to do with her involvement in raising awareness about the foster care system. Her speech dragged on a bit, but it was well prepared, and she was able to get some key points in while thanking some important people.

I looked over at Chloe and gestured as if I was throwing back an air drink. She got the message, and we were able to sneak away between awards and make our way to the foyer, where there was a bar. We both ordered a glass of Chardonnay and started making small talk about our week. Chloe is a kindergarten teacher. Based on how passionate she is about her job and her students, I assume she's the best teacher on her campus, if not in the world. She's always in a good mood, and always speaking positively about her school. Soon, Nora joined us in the foyer. Not to be left out, Alexis, clad in heels, ran in hilariously short strides to get to us as quickly as she could. I felt like it drew attention to her, and it embarrassed me again. I'm not an introvert, by any means, but I have yet to meet anybody as carefree and outgoing as Alexis.

We left Mark, Kyle, and Brett at the table. They were used to it by now. Usually Leon was with them, too. But of course, this evening he was sitting at a table with the other important husbands of the evening. Though our husbands don't have the most in common, they were probably just relieved one of Alexis's pretentious online dates wasn't sitting with them.

Alexis suggested we toast to our beautiful friend, even though she wasn't even in the foyer with us. We followed her lead, toasted, and continued visiting. Nora was quiet, but I assumed she was thinking about everything else she could be doing this evening, as I had been. Chloe was excited Spring Break was approaching. She said she needed that time to recharge for the end of the year. I knew from being a mom that after Spring Break, everything moves full throttle with events and testing and awards and talent shows. Chloe has always said Spring Break was her favorite. She felt the other breaks were a little long. But, of course, she felt that way. She was living her dream and working at her dream job. I do not use the word "passionately" loosely when I describe how Chloe feels about being a teacher.

I asked Nora if she was sore from our workout two days prior. We take classes together at the Y. We try to make it to Body Pump three times a week, but occasionally we throw a yoga class in the mix. This week there was a new release in our Body Pump class, and the lunge track was killer. Nora said she wasn't too sore, but she had been to a class without me two days before.

Ziah and Leon made their way to us and we all embraced and told her how proud of her we were. I turned around to see that Alexis had ordered us all shots. We all know it's a total party pooper move to refuse a shot when somebody has bought one for you, but it was a school night. However, I refuse to be the party pooper in this group. All of us refuse to play that role. So the next thing I knew, we were downing a shot of Patrón. (Seriously! Patrón on a school night?) I remember seeing Mark and Brett making their way to us.

And that's where my memory of the evening ends.

CHLOE

I was a little tired from the previous evening. I often only drink a few beers on work nights, but we had a fancy event the night before, and I drank a glass of wine, a cocktail, and took a shot. I needed to call and check on Steph, but I suspected she wasn't awake yet. She had been in rare form the night before. Class would start soon, and my little loves would join me at any moment. My check-in with Steph could wait until my conference period. I finished my Slim-Fast and looked at my phone. Brett had texted me a silly GIF about love, and I put my phone in my purse and started greeting the students.

One by one, they gave me a side hug and found their desks. I was always careful about hugging my little guys and girls. We had special training about not hugging students directly but could give them side hugs instead. This rule had been established to prevent any inappropriate closeness, and anything that could be misconstrued. Of course, I thought those reasonings were silly for me and my little five- and six-year-olds, but I'm a rule follower.

A couple hours into my day, I got a headache. I reached into my purse and grabbed some ibuprofen and saw there were several texts on our "GB" text thread. GB stood for Good Bras. Originally, our text thread had been titled "BFF," but then Alexis changed it to "Good Bras" after the infamous inside joke. The text thread had popped up while Ziah was in an important meeting once, and the title embarrassed her, so she shortened it to GB. I glanced over the texts and saw that Steph had said something, so I at least knew she was alive. We aren't supposed to be on our phones at work, so I put it back down and waited for my conference to read everything.

When my conference period came, I grabbed my apple and my sandwich and pulled out my phone to catch up.

"Good morning, bitches! Anybody else feeling like hell today??" Alexis had texted with typical Alexis enthusiasm.

Ziah responded, "Morning. I have a lunch meeting at noon with Lizzie. Ugh. Wish me luck. And no, I don't feel like hell. I drank a glass of water when I got home and took ibuprofen before I went to sleep. Besides, I didn't drink nearly as much as you and Steph!"

Nora chimed in, "Morning! I feel okay. I put today's makeup on top of last night's makeup. I feel like I have a Boy George vibe going. Lol."

"I've already been to hot yoga, and I kid you not, the room smelled like straight tequila when it was over!" Alexis sent with a laughing emoji.

Ziah said, "Oh, Lord! LOL! I bet it did! Steph? Come in, Steph. You alive?"

Alexis responded, "She's fine. She's probably already made Mickey Mouse pancakes, taken the kids to school, and had three cups of coffee."

"You're being pretty optimistic," Nora said.

Steph finally texted, "Uggggghhhhhhhhhh. Shoot me now."

Alexis replied, "There's our girl! Told you she was fine."

Steph continued, "Fine is a stretch. I feel like death. Lucky for me, it wasn't my turn for carpool. Mark is pretty pissed at me. I'm lying in bed, and Benjamin is running around the house doing God knows what. How can I parent when I can't function? FML."

"Yikes. I knew you'd be feeling it today. What in the world happened??" Nora asked.

"I took one of my freaking pills before the event!" Steph informed us.

Alexis replied, "Oh, shit."

Steph continued, "I planned on having two drinks, and then I forgot about the damn pill! Mark is being really short with me today. I don't recall what happened after we took that shot of Patrón."

"Which one? LOL!" Alexis said.

Steph sent a face palm emoji along with, "Shiiiiiiiiiiiiiit."

Ziah said, "Steph, I'm so sorry! I would have tried to rein you in had I known. I know the city makes you nervous, but I didn't put it all together."

Steph quipped back, "It doesn't make me nervous. It makes me anxious. They're two different feelings. I'm gonna go check on Benjamin. Gotta make sure he isn't playing with knives or something. Then I'm gonna give him a Melatonin and try to sleep some of this off. I'll check in later."

"I know they're different things. Sorry. I didn't mean to

offend you," Ziah wrote back.

Nora changed the subject. "Chloe? You okay?"

Alexis signed off by saying, "Good luck with Lizzie today, Z. By the way, your hair was ON. POINT. last night. Steph, I hope you feel better. I'm sure Mark will be fine when he gets home from work. Chlo, text when you can. Nora, I'll see you in a bit. Love y'all."

I winced when I finally caught up. I knew Ziah had unintentionally hit a sensitive spot with Steph. I hadn't realized Steph had taken a pill, or I would have tried to slow her down. But honestly, she seemed to be having such a good time. It was refreshing. She's a stay-at-home mom and getting away from the kids was important. Even though I'm a teacher and chose to surround myself with kids, I knew this was true. Brett and I had regular date nights so we could have time apart from Brady and Cooper.

I reread the last few texts and could tell Nora was trying to change the subject when she checked in on me. All my friends knew I'd be awake and at work and not able to text at that time. My conference period was almost over, so I quickly texted them back: "Hi! I'm good. I've got the hint of a headache, but other than that, I'm good to go. I'm sorry, Steph. I hate all of that for you. Mark will be fine later. He understands. Z, why are you having to meet with Lizzie??? Nora and Alexis, what in the world do you two have up your sleeves today? Don't you have to work, Nora?" Nobody had texted back by the time my conference period ended. I sent a quick "I love you" text to Brett and then put my phone back in my purse.

My littles came marching back to class, and we got to start a lesson on colors using Play-Doh. I always loved when we got to use Play-Doh, though I knew our janitors hated Play-Doh days. I don't like to disappoint anybody, so now on Play-Doh days, I usually stay a little late to pick up all the tiny pieces on the carpet.

Before I knew it, the bell rang for class dismissal. Cooper and Brady stormed into my room and asked when we were going to leave. I told them I had to clean up, and they could either help me or go wait in the cafeteria and work on homework.

Cooper is eight years old and in second grade. And my big boy, Brady, is ten and in fourth grade. I'm so lucky I get to work where they attend school—truly blessed is how I always described my life. I married my high school sweetheart, we had two healthy boys, my parents were both alive and healthy, and I had the best friends anybody could ask for. I felt as though I was sailing on a carpet of bliss, and I wondered when and if it would ever get ripped out from under me.

The boys opted to go do their homework, and I pulled my phone out before I got on my hands and knees to pick up tiny, colorful pieces of dough. There were several more text messages. I caught up.

Alexis had said, "Nora and I are meeting for lunch."

"We are discussing where Cyrus should attend school next year. Leon and I want him to go to public school, and Lizzie wants him to stay where he is. The issue is, if we decide he stays where he is, we have to re-enroll soon. So, the meeting takes place today. And of course, Leon is in Fort Worth and won't be able to be there. God grant me the strength…" Ziah sent.

Nora said, "LOL, Z. That sucks. How can one woman embody every quality we despise? And how can that one woman be your husband's ex?? Ugh. Leon definitely upgraded."

"#fucklizzie." Alexis always knew how to make us laugh.

Ziah replied, "LOL. Y'all are too much. It'll be fine. BTW, love that hashtag, A!"

Steph joined in: "Good morning. At … 2pm. Ugh. Melatonin worked! And the house didn't burn down. How did it go with Lizzie?" (A hilarious selfie of her curly hair looking completely wild and mascara falling in a ring below her eyes accompanied her text.)

Ziah answered, "It was less than perfect. We're gonna need to get the lawyers involved."

"Wait. I know a good lawyer…" Alexis texted.

"Ha! You're sweet. But I don't do family law. It's frustrating because she wants Cyrus to continue going there, but he is the only child of color in damn near the whole K-12 school! Since she's white, she sees him as white. She doesn't think he needs to be around anybody else that looks like him. And, of course, Leon will have to continue to pay for his education there," Ziah sent back.

Nora wrote back, "Vomit. I hate her. Steph, any word from Mark?"

"Yes. Every response to me is as short as possible," she replied.

"He'll get over it. You were just having fun. We aren't too old to deserve fun. Y'all know that, right?" Alexis encouraged.

Steph responded, "Yes. And he knows that. He's just pissed I forgot about the pill. I don't blame him."

Ziah said, "Well, you can't help it if you forgot."

Nora responded, "No kidding."

"Nora, where was Kyle last night? I remember seeing him at our table, but I don't remember seeing him in the foyer. I mean, for all I know, he could have carried me to my car! But I don't recall much of him," Steph wondered.

Nora replied, "He was there. Just doing typical Kyle stuff, playing on his phone and what not."

Alexis had a great idea when she texted, "Nora and I were talking about how we need a full day together when everybody's Spring Break rolls around. All of your kids are on the same schedule with that, right?"

Steph answered, "I believe so."

"Then when can you hookers all come over to play???" Alexis asked.

"Why don't we do it at our house? We can drink by the pool. Cy is on a different schedule than everyone else's, but we can make sure it's a day when he's at Lizzie's," Ziah texted back.

Steph followed with, "I'm in."

Alexis texted, "Perf."

"Yay!" Nora sent a happy GIF.

The conversation ended there. I chimed in that I was totally up for a pool day. Then I moved onto my text thread with Brett...

"How's your day, sweetie? I can't believe Steph last night! What a nightmare!" he had said.

I responded to him, "Hey, love. Day was great. The boys and I will be home in a little while. Play-Doh day! Steph is good now. Said Mark is pissed. I feel bad for her. I'll explain later."

I finished picking up every tiny particle of dough I could see, rounded up the boys, and we headed home.

Brett had big plans for us for the weekend. We left the boys with my parents and went to Hotel ZaZa. I loved when we got away together. Hotel ZaZa is where we got engaged, and now and then, Brett will surprise me with a trip down memory lane. He's a lot like the men in rom-coms, really. He's handsome, strong, extremely romantic, and he loves to make me happy. Early on in our marriage, we read about the five love languages, and believe me when I say that he knows exactly how to speak mine. As we checked into our room, we giggled like high schoolers. We set our luggage down, and he immediately pushed me down on the bed. We started passionately making out. I loved the way Brett kissed. He put his hand up my shirt and it felt like we were once again those newly in-love high schoolers all those years ago. I wondered what had gotten into him. Had he just gotten a multi-million-dollar listing? Was he going to tell me he wanted to have another baby? He was extremely passionate in the moment. I mean, he's always passionate, but this was next level stuff. After some amazing foreplay, we made love. I can honestly say it was one of our best love making sessions we've ever had.

After we showered and dressed, we Ubered out for dinner. I felt so connected to him. We needed this weekend. While at dinner, he got a text from Johnathan, his real estate partner. The downside to being married to a real estate agent is they are never truly off the clock. But I took the moment to check in on my texts. The girls were texting about our upcoming pool day at Ziah's. Steph said Mark was finally over her alcohol-pill fiasco. I was relieved to hear that. I knew all he needed was time. Mark isn't my dream husband, but he is good for Steph, and he's a great dad. Sure, he's sweet to her, and takes good care of her. My only real issue is that he leaves Steph too much. Mark has a full-time job as a successful insurance agent, but he also plays bass for a band that often travels on the weekends. Steph knows how much I hate that, but she seems fine with it, so I don't press the issue—to each their own. I just know that I would miss Brett way too much if he traveled as much as Mark does.

When Brett finished his conversation with Johnathan, our food came. Instead of ordering main courses, Brett and I loved to order several appetizers and try everything. I had been trying to eat better recently, and there was a lot of fried food in front of me, but I told myself our lust-filled workout an hour earlier must have freed up some caloric space for my day. When we arrived back at our room, Brett made a move on me again. Twice in one day was rare for us. I couldn't even remember the last time we had done that, but I wasn't complaining. Again, it was explosive and felt every bit as magical as when we had arrived. I went to sleep pinching myself. How did I get so damn lucky?

ZIAH

I dropped Cyrus off at Lizzie's early Saturday morning. My week had been pretty exhausting: I had a hearing, multiple deadlines to meet, another meeting with Lizzie regarding Cy's schooling, and an interview with The Dallas Morning News.

By the time the weekend had rolled around, I was very much looking forward to an overdue full day with my girls. Leon was home, but our home is big enough that nobody would ever even see him. He'd had a pretty tough week, too. He'd lost one of his favorite patients to heart failure. Being in the business as long as he's been, it's rare for him to choose favorites. But this little pug mix had something about him. And his owners were the sweetest elderly couple. They'd always bring Leon muffins and cookies and Starbucks anytime they had an appointment. I knew it had hit Leon pretty hard, so I felt this weekend actually worked out well with timing. The perfect healing for Leon's broken heart would be March Madness.

Alexis was the first to arrive. She looked so beautiful. Her swimsuit fit her perfectly. She looked like she should be on the cover of Sports Illustrated Swimsuit Edition. Her long blonde hair was pulled up into a messy bun, and she had on minimal makeup. Her yoga body looked amazing. I preferred Alexis like this. Not a lot of makeup and not a lot of effort. I wish she knew just how beautiful she was without all the fillers and surgery. But she doesn't listen to us girls. I mean, I'm as guilty as the next woman when it comes to Botox. But it stops there. I modeled to put myself through law school, so I've always embraced my natural looks. (Other than the wrinkles— nobody's got time for that.)

"Hey, Z! I brought the wine!" She did a little dance as she held two bottles of white. She and I both knew that wouldn't be enough for us, but she also knew I had a fully stocked bar. Alexis and I were close. She always made me laugh. She was so full of life and so vivacious. I envied her lack of responsibility. The only thing she was responsible for was showing up to her workout classes on time and finding different guys to date. Oh, and taking care of her dog, Gibbs. I liked Gibbs, too. He was an adorable Goldendoodle, and since Alexis didn't have any children, she considered him her baby. Leon liked Gibbs, too. Alexis would drive to Fort Worth so Leon could be Gibbs's veterinarian. Leon appreciated that level of loyalty. He also appreciated how real Alexis kept it. She was a ball of fun, but she wouldn't hold back on giving you her advice. We always felt she missed her calling to be a therapist. Or to be on the Bachelorette. Alexis and I are also close because she was one of my first clients. We were already best friends, so it seemed obvious she'd use me, but it was a big case, and I was pretty green as a lawyer. She took a chance on me, and it paid off. Literally.

I was fresh out of law school, and Alexis was working for an architect. Her dream had been to become an interior designer and working for this particular architect was a good foot in the door. After working for him for several months, he started making uncalled for, sexually suggestive comments to her. She's a pretty tough cookie, so she flat out told him to stop. But he didn't. It only got worse, and it came to a head when he physically threw her on his desk and put his hand up her skirt. She scratched him with her fake nails, screamed "No!" repeatedly, while he continued to say, "Come on, baby. You know you want it as bad as I want you." But Alexis didn't. And she wasn't going to stand for his bullshit. She physically fought him off and called me the next day. Together, we took his ass down. She won a large settlement and has been living off it ever since. She knows the amount of money she won isn't enough for her to live off forever. But she figures she'll marry somebody rich by the time she runs out.

"Pour me a glass!" I said. She knew where the bar was, and we are close enough for her to help herself to anything. She walked over to the patio furniture where I was sitting and handed me my glass. We toasted each other, excited for the rest of our girls to arrive.

Soon after, Nora arrived. She almost walked into a pillar as she was looking at her phone.

"Nora! Be careful! And besides, no phones on girls' days!" Alexis yelled.

Nora looked totally distracted, but she looked happy. She set her phone down on the bar and walked over to us.

"Why aren't y'all in the water yet? It's a heated pool, you chickens." she said.

And just then, Alexis went running full speed across the lawn, yelling, "CANNONBALL!" She jumped in, holding onto her long legs. We barreled over, laughing. She truly was the life of the party.

Nora and I got in, too. She started telling us about her work week. Nora is a labor and delivery nurse, and she usually always has all kinds of sweet stories. Our favorite stories are about the awful baby names people choose, though. She didn't have any good ones this week. Just as she was telling us about a mom who was cursing out her husband during delivery, Chloe arrived.

"Hey, Chlo!" Nora said.

"Chloe!" Alexis shouted.

"Hey, girl. Come on in. You know where the bar is! Grab you something and join us. The water feels amazing."

Chloe got in and we asked how her Spring Break had been going. She was happy to have the break to rejuvenate, but nervous about Brady's testing that the state required. She told us about her recent getaway with Brett. Nora sighed and said she wished that Kyle was more like Brett.

"He's so into these stupid games on his phone and work. I swear, if I went back in time and told myself I'd end up marrying an accountant who plays video games in his spare time, I would have laughed in my face," she said.

I didn't care too much for Kyle as Nora's husband. He was a nice guy and all, but he wasn't her perfect match. Nora was completely fabulous, and Kyle was, well, boring.

Steph's arrival broke the awkward mood that had been created by Nora basically calling her husband a dork. She was late as usual. Steph never arrived anywhere on time, but you better believe she'd have a reason for it. All of us had stopped even bringing attention to her tardiness. Unless it was something extremely important, it didn't matter anyway. She looked a little disheveled, though she was wearing a beach hat and a cute coverup. I assume if I ran late everywhere I went, I'd look a little disheveled, too. Steph awkwardly shuffled into the pool, and Alexis asked her what in the world was going on. "I'm sore!" she said. "Nora and I had a killer workout class yesterday, and it's kicking my ass today. Not to mention chasing around kids all day since it's Spring Break."

"We're getting old, y'all," Alexis chimed in.

"Oh, shut up! You're five years younger than me," Steph said.

"Well, we are. I cannot believe I'm thirty-five. I feel like I'm eighteen."

"And you act it, too!" Nora jabbed.

We all laughed, including Alexis.

"So who has a good story for us?" I asked. "It's been too long since we've been together without the men!" I asked.

"I do!" Chloe said. "Brett just got a huge listing in Highland Park. If this sells at listing price, it'll be huge for him."

"That's great, Chlo!" Steph said. We all oohed and ahhed over the details.

"Oh! I'm dating somebody!" Alexis excitedly yelled. "He's a plastic surgeon, so we might as well just get married now, right?"

"Man, I miss the dating days," I said. "I mean, Leon is my perfect man. I just miss all those feelings. Even the 'is he gonna call, or isn't he?' feelings. I envy you, Alexis. Hold onto this time while you can. Next thing you know, you'll be fighting with your hubby's ex-wife about everything under the sun."

"Tell us about him, Alexis," Nora urged on.

"Well, he's about 6'3." He has an ex-wife but no children. He owns his own practice in Preston Center. He has a dog, and you know I love that! He visits his mother every other Sunday. And he really likes me. We've been out four times, and he laughs with me a lot. I never feel like I'm too much around him. And y'all know I'm a little much for some guys."

He sounded great, but so many of Alexis's men did. It always started off like this and then ended when she got scared. Or it ended because they were pretentious assholes. That, too.

Right as Steph was telling us a funny story about her kids, Leon walked out onto the patio.

"Hey, Leon!" Alexis said. "You know the rules—no men allowed! And no phones, either."

I noticed he was holding my cell phone in a way that told me somebody waited on the other end of the line. Worry started consuming me. I hustled out of my beach-entry pool and wrapped my torso in a towel. I looked at his face intently, trying to read him. When I got close enough to him, he said, "It's Sherry. There's a situation."

We use the word "situation" when there is a foster child needing to be placed, and we've been called for placement.

"Shit," I said. I didn't mean it like that was a bad thing. I just hated the timing. But I love getting placements. I grabbed the phone from Leon and we both walked inside.

"Hey, Sherry. What's the story?"

"Well, he's four months old. Dad is in prison. Mom is in custody for child endangerment. His name is Tommy. He's got a broken tibia and possibly some broken ribs."

My heart sank. We had gotten a lot of children with bad backstories, but a helpless baby having broken bones hit me hard.

"Who is next in line to get him?" I asked.

"Grandma is working to get him, but it will probably take a month, at least. If she even gets certified."

"Who would be next?"

"They're trying to find some extended family, but basically all of his immediate family has a rap sheet."

"Okay, let me talk to Leon and I'll get back with you in five minutes." I looked at Leon before I even hung up and he nodded his head yes.

"Sherry? You still there?"

"I'm here."

"We're in. When does he arrive?"

"We'll get him to you at about six this evening. You still have the crib from Mason, right?"

"Yes," I said. I felt a pang of sadness at the mention of his name. But that was all part of fostering: these sweet souls come into your life temporarily; you love them with all you have, and then they leave. You can only hope you've left an impression on their lives, and they'll be better for the time they've spent with you.

I hung up with Sherry, hugged Leon, and he said he'd get the room ready, so I could get back to my pool party.

I got back in the pool and told the girls what was up. They were appalled at the broken bones detail and ecstatic that we were getting Little Tommy. I saw a single tear roll out from under Nora's sunglasses and down her cheek, and then I thought of her loss.

NORA

Ziah's pool party was a much-needed break from the real world. Any time we are all able to get together with nobody else around is sacred. Ziah got a call for the placement of a four-month-old baby boy while we were there. I don't know if anybody else put it together, but my baby would have been four months old right now. I caught myself getting teary but shut it down quickly. I didn't want to make it about my pain when this was about Ziah and Little Tommy.

The thing about miscarriage is that everybody else seems to forget about it. Everyone but the mother. Heck, even Kyle seems to forget it happened. It didn't affect him the same way it affected me. And quite frankly, I think the difference in how we've experienced the loss has driven a wedge between us.

I'd never been pregnant before, and it seemed like the next step in our marriage. I'd longed to be a mother for quite some time, and I knew Kyle would be a good father. He'd have our child watching every Star Wars movie before they could even speak, I'm sure. We tried for about five months before we finally had a positive test, and I was ecstatic. I did everything I was supposed to do and avoided everything I wasn't supposed to do. We chose a name for a boy and a name for a girl. I went in for my first appointment, and all was well. The reality that I was going to become a mother felt overwhelming in the best way—it was all I could think about. I told the GBs and our families. The girls were over the moon for me—for us. I knew that they didn't love Kyle as my perfect match, but they knew he was a great man and that he'd be a wonderful father.

When my second OBGYN appointment arrived, I went alone. I was twelve weeks, which was approaching the safe zone. But when the nurse put the doppler on my belly, she had difficulty finding the heartbeat. She assured me twelve weeks was still early to hear it through the doppler on the outside, but she thought Dr. Spurrier would probably walk right in and find it. The weird thing about OB nurses and labor and delivery nurses is that, as similar as we all are, a mother gets passed from one to the other after her baby is born. Though both of our goals are to take care of the mother and the baby, we have two distinct roles in the process.

I wasn't familiar with this nurse, but I had worked with Dr. Spurrier several times in the delivery room. When she came in and also struggled to find the heartbeat, I wished, in that moment, that I hadn't told Kyle it was fine for him to work, and this appointment would be no big deal. Dr. Spurrier stayed optimistic and sent me to get a sonogram for reassurance. I walked down the hallway into the ultrasound technician's room, which felt more like a massage therapist's room. The lights were dim, it smelled of essential oils, and there was peaceful music playing. Vannah was the woman's name. She had me get up on the chair, and she reclined me back pretty far. She put the gel on my stomach, and I watched her screen as she moved the camera all over my pelvis and stomach. I know what a baby looks like on a sonogram. What I saw on that screen was not a thriving, wriggling baby. What I saw was what looked like a withered pile at the bottom of my uterus. In the sweetest voice, Vannah said she needed to go get Dr. Spurrier, and she'd be right back. Of course, I knew what was going on. Dr. Spurrier came in and told me that the baby hadn't made it. I didn't hear much else, other than that I had probably miscarried around nine weeks, even though here I was at twelve. Since I'd had no signs of miscarriage, she wanted me to come in for a D&C the next day. I was shocked. I walked out of there as pale as a ghost. I sat in my Explorer and the tears started streaming. I called Kyle, and he didn't answer, which pissed me off. Next, I called my mom. She cried with me. Kyle beeped in and I yelled to him what had happened. Instead of being the consoling, strong husband that I needed in that moment, he was quiet. He told me he'd come pick me up, but I told him I was fine and not to leave work. I would see him at the house later. I then called Alexis. She's not my most maternal friend, but she is the most real—and the funniest. She offered to come get me, just as Kyle had done, but unlike my reaction with Kyle, I took her up on her offer. I got in her jeep and we drove to Rodeo Goat for burgers and a drink. She listened to me cry and told me everything would be okay. But other than saying it would be okay, she told me that it fucking sucked. And that's why I chose Alexis. I knew she wouldn't sugarcoat anything, and she'd say it how it was. And it did suck. Big time.

I was excited to get back to my phone after our pool party

at Ziah's. Lately, I had been a bit too tethered to my phone, though I hoped that nobody else noticed.

The universe had been playing some weird games with me. My ex-boyfriend from college, Andrew, whom I hadn't seen or spoken to in over fifteen years, recently started following me on Instagram. When I saw the new follow, my jaw dropped to the floor. Andrew was the one I thought I'd marry. I considered him the love of my life. I adored his family, and they adored me. The same goes for my family. We'd dated for three years. He's two years older than me, so when he graduated and got a job, he had to move, and I was still in Fort Worth finishing up nursing school. His new job took him to Austin, and the long-distance thing took its toll on us. I remember as we sat in his truck, making the decision to go our separate ways, I said to him, "Maybe we just found each other too early. Maybe there are other things we are supposed to do, and the universe will bring us back together when the timing is right." He'd cupped my face in his hands and kissed my forehead.

"Hopefully, eventually," he said.

I was heartbroken. It was the saddest I had ever been in my life. Compared to my miscarriage, I was even more broken during that time. That sounds awful, but I was young and hadn't learned how to cope with pain and loss. Everybody thought Andrew and I would get married. When it didn't work out, I decided the easiest thing to do would be to completely cut him out of my life. There was no way I could be his friend; it would absolutely kill me to watch him go on in life without me by my side. Even the girls cut him out in support of me.

I'd heard he had gotten married to a girl he met in Austin, but that's about all I knew. I never asked about him, because I knew my heart didn't want to know the truth. Was he a dad? Was he still in Austin? Was he still married? Was he happy? And did he ever think about me like I did of him? Did he have dreams about us like I did? I knew I couldn't handle any of those answers.

But when he suddenly followed me on Instagram, I got butterflies in my stomach. *Why would he do that?* I thought it must have meant that he wanted to see what I was up to. I followed him back, and that was as far as it had gone for the first week. Soon enough, he started "liking" my photos. One photo he liked was a candid photograph that Steph had taken of me last summer by the pool. I was in a swimsuit, laughing, and not looking at the camera. Liking this photo had surely taken effort, and it sent a clear message. He had to have scrolled through months of photos to get to that one, and by liking it, he was letting me know that he'd taken the time. One evening when Kyle was already in bed playing on his phone, I opened Instagram and sent a direct message to him. "Hey, you. What in the world are you up to?" it said. I knew it was innocent enough. Kyle couldn't really get mad at me for that. I thought it weirder that we hadn't run into each other sooner. After I sent the message, I went to bed. I even fell asleep with a smile on my face for the first time in months.

When I woke the next day, I had a message in my Instagram DMs.

"Hey, stranger. I got transferred to the metroplex recently, and I'm just trying to get all settled in. I hope you're well, Nori."

Andrew was the only person to ever call me Nori. I had always given him a hard time about it, because it didn't shorten my name at all. It simply changed out a letter. He said he didn't call me that to shorten it. He called me that because he was the only one who did, and it was a special name just for him.

When I read the message, my stomach dropped. An odd feeling washed over me in finding out he was in the metroplex again. I felt as if I was going to vomit. The only way I had been able to move on from Andrew was to think I'd never see him again. And I say "move on" instead of "get over," because I never truly got over him. I've always resonated with these John Mayer lyrics: "Moving on and getting over are not the same, it seems to me." Those words ring true for my relationship with Andrew. Well, from my side, at least.

I threw my scrubs on, slapped on some makeup, and headed to work. *Should I write him back or not?* I wondered. It felt a little like I might be playing with fire. But I kept reminding myself that it was innocent enough. I really could've used some advice from the girls in that moment, but it was too delicate a situation to get anybody else involved. When I pulled up to the hospital, I pulled open my DMs again and wrote back, "Wow. Crazy you're back." I hit send and sat in my car, thinking about how simple that statement was, but also how complex it was at the same time.

Our messages grew more frequent, but I still didn't feel terribly guilty when I thought about Kyle. For all I knew, playing his phone games was his version of the same thing, a distraction or a harmless interest of sorts. Andrew was giving me attention I hadn't received in a while. And just as so long ago, something about Andrew pulled me like a magnetic force. I never could resist him.

I remember the first time we made love. We were in college.

He had taken me to meet his parents during Thanksgiving break, and we stayed the night at their house. We slept in his childhood bedroom. His parents thought I'd be sleeping in the twin bed, and Andrew would be sleeping on a pallet on the floor. I had actually thought that, too. But Andrew had climbed up into the bed and started kissing me. My throat always felt like it sank to my pelvis when he kissed me. We had made out several times before and messed around a lot, but something felt different this time. While he was on top of me, he pulled away and moved my hair out of my face. "I love you, Nori. I've never felt this kind of physical pull that my body has towards you ever before. It's like if you're in the room, I need to be as close to you as possible. I can't help it. I love your laugh. I love your smile. I love your drive. I love your humor. I can't think of a single thing about you that I don't adore."

I told him I loved him, too. Since we were in a twin bed and at his parents' house, I stayed clothed. He moved my panties to the side, and we had the most amazing sex of my life. And that's how it always was with Andrew. He was full of loving words towards me, and our lust was just as strong as our love.

The feeling I had being away from my phone during the pool party scared me. It made me realize just how excited this whole thing had gotten me, and how involved in it I had become. When he had told me all those years ago that he had never felt that type of physical connection before, I knew exactly what he was talking about. We were completely magnetic to each other. I equally worried and hoped that the case was still the same today.

I opened my Instagram and quickly read through his messages. There was normal talk, but then a message that really got me: "I miss you, Nori."

Was he talking about today, because I hadn't replied? Or was he talking about all the time? I let my heart win the battle over my head and I typed out, "I miss you, too."

ALEXIS

I had just gotten in from walking Gibbs and checked all my messages. Checking messages is a bit of a chore. I have just about every social media and dating platform possible, and I have all notifications turned off, so my phone battery doesn't die two hours into my day. I had been on four dates with a plastic surgeon named Dave. I felt like it could possibly go somewhere, but we certainly weren't exclusive. I wasn't about to cut off all other possibilities after only four dates.

I opened my Snapchat to see if there was anything new, and I was shocked to see Brett on there as somebody I might know. Chloe's certainly not on there, and I'm surprised he is. I hadn't taken him for much of a Snapchatter, but he is a hell of a real estate agent, and networking is a big part of that business. I chose not to follow him, because I don't want to see all the newest listings. I just use this as a source to meet people. Oh, and to use fun filters. I moved onto my other apps, but there was nothing groundbreaking. A few DMs here and there from guys who I pegged as typical Dallas douchebags.

I put some mascara on and a little lip gloss, told Gibbs I loved him, and headed out of my apartment.

I had plans to work out and then meet up with Steph for lunch. She was going to leave Benjamin with her mother-in-law, and meet me at Smithy for a cocktail, lunch, and some much needed one-on-one time.

I got to the Y and almost fell over dead at what I saw when I turned the corner. Or who I saw, rather. It was Andrew. Andrew had been the love of Nora's life. I couldn't believe my eyes. I put my head down to avoid him and hurried to the women's locker room. I leaned against the wall and wondered what the hell I should do. I wondered if I should talk to him, or if that would be a betrayal to Nora. He looked really damn good. I didn't know Andrew as well as the other girls, because I had come into the picture towards the end of "Nordrew."

Here's how we are all linked: Ziah and Nora had gone to high school together, and Chloe and Steph had known each other from working at Gap. Steph and Nora met at Texas Christian University. I met Nora in a yoga class, and we immediately hit it off. I'm the youngest of the group. And if I ever forget that detail, Steph will remind me. She's always making me feel immature, shushing me, and speaking to me in a condescending tone. Nora assures me it's not intentional, and it's more of an insecurity within herself. But insecurity or not, it pisses me off. I'm not a sensitive person, so the fact I even pick up on it means it's pretty damn evident.

I started thinking maybe it wasn't him. Why would he be at the very Y where the girls and I are members? There are a million YMCAs. Hell, there are a million in Dallas alone! Why would he be here? I thought he was in Austin. As my mind raced, I realized how ridiculous it was for me to think it would have been Andrew. I walked back into the main gym, and I didn't see the guy I had thought was Andrew, so I lunged my way to the elliptical, put in my AirPods, cranked up my Missy Elliott Pandora station, and started going. I was starting my second mile and midway through "Air Force Ones" by Nelly when I felt a tap on my back. I was irritated because I loved that song, but nevertheless I pulled out my AirPods and slowed down.

Holy shit, I thought—it was Andrew. In that split second, I wondered if he could read the exact "holy shit" expression on my face. Then I remembered my fresh Botox and realized he probably couldn't discern any type of expression.

"Whoa! What the hell are you doing here, stranger?" I said to him.

"Hello, Alexis. Fancy seeing you here."

"Wow. Forgive me. I'm just… surprised to see you. Seriously, what are you doing here?"

"Working out! Duh." He laughed. "No, really. I've been transferred up here. I knew you lived in Dallas but didn't realize we'd be in such close proximity. There are a million Ys in Dallas. What are the odds we'd end up at the same one? Must be the universe," he said. I wondered if he could see that the blood had drained from my face beneath my spray tan. It was as if I had seen a ghost, and the ghost was telling me he was here to stay.

"Awesome. Is everything going well with you?" I hoped that question translated to, "Are you still married?"

"Things are going amazingly well. I was a little lost when I first got here, but I feel like I'm happier now than I have been in a long time. Let me tell you a little secret." He put his hand to his mouth and whispered: "Austin is weird."

Damn, I thought. He wasn't taking the bait.

"Well, I'll let you get back to your workout, Alexis. It's so great to see you. Hey, listen. Maybe we can all get together sometime. I'd love to catch up. Are you on social media?"

"Ha!" I laughed. "I'm on every social media platform in existence. Still trying to find that perfect guy! You got any friends for me?"

"Well I see not much has changed," he laughed back. His dimple in his right cheek was prominent, and I couldn't believe how good he looked. Nora would absolutely melt if she saw him.

I wondered if when he said "all get together sometime" he meant him and his wife and me and whoever, or if he meant the girls and him.

"Well, listen. I'm on Instagram. What's your handle? I'll follow you and we can at least connect there. That's the only social media I've got."

I told him my Instagram handle and that I'd hopefully see him around sometime. I didn't start back on the elliptical. Instead, I hurried to the locker room and texted Steph.

"SOS! 911! We need to meet for brunch instead of lunch. Meet me there in 30?"

Steph responded, "Everything okay? Let me see if Gayle can take Benjamin earlier than planned. Hold on."

"Yes. Sort of. Maybe. I don't know. We've got a major discussion to have. I'm tempted to call in reinforcements and see if Z and Chloe can meet us, too."

Steph replied with, "What?? Why? What about Nora?"

"It's about Nora. But we'll just stick to you and me for now. You can help me navigate this, and then we'll decide if the others need to be involved. Just let me know if you can meet me earlier. I'm going now because I need a drink. If you can come earlier, come. I'm going now either way," I said.

"Leaving in 5," she wrote back quickly.

Steph pulled up to Smithy as I was walking in. Instead of waiting for her in the parking lot, I went ahead and got us a shaded table on the patio and asked the hostess for two mimosas. I knew it wasn't her job, and she probably wasn't even old enough to serve alcohol, but she'd pass the message onto our waiter or waitress quicker than if we waited for them to come ask. I needed a drink, like, right that second.

"Hey. What in the world is going on?" Steph semi-whispered as she set her Tory Burch tote on the other chair. I had always loved that bag, but she used it as a diaper bag for so long that it was hard for me to see it as chic anymore.

"You are going to shit your pants!" I exclaimed.

"Shhhh! Alexis, you can't talk loud like that in public."

I refrained from rolling my eyes because I knew that would be an immature reaction in Steph's opinion.

"You'll never believe who I ran into at the Y ... ANDREW!" I said.

The waitress set our mimosas down and started politely asking something, but I interrupted her and asked if she could give us a few more minutes. I took a huge swig of my mimosa through my straw. (I had a love-hate relationship with straws. I hated the wrinkles they could cause, and that they were bad for the environment, but I also hated gulping out of a glass and ruining my lip gloss.)

Steph squinted her eyes, looking at me intently, and I could tell that she was thinking that maybe I had seen someone who *looked* like Andrew. After all, I'm only thirty-five years old. Maybe I don't know how to tell who somebody fucking is. Ugh.

"Steph. It was Andrew. He stopped me while I was working out and said he's been relocated up here for work. He's like, *here* here. Not just visiting. He got my Instagram handle to stay connected and said maybe we can all do something together sometime."

"Who all? Nora all? I'm so confused right now. He's married still, right? God, Alexis. What do we do?" Steph took a big swig of her mimosa, too.

"You don't have a pill in your system, do you?" I asked. I could tell we'd be having a few drinks, and I didn't want a repeat of Ziah's award night.

"Hell no. Though with this information you're feeding me right now, I might need one!" she said.

"Same, girl. Same," I said as I took another large sip. I was already ready for a refill.

Over the course of our brunch and multiple mimosas, we decided not to tell Nora about this revelation. It would be too hard on her. She was a strong woman, but Andrew was her weakness. I've never known two people more perfect for each other. Honestly, she and Andrew were a better match than Ziah and Leon, and Steph and Mark, and even Chloe and Brett. And they were definitely a better match than Nora and Kyle. I always imagined that if Nora and Andrew were celebrities, they'd be like Brad and Jen—so many people would be rooting for them to get back together.

Nora met Kyle through her cousin several years after she and Andrew broke up. She had dated a handful of men since Andrew, but nobody too seriously. When she and Kyle started dating, she found his nerdiness charming. He made her giggle, and he was an extremely kind person. We all saw that, and we all liked him. We just didn't like him for Nora.

After brunch, I got in the Jeep and opened my phone. I had a couple of texts from Dave. I sent him a selfie of me making a kissy face. He wanted to have dinner that evening. I felt like we had been on enough dates that I'd finally give in and have sex with him that night. Besides, I'd been without for a while, and a little sex would do me good after the stress I had dealt with that morning.

After solidifying our plans, I tabbed through my other apps absentmindedly. Sure enough, I had a new follower on Instagram. I clicked on Andrew's profile and scanned through a few photographs. I didn't see his wife in any recent photos, but I'd do more research on that when I got home. I scrolled back up to the top and noticed under his name it said "Followed by" and then my eyes almost bulged out of my head when I saw nora.tcu.

"What. In. The. Actual. Fuck?" I said out loud to myself.

CHLOE

I was happy to be back in my school routine after Spring Break. Nothing made my soul feel better than being with my students. Actually, that's not true—there are three things that make me happier: time with my boys, time with my girls, and time with Brett. Brett was always telling me I didn't need to work. He made enough in real estate that I could stay home. But being a teacher was truly good for me. I loved my students, my students' parents, and my coworkers. I couldn't ask for a better job.

But although I was sad that the end of the year was approaching and I'd have to bid farewell to this group, the girls and I had a summer trip booked that I was looking forward to. We always took a summer trip together without our kids. We've done the mountains, the beach, the city, and even just a long weekend at Ziah's house before. This year, we were going to a beautiful resort in San Antonio. It's in the Hill Country instead of the heart of San Antonio, so it's better for Steph. Alexis would text us unexpectedly now and then with an official countdown. This morning, she texted, "T Minus 63 days, 4 hours, 43 minutes, and 8 seconds."

That text started a thread of texts between us. Of course, I could only chime in briefly before the bell rang.

"So pumped!" I said, sending a GIF of the Golden Girls hugging each other.

Steph sent a Friends GIF of Rachel and Phoebe jumping up and down clapping, and then Ziah sent a GIF of a bra that made me laugh out loud.

I texted Brett to have a good day before I put my phone away for the morning.

Today, we got to use shaving cream on the desks. The students loved this activity, and it had the bonus of cleaning off glue that had accumulated on the desks, so it was a win-win for everybody.

We talked a little bit about Easter, but I knew I had to be careful with what we discussed. As a teacher, we had to be careful not to impress Christian or other religious beliefs onto our students. And as I said before, I'm a rule follower.

When my conference period rolled around, I pulled out my protein shake and my phone. There were a lot of text messages I needed to catch up on, a few from Brett and a lot from the girls. I opened Brett's texts first.

"Hey, baby," the first one read. Brett rarely called me baby. He called me several pet names, but baby was reserved for when he was really excited or feeling overly affectionate. "Hope you're having a great day with your students! I got another big listing today! We'll have to celebrate later tonight! Love you!" He followed the string of messages with a silly love GIF.

"Yay! So excited for you! Day is going well. Love you," I wrote back. Then I opened the GB group thread.

Ziah started: "Wish me luck again, gals. We have a family interview with Cy's potential new school in a bit. Also wish me luck that Tommy sleeps through it! I don't want Lizzie to ask to hold him. Ugh."

Nora replied, "Wait. New school? If it's public school, why do you have to interview?"

Ziah answered, "After meeting with the lawyers, we all decided to meet in the middle. Our main issue with the current school is the lack of diversity. And Lizzie's concern with the school we liked was it not being 'good enough,' which translates to 'public,' in her opinion. Some of my colleagues have children attending this new school, and it is diverse and private. So hopefully it all works out."

I always hated when people thought that private school was better than public school. But at least Ziah knew that it wasn't. I was happy that she and Leon knew the truth.

Steph said, "Good luck, Z."

Alexis chimed in, "Y'all. I slept with Dave."

Ziah responded, "LOL. How was it?"

"Wow. Talk about a change of subject!" Steph said.

Alexis replied, "Bad bad bad. So bad. I can't even."

Nora said, "OMG! I'm dying!"

Alexis continued, "I really had high hopes for this one. Oh well. More fish in the sea, I guess."

"Did you break it off with him?" Steph asked.

"I'm just ignoring him. He'll get the hint," Alexis informed.

Ziah said what I was thinking: "Girl. You need to face the music and break it off. You can't ignore him."

Alexis wrote back, "But I don't wanna!" She added a GIF of a child throwing a tantrum.

Nora said, "You do you, Alexis. If you don't want to talk to him, don't. I've come to realize that we only have one life, and we can do with it what we wish. It's too short to compromise."

Alexis responded with, "It's too short to compromise is exactly right—if you know what I mean! And in the meantime, I WILL do me. Perfect advice for this situation, Nora. Thank you."

"OMG, Alexis! LOL!!!" Ziah wrote.

Steph asked, "Nora, you been doing a lot of reflecting lately or something?"

Nora responded with, "No. I just think that we aren't getting any younger, and if we don't want to do something, we shouldn't have to. And in the same sense, if we want to do something, we should go for it."

That's where the thread stopped. I wondered if the other three were side-texting about what in the world could be going on with Nora.

"Hey, hey! Ziah, have you had the interview yet? If so, how did it go?" I asked.

"We had to reschedule. Tommy is extra fussy today, and I'm taking him to the doctor," she quickly responded.

Steph replied, "Oh no! Hopefully everything is fine with little T. Benjamin got a hold of a Sharpie while I was showering and drew all over the kitchen wall."

"Oh no, Steph! That's awful! Google the toothpaste method. It works." I replied.

"Nora, what a great way to look at life! Love it!" I said, not wanting to have ignored her previous philosophizing.

I switched over to my thread with Brett and asked what he wanted to do for dinner.

"Hey, babe. Johnathan and I have to go check out the new listing, and the couple won't be home until 7. It's gonna be a late evening for me. Go ahead and feed the boys, and I'll be home as soon as I can."

"Sounds good," I replied.

I hated his late evenings, but it was all part of the business. Besides, after I got the boys in bed, I could binge some Bravo.

By the time my workday ended, I decided to swing through fast food for the boys and me. They voted on tacos, so we grabbed some and headed home.

After dinner, I got my pajamas on and snuggled into my cozy bed. We kept the thermostat on sixty-four degrees in our room, and our bed felt like a cloud. It was one of my favorite places. I had just turned on the television, when Brett called.

"Hello?" I said.

There was nobody there. I could only hear breathing on the other end. *He must be on his way home*, I thought.

A couple of minutes later, just as I was laughing at Andy's facial expressions on Watch What Happens Live, my phone pinged in a text message: "Sorry, babe. I butt dialed you. Will probably be home after you're asleep. Love you. I'll kiss your forehead when I arrive."

The next morning, I woke with Brett spooning me. His soft breath felt comforting on my neck. In the twenty-two years we'd been together, we didn't often sleep apart. Usually only on my annual GB trips and his golfing buddy trips. He was definitely my safe place.

We had started dating when we were both seniors in high

school. We lived in a small town southwest of Fort Worth. Brett followed me to college, but he dropped out after our first semester. He decided to get his real estate license, which was one of the best decisions he's made. We moved in together, and I worked at Gap, while he became an assistant for a real estate agent. He wanted to observe how the business worked before he dove in—another smart move by my man. Gap is where I met Steph. We all got introduced to each other during that time in our early twenties. It's odd because I don't remember the details of meeting everybody. It's like, when we were all together, it just seemed that it had always been that way.

I rolled out of bed and got ready for work. I tried to be quiet for Brett's sake, but I made sure the boys were awake across the house. When I got to the kitchen to make them breakfast, I saw some notes about Brett's new listing on the island, which indicated that he stood to make a $50,000 commission if he closed this deal. I was so proud of him. He worked his ass off to provide for us. He was constantly staying ahead of the competition with advertising and social media. With a smile on my face, I hurried the boys out the door and headed to school.

ZIAH

Adjusting to having Tommy with us wasn't hard. He's a very sweet four-month-old. He was born premature, and he's more like a two-month-old than a four-month-old, really. The premature birth delayed his development, but it's also likely that his life's circumstances have further delayed it. Of course, waking in the middle of the night to feed him took a little time to adjust, but that was the only struggle. And Nina is always more than willing to help in any situation. Nina is our maid, but I hate that word. She's more like a live-in friend who assists us where needed. She is certified to babysit our foster kids, and we are forever grateful for her. She takes some of the midnight feedings anytime we have a baby with us, when I have a work meeting or some other function early the next day. Nina is one in a million.

I recently had been named keynote speaker at the Foster Care Awareness Month Gala to be held at The Anatole in May. I needed to let all the girls know that they could attend if they wanted. I always felt torn when it came to inviting them to these events. I wanted them to feel like I wanted them there—and I did. But I never wanted them to feel obligated to come. Sometimes I had the feeling that Steph would rather skip out on some, but she hadn't yet.

The event would take place on a Saturday night, which was better than the last event. I knew there had been some huffing and puffing about the last one one falling on a school night, and then Steph ended up overdoing it.

I find it difficult to understand Steph's anxiety, but I tried my best to be sympathetic. I knew that she was hypersensitive to my being uninformed about it, so I worked to educate myself more since the last time we had talked about it. I'm a firm believer that if we can all get outside of ourselves and empathize with others, we are all better off. The research I did really opened my eyes. I had no idea how intense it could be, and how it could truly come out of nowhere. I learned that there are specific triggers for certain people, and other times there doesn't have to be a trigger. I also found that diet and alcohol can play a role. I wondered if Steph knew this. She's so sensitive about her mental health that I really didn't want to discuss it with her.

I worded my text to the girls in a delicate way, hoping that they'd get the hint that they didn't have to attend if they didn't want.

"Hello to my GBs! Real quick, just wanted to let y'all know that I have a thing at The Anatole May 4. It's a foster care thing, and I don't want you to feel obligated to attend. Seriously, NBD."

Nora replied, "Ugh. I'm about to send the dorkiest text response ever. You ready?"

"Sure?" Ziah responded.

Nora said, "Kyle has a Stars Wars thing he asked me to attend that evening months ago. It's a whole 'May the fourth be with you' thing."

Alexis said, "Yikes, Nora. Z, I'll be there."

Chloe responded back, "Let me check with Brett, and I'll let you know ASAP."

"Oh, good. That's a Saturday. Better than last time. I'll definitely be there. Let me make sure that Mark doesn't have a gig. If he doesn't, he'll be with me for sure," Steph texted.

I was happy that Steph was coming, but I didn't appreciate her little jab about the last event—I didn't make her come, nor did I make her drink so much, and I certainly didn't make her take an anxiety pill. But that's the way Steph is; she's a blamer—a passive aggressive blamer. We've all taken the brunt of it, and we've all witnessed Mark take the brunt of it. But she's hardest on Alexis, though I was always proud how Alexis never let it affect her.

"Alexis, you bringing a plus one?" I asked out of curiosity. I hadn't heard much about her dating life since she'd broken things off with the plastic surgeon.

She responded with, "Nah. You girls got all of the guys who are worth a damn."

Nora sarcastically texted back, "Really, Alexis? You wanna go to a Star Wars Convention? LOL!"

I didn't like Nora talking so dismissively about Kyle, but she tended to do that a lot. I wasn't Kyle's biggest fan, but he was a nice guy. And like it or not, she married him. We all knew that Nora was one of those people with a "the one that got away" story. *Her college boyfriend had really been the one*, I thought. But for one reason or another, the stars hadn't aligned for them, and they had been pulled in two different directions.

My thoughts were interrupted by a call from Leon.

"Hey, baby," I answered.

"Hey, sweet lady. What you got going on today?" he asked.

"I have a meeting with a client in a bit, lunch plans with Alexis, some paperwork at the office, picking up Tommy's prescription, and then I'm meeting Lizzie to get Cy."

"Bless you."

"Yeah. You owe me for sure," I said.

"Well, I'll pay you back tonight. How about that?"

"Mmm. Sounds like a plan. See you tonight, baby." I replied.

"I love you, sweetie. I'll see you later," he said in his smooth, deep voice.

I hung up the phone and again wondered how a man so damn smart and fly could have chosen a woman like Lizzie at one point. I loved that Cyrus was a product of their marriage, but really, Leon? I just didn't get what he'd seen in her.

I made it to my meeting ten minutes early, which to me, is right on time.

I was excited about my lunch date with Alexis. We hadn't had time just the two of us since my pool party when she had been the first to arrive. Everybody needs a friend like Alexis; she is a bright light in this dim world. When she walks into a room, she commands everyone's attention. She's gorgeous, loud, hilarious, and she exudes positivity. I met Alexis through Nora, and Nora met Alexis in a yoga class. The story goes that the two of them were next to each other, and when it was time for the Happy Baby pose, another woman in the class had passed gas. This wasn't completely out of the ordinary, but it cracked Alexis up. When Alexis couldn't contain her laughter, Nora started laughing. They said that the fact that they weren't supposed to be laughing made them laugh even harder. Tears ran down their faces, and they rolled up their mats and ran out of class before it was over. They decided to go grab a bite to eat together, and the rest is history. It's funny to hear them retell the story, because they always have tears streaming down their faces when they detail the instructor's reaction to their laughing.

I finished my meeting and got in the Range Rover to head to Mi Cocina. Alexis wasn't there yet, but like I said, ten minutes early is my forte. I got us a booth and ordered her a margarita and a water with lime for me. I had my mouth full of chips and salsa when Alexis walked around the corner.

I stood up to hug her, and she squeezed my butt cheek. This was such an Alexis move. She looked a little different from the last time I had seen her.

"Filler in my cheeks," she said.

"I'm sorry?" I replied.

"I know. I look different, and I can tell you're wondering why. I got filler in my cheeks. It'll settle in about a week. Don't worry," she said.

"Well, I guess I'm not good at hiding my feelings through my facial expressions." I laughed.

"You know what that means, Z? Time for more Botox!"

She was actually right. I was a little overdue but hadn't had time since Tommy's arrival. We chatted some more, and I could tell something was bothering her. She wasn't her flippant self.

"What's up? You seem a bit off today," I told her.

"Ugh. I am. Z, I need to tell you something, but I don't know if I should. There are so many reasons why I don't know if I should or not. One reason is that I feel like I'm making assumptions, and the second reason is that once you know this, you'll be burdened with it like I am."

"Oh, Lord. Did somebody kill somebody? Are you talking to me as your lawyer right now? Or your friend? You know I don't deal with cases like that." I was half-joking, but her serious tone scared me.

"Girl, I almost wish it was something like that," Alexis said.

I could see that she was shaken. She pulled out her phone, scrolled through some stuff and showed me an Instagram profile.

"What exactly am I looking at here?" I asked.

"Look closer, Z," she said.

I looked at the name and the photos and realized it was Andrew—Andrew as in Nora's Andrew. And he looked damn good.

"Okay. It's Andrew. What's going on? Damn, he looks fine," I said.

"Ziah, he's been transferred to Dallas. He's like ... here. I mean, not here at Mi Cocina. But he's around. I ran into him at the Y. And you're right—he's super hot."

"Okay. Does Nora know about this? I don't know that she'll want to know, honestly. Let's think this through."

"Take a look at his followers," Alexis said, and she put the phone back in my hands.

I saw that Nora followed him.

"Oh, shit. What the fuck? Alexis! What the fuck? I thought she hadn't seen him or spoken to him in fifteen years!"

"So I ran into him at the gym and he asked for my Instagram handle. It's the only social media platform he has, so I don't think he realized that I'd be able to see that Nora follows him and he follows her. I spent almost an entire day trying to figure it all out, and I found that he's liked a lot of her old photos. But he hasn't had his account for long, so he must have looked through her profile and scanned through tons and tons of photos. It's so bizarre, Ziah. I remember Nora telling me that when they broke up, she wondered if the universe would ever bring them back together. Do you think that's what the universe is doing here? Is this it? I'm freaking out."

"Okay," I said. "Calm down. Do any of the other girls know about this?" I asked.

"Steph knows he's in town. But she has no clue that they've been in contact. If you think it through, Nora has been acting a little different for a couple of months. Even at your last award event, she was a little off. And at your pool party, she was, like, glowing or something. And then she's texted some weird shit lately about life being too short. Do you remember?"

"Okay. Calm down," I said.

"Z, you just said that. And you know I don't do calm very well," she spewed back at me.

"I don't know what to do. I'm going to have to think this through. We don't need to make any sudden decisions. I wonder if we should talk to the other girls. No. No. I don't think so. Okay, you've had a little time to process this, but you don't seem to have a clear handle on how to navigate this situation," I continued.

"Hell no, I don't know how to navigate it. That's what you're doing here. Of all of us, you've got the best head on your shoulders. I would say that Nora was in a tie for that spot, but lately, I'm thinking not. Steph is a little too judgmental to handle these details, and Chloe is too busy thinking the world is all rainbows and butterflies to deal with a conflict like this. She's not built for conflict. This is up to you and me, Z. Now then, what are we gonna do, boss?"

"Oooh, no you don't. Don't put this on me. Okay, let's take a deep breath. How about we enjoy our lunch, let me go home and process it, and then we will regroup. Sound good?" I asked

"Whatever you say, boss," she replied.

"Stop calling me that. Now pass me your margarita."

STEPH

It had been a while since I had felt any sort of anxiety approaching, and I'd been feeling like I was in a much better place lately. Mark hadn't been traveling with the band as much, and Gayle was sure to let me know that she'd take the kids whenever I needed some time to myself. I knew I'd end up taking her up on that offer during the weekdays in summer because all three would be home all day with me. But with only Benjamin home during the weekdays for now, it was fine. I suspected that Mark had talked with Gayle, and that's why she volunteered. He was always looking out for me, and his mom was an absolute saint. Mark was very hands-on with the kids when he got home from work, and he was sympathetic to me as a stay-at-home mom. I knew I had the option to work, but raising the kids at home was something I was passionate about. Mark's mom had done it for him and his sister, and my mom had done it for me.

Occasionally, I'd have to take one of my pills before Body Pump class with Nora. I found that if I didn't have a big enough breakfast or drink enough water, my nose would start tingling in class, and anytime I felt a tingle anywhere, I got scared an attack was approaching. And one of the many frustrating things about anxiety is that if you start getting anxious about having an attack, then you'll trigger one.

I met Nora in class and had been right on time. She already had my station all setup for me but was impressed by my punctuality. Every time we'd met there, since I had lunch with Alexis, I was terrified that we'd run into Andrew at the gym. I wasn't sure what Nora would do if she knew he was in town. I was conflicted having the information. Should I tell her or not? I ultimately decided that this was Alexis's thing. She's the one who had seen him and talked to him. She could decide what to do with the information. I had already planned that if we saw him, I'd act just as surprised as Nora genuinely would be.

I always hated the warmup at the beginning of class. It's my least favorite track, and it's the longest. I started dripping sweat from my elbows and I made a funny face at Nora. We always enjoyed class. The other people usually rolled their eyes at us, but I chose to ignore it—class was one of the few places where I felt I could completely let loose.

When we finished with class, we decided to send a goofy photo of ourselves to the girls. Nora had Snapchat on her phone for the funny filters, so she opened the app. We took a funny selfie with mouse ears, and she sent it.

We left the Y and headed to Starbucks around the corner to grab a cool-down drink—but it was really just an excuse for us to spend some more time together. I ordered a Jade Citrus Mint Green Tea, and Nora ordered a Mint Majesty Herbal Tea.

As I sat across from her, I noticed how happy she was. She'd pulled her fine brown hair back in a ponytail, and a cute floral headband held back her loose hair. Her Lululemon outfit was both fashionable and practical. She smiled often as we chatted about mundane things. I couldn't dare break her bubble of bliss by letting her know that Andrew was back. She finally seemed to be in a good place since the miscarriage.

Our phones buzzed and we knew it must be the girls responding to our photo.

Ziah texted first: "Y'all are so adorable! Hope y'all are having fun!"

Alexis replied with, "Love y'all! T Minus 47 days, 22 hours, 23 minutes, and 2 seconds!"

I loved when Alexis gave us a countdown to our trip. It reminded us that we had something fun to look forward to together. I mean, the group would be together May Fourth, except for Nora. And besides, those events don't count as get togethers. Those are fancy events where we don't let loose, except for the last one. But I had learned my lesson from that. And there was no way Mark would let me get in that form again. It had taken him a while to get over the last time. I told him that with my anxiety, I needed his help at events like that. We had a long heart-to-heart, and both of us came out with a good understanding of the other's feelings about the situation.

Nora's phone buzzed again, and I instinctively checked mine. I hadn't received a message. It must have been Kyle on her end. She suddenly said she needed to go. I didn't get why she'd need to leave so soon when she had the day off, but I wasn't going to question her. As I mentioned, she seemed so happy finally.

On the day of the event, I strutted down the stairs in my gown I'd rented online for Ziah's award ceremony. It was a one-shoulder number with black lace; it fit my body perfectly, and I knew it. I wore my hair down with my natural curls tamed, with one side pinned back tightly. Mark's jaw dropped and when I reached him, he spun me around, dipped me, and kissed my lips sweetly.

"You're amazing," he said.

"Well, thank you, kind sir. You don't look too shabby yourself," I replied.

"I mean it, Steph. You're absolutely amazing. I'm one lucky fella to have you on my arm for life. Also, I can't believe you're on time."

I slugged his arm and he kissed me again. This time, filled with passion. I started getting flushed and I pulled away. "Hey, now!" I said. "We were on time. Keep that up and we'll miss the entire event." I knew I had kissed off all my lip gloss, but it was worth it. I could reapply in the car.

I didn't take an anxiety pill this time, but I did bring one with me in my purse. The Anatole didn't usually make me anxious. The girls and I had been there for a weekend in the summer, and since I felt familiar with it, I felt more confident about being there. I also felt ultra-confident because of my dress and hair.

When we walked in, I was surprised to see Nora sitting with Alexis. Brett and Chloe were there, too. I got excited because Leon was at our table, which meant that after Ziah did her thing, she'd be joining us, as well. The only one that wasn't there was Kyle.

When we approached the table, Alexis said, "Day-um,

Mama! You look gorgeous! I am completely envious of your hair right now. It's absolute perfection, Steph. This is one of your best looks. Like, seriously. I feel like you're more beautiful than any bride I've ever seen right now. No offense to present company, including you! Ha!"

Chloe and Nora complimented me, as well. I returned the compliments, and we sat down. Everybody looked fantastic. I still wasn't sure why Nora was there, and my curiosity got the best of me.

"Nora, I didn't think you were coming. Aren't you supposed to be dressed in a gold bikini with two buns right about now?" I joked.

"Kyle had two tickets, and his nerdy accountant coworker wanted to go, so I told him it was fine. He knew it wasn't my thing anyway. Besides, I'm glad to be here with you guys!"

Brett made small talk with Leon about the real estate business, and I could tell that Leon was only pretending to care.

I interrupted the two of them to save Leon. "How's Little Tommy doing, Leon? Ziah had explained to us that since he's so young, he didn't need any casts for his broken bones or anything. Is he healing properly? I feel bad that I haven't asked her lately."

"Oh, man. That little guy is something else," he said. "He started smiling at us this week, and you know Z and I turned into puddles. He's doing great physically. He's a little behind where he should be, but man, he's awesome."

Leon was an incredible man with a heart of gold. He was a veterinarian, but he never introduced himself as a doctor. It was always just "Leon," "Leon Green," and sometimes "Ziah's husband." He wasn't the least bit pretentious, even though they lived in a house bigger than all of ours. Leon and Ziah didn't like to talk about status or money. They donated substantial amounts to charity every year. Occasionally they'd donate to a political campaign. And we all knew they had to pay Lizzie a ton of money every month, plus pay for Cyrus's education.

Brett and Chloe were all cuddly with each other, which wasn't out of the norm. They'd been together for all these years, but if somebody had just met them, they'd probably think they were newlyweds. There was champagne on the table, but I decided I better not drink anything at all. If I ended up needing to take that pill in my purse, I didn't want to have alcohol in my system.

I glanced down at the table and noticed brochures about foster care awareness. I picked one up and skimmed through it, finding it interesting. I envied all that Ziah was able to do. But she and I lived in two different worlds. Between Ava's dance schedule and Logan's basketball tournaments, and Benjamin being Benjamin, I didn't have time for other activities. Ziah only has Cyrus, who stays with them every other weekend and every Monday and Tuesday. It's different. I'm happy that people like Ziah exist. And I know that I contribute, too—just not in the same way.

Ziah walked on stage in a royal blue dress with wide, pointed shoulders. Her legs looked amazing, and her dark skin glistened. Her hair had been plaited into cornrows that led up to a high braided bun. She looked flawless. She began her speech with some statistics that surprised me. She said there were over 29,000 children currently in foster care in Texas. She also said that over one thousand kids will age out this year, turned loose with no support system because they are adults in the eyes of the law. This is when they're likely to become homeless, turn to drugs, enter into prostitution, or other forms of illegal activity. Her speech was everything it should have been as keynote speaker: informative, interesting, eye-opening, and well delivered. At the end of it, she talked about all the different ways that we can help, especially highlighting that it isn't necessary to become a foster parent to help the system.

Up until that point, I really hadn't thought through it all in depth. I had always assumed that you could either be a foster parent or not. And I knew that my family wouldn't be good candidates. But her speech cracked my heart open in a way that I hadn't felt before. I knew that I wanted to find out more about the issues these children faced with aging out. It just seemed so unfair. I looked at Mark, who had been listening just as intently as I had been. He caught me looking at him, and he gave me a wink.

When Ziah made her way to the table, we all hugged her and fawned over her. She told me I looked "smoking," and I gave the compliment right back to her. Nora told her about how she had gotten out of the Star Wars thing, and Alexis asked if there was a bar in the front. I immediately told Alexis that I wouldn't be taking any shots and requested she not include me if that's what she was thinking.

We all sat, visiting together while Alexis made her way to the bar, and I took in the moment. These were my best friends in the world. We were a diverse group of women with vastly different husbands—but man, how lucky were we? Ziah was changing the world and had an amazing husband who was doing wonderful things for animals. They had an awesome son—and a sweet little baby under their care at the moment.

I had everything I needed in Mark and the kids. Alexis was still chasing the rainbow for the pot of gold, but she sure was having a hell of a lot of fun on the hunt. Chloe had her dream job, healthy children, and her high school sweetheart. And Nora finally seemed happy. I didn't know if it was the fact that I was 100% sober at one of these events for the first time, but I felt like I was seeing so clearly. These women truly were comfortable, supportive, lifted me up, and made me seem better than I was. They really were like a hell of a good bra.

NORA

My shift had just ended at the hospital and I stopped to look at myself in the mirror. My hair was messy, and I looked tired. But I also looked younger. My skin was looking healthier than it had in a long time, and my Botox from two weeks prior had done me good. I felt butterflies in my stomach—butterflies that had become a part of my daily life over the past several weeks.

Andrew and I had been talking every day. What had started as innocent communication had taken a scandalous turn recently. Instead of just sending messages through Instagram, we had started talking on the phone during the day. When we were able to coordinate a work break, we'd sneak in a quick conversation. He made me feel so young again and so alive. When I tried to think of the last time I'd felt that way, I realized it had been before we broke up. Something had died inside me when he left, and I had moved on without that piece of me. In retrospect, I can see that I should have gone to therapy. The day that Kyle proposed to me, I was still thinking about Andrew. I knew that Andrew was my soulmate, but I had heard that he had gotten married. If he moved on, then I figured the universe wasn't going to bring us together again, as I had hoped when he left. So I said yes to Kyle. I don't mean to make it sound like I settled for Kyle, because he is a wonderful man. He'd give the shirt off his back to anybody in need. He loves animals, which is why we have three rescue cats and one pain in the ass, yappy dog. He is handsome, but I wouldn't say that he exudes sexiness upon a first impression. He's thin and doesn't tan. When we go on vacation, I have to cover him in sunscreen, so he doesn't turn into a lobster. He is funny—I'll give him that. But we don't have a lot in common. He is very nerdy, and we don't share a lot of interests. When Pokémon Go came out, he ran all around the city, trying to catch whatever it is you catch. He loves the Star Wars, Harry Potter, and Lord of the Rings franchises. I've never read any of the books or seen any of the movies. My favorite movie is "Lonesome Dove," though it was really a miniseries, to be exact. It's also my favorite book. When I was young, I thought I'd marry a man like Augustus McCrae. Kyle is the polar opposite of Gus. I tried to watch it with Kyle once, and he fell asleep before the water moccasins scene. It was one of the saddest parts, and I looked over to see his reaction, and he was out like a light. I stayed up for several more hours to finish it by myself. He never even budged.

I let Kyle plan our honeymoon and surprise me. I was hopeful for somewhere tropical—an all-inclusive resort somewhere, where we could spend our days listening to the ocean, sipping on banana daiquiris, snorkeling over a beautiful reef, or even swimming with the dolphins. The wedding planning had exhausted me, and I was ready to completely relax with my groom. To be clear, I was happy with Kyle; we were in love. And I still have a tremendous amount of love for him. I just think that we've fallen a little out of love over the last year.

When we boarded our flight for our honeymoon, I had to refrain from looking at our boarding passes or reading the monitors. I even had to put headphones in as soon as we sat down, so I wouldn't hear the captain announce where we were headed or how long the flight would be. Kyle was so excited to surprise me, and I found it adorable. I was surprised when we began landing after only a couple of hours, but I knew that the flight to The Bahamas was pretty short and so was Mexico. I still went along with the secret and didn't cheat. When I noticed several children getting off our plane, I was confused. I reasoned that maybe we were in The Bahamas, and these families are going to a family friendly resort. And that's when I noticed mouse ears. *Oh, dear heavens*, I thought. *He didn't.*

But he certainly did. He had planned our honeymoon for Disney World.

I love Disney World. I love the magical feeling of being there, I love the characters, and I love the happiness. What I don't love is Disney World as a honeymoon. All I wanted to do was lay in a lawn chair in my bikini, have sex with my husband in our bungalow, eat at all-you-can-eat buffets, drink whatever my heart desired whenever my heart desired it, and relax. Disney World doesn't exactly exude relaxation, and waiting in lines for hours sounded like my own personal hell in that moment.

But Kyle was so excited and proud of himself for surprising

me—oh, he surprised me, all right. I found him adorable when he was proud, and I know he worked hard on all the plans, so I went with it. But I'd be lying if I said I wasn't extremely disappointed. It wasn't what I had dreamed of at all. I broke honeymoon protocol and texted the girls. They all put a positive spin on it, but they knew me better than that. I had so wished that Kyle had enlisted their help with this, as he had done with my engagement ring. (Thank God for that, by the way! Otherwise I'd be wearing a heart-shaped diamond with the words, "After all this time? Always." inscribed on the inside. It sounds romantic, but it's a quote from Harry Potter.)

I did as much relaxing as I could on our honeymoon, and Kyle agreed to relax by the pool every evening, which was nice. We still had great honeymoon sex every night—it just wasn't in a romantic bedroom with our towels folded in the shape of a swan on our bed. I never let on that I was disappointed in the trip, but I cried in the bathroom on the first night. I wondered if somebody could get this important trip so incredibly wrong, was he really the one for me? I knew the answer to that even then, but I shut it down.

Back at the hospital, I pulled my phone out and called Andrew. I had learned through our conversations that he and his wife, Claire, had separated. She had stayed back in Austin when he got transferred, and they were on a "break" to see what they wanted to do moving forward. We rarely talked about her or Kyle because we were so consumed with talking about each other. We had shared that talking about our spouses with each other made us both feel a little jealous, so we opted to leave them out as much as we could. Andrew had mentioned meeting up, and the thought both aroused me and terrified me. I didn't know if I was ready for that. I knew what he and I were like around each other. The magnetic force is undeniable, and I wasn't sure if either one of us were strong enough to resist it.

Our conversation was short and sweet—we didn't have much time to visit, but we got some giggles and blushes in. He asked me if I ever thought we'd meet up, and I replied, "Hopefully, eventually." The thought gave me a rush. When we hung up, I started my Explorer, and I ruminated on that answer on my short drive home. "Hopefully, eventually" said so much in just two words.

I pulled onto our street and noticed how lovely all the surrounding homes were. We were lucky that Brett had been able to help us find our adorable home in Lake Highlands when he did. Houses had moved quickly, and he'd told us about it the day before it hit the market. He made double commission because he was the listing agent as well as the buyer's agent. It was a fairly small deal for him, but he knew exactly what we were looking for and found this house that had everything on our wish list. It was also in a great neighborhood and zoned for the same school where Chloe taught. That was something important to me when we ever did grow our family.

When I walked into the house, I realized that Kyle wouldn't be home for another hour or so. The short talk with Andrew had gotten me a little hot, and something came over me that I couldn't really explain. I went into my bedroom, took off my scrubs, put on some fresh Chapstick, let my hair down, and took a naked photo in the mirror. Before I had time to change my mind, I sent it to Andrew.

Holy shit. I can't believe I just did that, I thought. I felt invigorated. I felt sexy. I felt a bit like Alexis!

I hurried to put on some regular clothes and started dinner. While the oven was pre-heating, I turned on my favorite Chris Stapleton album. The song "Either Way" came on, and it stopped me in my tracks. It felt like a reflection of my relationship with Kyle lately. I sat on the arm of the couch and listened. I felt a pang of sadness for the life I had hoped for with Kyle. Was he happy with me? He hadn't shown any true signs one way or another. We had still been making love, but there was no real spark outside of those moments.

When the oven loudly alerted me that it was ready, the song ended. I snapped back into reality. I put the lasagna in and set the timer for one hour. I hated that some frozen meals took so damn long to make, but then again, frozen meals kept me from cooking. I grabbed my phone and suddenly I could hear my heart beating. I opened Instagram and Andrew had responded.

"Oh, my God, Nori. You're even more perfect than I remember. I've got to see you soon."

His reply made me feel really good. And it made me really want to see him, too.

"Where can we meet and when?" I replied. Every message I sent him gave me such a rush.

He immediately said, "You said you're off Mondays, right? I don't know where we can meet and be sure nobody will see us. Do you?"

"Monday. Let's meet in Arlington at 1. It'll be a little bit of a drive for both of us, but worth it. There's a Target right off I-30. Nobody we know would ever be there. Park in the back of the parking lot and let me know when you arrive. I'll do the same." I hit send with shaking fingers. I surprised myself at how assertive I was with this plan.

"Deal. I'll play hooky from work. I can't wait, Nori. I really can't. My heart is beating so fast thinking about touching your hand," he said. "I don't know if I can resist anything else. It's gonna be a huge struggle. I'm just letting you know."

Ugh, I thought. *What the hell have I gotten myself into?* The universe was doing what I had always hoped it would. I just didn't think it would happen right now. *Funny timing, but thanks?* I said to nobody as I looked up at the ceiling.

And then this new, risky version of myself did something that really made me feel like Alexis.

"Return the favor with the pic when you can. ;)" I typed out.

ALEXIS

"T Minus 23 days, 2 hours, 44 minutes, and 46 seconds, Babes!"
I texted the girls.

I grabbed Gibbs's leash and he ran to me and sat, then shook my hand, and I pet his scruffy head. He was the cutest dog I had ever seen. I had paid way too much for him, but he didn't shed, he was brilliantly smart, his bark was loud enough to scare a possible intruder, and aside from the girls, he was my best friend. We took our normal route, which kept us close to the apartment complex and in plain sight. After having been pinned down by a man who shoved his hand up my skirt years ago, I had tried my best to be smart about being alone. I never told the girls this, but that's another reason why I wanted to find Mr. Right: I was tired of having to fend for myself and protect myself.

Do not get me wrong—I am a strong, independent woman, and I could live happily ever after alone. But I'd love to have that strong, protective partner by my side. I'd also like to have somebody to laugh with every day, cuddle with, dance with in the kitchen, and eventually to have a family with. The girls don't think I'm ready to settle down, but the truth is, it's not the settling down I'm against. It's the settling. I watched Nora settle, and I can see how it's changed her. I want to be swept off my feet and find somebody who is the whole package. I want the kind of love that's in the movies. I want what Brett and Chloe, Leon and Ziah, and Steph and Mark have. I'm good at reading people, and I can tell that, at times, the girls are envious of my singlehood and my freedom. But in truth, I'm jealous of them. The grass is always greener, right?

Gibbs and I finished our walk and then came back into the apartment. I checked all my apps and saw that Nora had posted a beautiful selfie on Instagram. Nora never posted selfies. In fact, all the ladies gave me a hard time for my selfies. Sure, it was okay if somebody else was in the photo. But a true selfie alone was not like Nora at all. I looked to see who all had liked the photograph. There were forty-eight people. I scrolled down and saw that, sure enough, Andrew was one of them. *What in the world was going on with these two?* I wondered. I texted Ziah to update her. She was the one who would help me decide what to do. As for now, we had decided to sit back, observe, and remain idle.

I decided to take Gibbs on a Starbucks run with me and then spend the day at home. When we returned with his Puppuccino and my iced coffee, I plopped down on my West Elm couch. I loved the way that I'd decorated my apartment. I'd carefully selected every single detail, and I took pride in it. I'm talented at decorating, and that's another reason why I hate that asshole who harassed me. He ruined that for me. Sure, I could find another job, but that whole fiasco had knocked the wind out of my sails.

I decided to look on Bumble and see if there was anybody worth a damn that I hadn't seen yet. I saw a few guys that I hadn't seen before, and one was really hot: "Dean, 37." I was used to forty and older, but I liked the idea of someone closer to my age. I scrolled through his photos and liked what I saw. He had a beard, but not a bushy one. There was a photo of him on the beach, as well as one of him hiking. He looked adventurous, which I liked. He had a good physique, but he wasn't too showy about it in the photos. His biography read the hook line to one of my very favorite Mase songs, "Tell Me What You Want." I sang the words as I read them. In my mind I sounded just like Total as I sang their part. I reread it again and got lost in the song for a moment before I focused back on his profile.

I giggled out loud and realized I was smiling from ear to ear. I imagined that most women who saw that wouldn't have a clue what in the world he was talking about it, and would swipe left, because it seemed weird. But to me, the introduction couldn't be any more perfect. I swiped right.

I went into the kitchen and microwaved an egg. This was a trick that Steph had taught me, and I found it to be absolutely genius. I poured lemon pepper all over it, sat down with my coffee, and savored every tangy, peppery bite. The girls thought I was crazy, but I love lemon pepper on just about anything. Sandwiches? Lemon pepper. Pizza? Lemon pepper. Eggs? Lemon pepper. Biscuits? Lemon pepper. I loved it. After I finished eating, I went back to my phone and saw that Dean had swiped right on me, too. I wondered how many girls missed out on him because they didn't know who Mase was.

"Love your bio," I said.

"Ha! Thanks. You familiar with the song?" he replied.

"Only every single lyric," I responded.

"My buddy made me sign up for this app, and I told him I would. I haven't taken it seriously, really. You're the first one who has known the song. I'm impressed."

"So since you skipped out on your real bio, what's your story?" I asked.

"I'm a golf course manager."

Wow. That's a position I'd never dated before, but it sounded like it could be fun. It didn't sound pretentious like the other guys that I had met online. I tended to go for doctors, lawyers, realtors, oil and gas guys, and other big money makers. And obviously, they hadn't worked out. All the girls' husbands enjoyed golfing, so maybe we could all have a group date sometime if this went well.

"What about you? What's your story?" he asked.

"I live with my dog and lead a very important life, according to him." I said.

"LOL. Well, Alexis. Do you want to meet for a coffee sometime? Like I said, my buddy made me sign up for this, and I'm not good at it. But I'm less awkward in person."

"I'd love to. Let me know when you're thinking, and I'll check our schedule." I replied.

"Our?" He asked. I assumed he was wondering if this meant I had children.

"Yes. I told you I live with my dog."

"Ha! Okay. How about Thursday?" he replied.

"Just let me know what time and where and I'll be there."

I closed out the app and smiled. I liked this Dean guy so

far. He seemed fun. And I liked how we skipped a bunch of insignificant back and forth and got straight to the point of setting up a date.

The girls started texting right about then.

Chloe said, "Schooooooooool's Out For Summer!"

Ziah responded, "OMG! Go, Chloe! Another outstanding teaching year in the books! I'm sure that every single child is better for their time spent with you, my sweet friend."

Steph added, "Is it bad that I'm not celebrating? Ava and Logan will be home all day every day unless they have camp. These 23 days can't go by fast enough. Ava is about to be 13. Lord, help me."

"Update on Little Tommy: He's going to his great aunt's in two days. We are going to miss the hell outta that little dude. The little ones are hard, man. Ugh. Here comes my Zi Cry again, as Leon says," Ziah said.

Nora replied, "Oh, Z. I'm so sorry. I don't know how y'all do it. You guys are truly amazing. I hope that Tommy is shown the love that he deserves from his family moving forward."

"Thank you, Nora. All we can do is love them and love them big while we've got them. Our goal is always for them to go to family in the end and not get stuck in the system. But we pray that he is taken care of, that God wraps his arms around him tightly, and that he doesn't go back to foster care. Unless, of course, that's what's best. Damn, this is a hard thing. I would ask if we could do drinks tonight, but I want to spend every moment with little T," Ziah responded.

Steph texted, "Damn, Z. I'll be thinking about y'all. Please tell Leon we're thinking of him, too."

I chimed in, "Bummer. I always hate this part, Ziah. (Except for that one time when that little shit Jackie left. LOL, remember that?)"

Ziah answered, "LOL. Alexis, you always know when and how to bring the comic relief. Yes. How could I forget? Jackie was the one who gave me a run for my money. But she just needed extra love."

"Let us know if you need anything, Ziah. We can bring some wine over after he leaves if you'd like," Chloe said.

I added, "Well this just means we are all needing this trip more than ever. It'll be the perfect break for us all."

The conversation died down. I opened Bumble again and sent Dean another message: "How about tomorrow instead?"

"Wow. Sure. But I work at the club tomorrow. Can we do dinner instead of coffee?" he replied.

"Club?? Oh, God. Are you a bouncer? Please don't tell me you're a stripper."

"Ha!!! The country club. The golf course. I like you, Alexis. You're fun. How about tomorrow at Hillstone?" he asked.

"See you there. Wait. Are they dog friendly?" I joked.

"LOL. See you tomorrow, Alexis," he said.

I went to bed that night feeling giddy. I hadn't really felt like this in a while. Even with Dr. Dave, the plastic surgeon, I hadn't felt this kind of match. It felt like Dean was more on my level. Usually, I wear the pants in my online relationships, and I hold all the cards. But that night, I kept checking to see if Dean had written anything else, which he hadn't. It was totally against everything that I stood for to do what I did next, but I did it anyway.

"Goodnight, Dean. I'm excited to see you tomorrow," I

wrote.

He immediately responded, "Wow. I was just thinking about you. I'm excited, too."

I fell asleep cuddled up to Gibbs and slept better than I had in a very long time.

CHLOE

Saying goodbye to my students was always hard. Kindergarten graduation is a tearjerker every single year. I always felt that summer break was a little too long, but I was looking forward to some time off with the boys. We also had our GB trip approaching, and we were continuing to count down the days. Usually the boys and Brett and I go somewhere for a getaway, but Brett had been having his most successful year to date, so I couldn't ask him to put things on pause. Staying home made me feel good, because I was able to make sure the house stayed clean. The boys were old enough now that they could at least help me with laundry and trash. Brett worked so hard, it only seemed fair for him to come home to a nice, clean home. I was able to join Steph and Nora at their Body Pump classes, which also made me feel good for Brett's sake.

It had been about a week since Little Tommy had left Ziah and Leon, and I knew I needed to check in on her. She and Leon always handled their foster children leaving with such grace. Ziah was so busy that she just kept right on ticking. And they had Cyrus for an extended period, since it was summer. But I still wanted to touch base and let her know I was thinking about her.

"I've been praying for you, my sweet friend. I hope you and Leon are doing okay with the transition," I sent.

She replied, "You're so sweet, Chlo. Leon and I are doing fine. We just pray that Tommy is in good hands."

"Man, Z. You're who I want to be when I grow up," I responded.

"I hate to break it to you, but you're grown. And you've got it all, girl. Your boys adore you, Brett is everything you could ever hope for, and you have your dream job. You've got it all. Plus, you touch more lives than I could ever dream of," she sent back.

"I cannot wait for our trip!" I sent. Then I swapped over to our group text. "Alexis! Where are you with our updated countdown?!"

"Sorry. I've been busy lately. I've been seeing somebody new, and I think y'all are going to love him! But the official countdown is T Minus 16 days, 21 hours, 43 minutes, and 9 seconds," she chimed in.

Ziah replied, "Yay! I need this so badly! Cannot wait to sit around giggling with y'all!"

Steph said, "Oh, man. I can't wait! Benjamin, Ava, and Logan are already over the chart of chores I've created for the summer. But today we are going shopping, getting everyone's hair cut, and then getting snow cones. (If they complete the chart, that is! Ha!) I'm glad to have them all home, but I am definitely looking forward to our getaway! This hotel sure doesn't know what they're in for! And this mama needs a tan!"

"Alexis! Tell us about this guy! When do we get to meet him??" Nora asked.

"I don't want to jinx it," she quickly typed back.

"What?? You always spill the tea! This one MUST be different if you're staying mum about him. I'm with Nora, though. When can we meet him?" I responded.

Alexis replied, "I don't know. Soon. Find us something to do, and we can have a couples' date or something."

I had the perfect idea. Brett's real-estate partner, Johnathan, was going to be coming over that Friday with his husband, Blake. Brett and I were having them over for dinner because we hadn't done anything with the two of them together in quite some time. It was my idea because I adored Johnathan and Blake. I didn't think that Brett would care if we turned the whole thing into a barbecue get-together with Steph, Mark, Ziah, Johnathan, Nora, Kyle, and Alexis and her new guy, plus all the kids. I couldn't recall the last time that all our kids had been together, so this would be the perfect way to officially kick off the summer.

I texted Brett to make sure he was okay with changing the plans a little. He immediately responded that it was fine, and he'd let Johnathan know. I knew Johnathan and Blake would be fine with it, because they adored the girls.

I loved entertaining, and the thought of it all excited me. I texted the girls and crossed my fingers that everybody's schedules would allow this to pan out as I had hoped.

"I have a perfect plan for how we can meet this mystery man! Let's have a BBQ at my house Friday! Kids invited! Plus ones invited! Gibbs invited!" I texted. Alexis said she'd check with her plus one and get back to us ASAP, but either way, she and Gibbs were in.

"You mean we can't bring Punkin'? I'm so hurt," Nora sarcastically wrote.

We all knew she didn't care much for her and Kyle's little dog. She liked the cats all right, but the little dog was more of a one-person dog, and that one person was Kyle.

"Count Leon, Cy, and me in! Let me know what to bring, Chlo! I'm excited!" Ziah said.

"How sweet, Chloe! I need to check our family calendar in a bit and make sure Mark doesn't have a gig, but the kids and I will be there for sure. The kids will LOVE seeing Gibbs! And all of you, of course. Ha!" Steph replied.

I was pumped. At least all the women were in. I really hoped that Alexis's new guy could come. For her to say that she didn't want to jinx it was out of character.

"Z, nobody needs to bring anything. Y'all just bring your fine asses and your families!" I said. Any time I cursed, I felt a little like Alexis. We all liked to channel our inner Alexis now and then.

Our conversation died down and I texted Alexis separately

"I really can't wait to meet this guy. I'm getting happy hands just thinking about it. I hope he can come Friday," I sent. Happy hands were what we called it when I got excited about something and couldn't help but shake my hands in delight and excitement.

"He's in!" Alexis replied. Then she let the group know. Everybody was ecstatic.

I was happy to start planning it all. I tried to stay busy in the summer because sitting around too much made me miss the classroom. I checked the time and asked Nora and Steph if they were doing Body Pump later. It turned out that they were doing the late afternoon class, so I decided I'd meet them there. The boys could swim while we took our class, and it would be good for them, too.

When the boys and I got to the Y, I sent them out to swim while I went into the studio. Nora was there, but Steph wasn't. No surprise, since Steph was always late. Nora already had hers and Steph's station set up and was working on getting mine set up. I took over and got all my different weights laid out.

"So what do you think about this guy of Alexis's?" I asked.

"I don't know, but I am so excited to find out about him. It's unusual for Alexis to be so serious when talking about somebody to us. I can't wait for Friday. Thank you for hosting, by the way," she gave my arm a squeeze.

"No problem. You know I love having everyone over. And it's been a while since you guys have seen Johnathan and Blake. I haven't even seen Kyle in a while. It'll be nice for the guys to catch up," I replied.

Just then Steph walked in. She looked cute with her headband on and her curly hair in a bun.

"Ugh. Sorry I'm late. I couldn't find my keys, then I took a drink of my water and the lid wasn't on all the way and it spilled all over my shirt. So then I had to change, and now, here I am. I swear..." and she shook her head. "Thanks for setting me up, y'all."

The workout was particularly hard because I hadn't been in a while. The squat track killed me, and then by the time the lunge track came around, my legs were involuntarily shaking. I was ready for it to be over, but I wasn't a quitter. I kept seeing the prize at the finish line—a tight ass. The older we got, the saggier the cheeks got, and the harder it was to maintain a fit figure. I felt I owed it to Brett to look good, and I owed it to myself. I pushed through and then it was finally over. During the cool down, I meditated a little bit. I used the quiet time to thank God for all that I had. I thought about Brett and the boys, and calmly stretched each muscle. I was blessed beyond measure, and my quiet thoughts were consumed with appreciation.

As the girls and I put our weights back, we talked a little bit more about the approaching BBQ. Everybody expressed excitement. Steph said that Mark didn't have a gig, so he'd be there. I was happy to have one hundred percent attendance and did my happy hands again at the thought. I absolutely loved playing hostess. We gathered the boys and Ava from the pool, and then we bid each other farewell.

ZIAH

Friday finally rolled around and I couldn't wait for Chloe's barbecue. Leon looked sharp in his coral shirt, khaki shorts, and hat. And Cy looked like a mini Leon. I wore a floral romper, and even though Chloe said not to bring anything, I made Leon's favorite blueberry peach cobbler, and brought a gallon of Bluebell ice cream. I was curious to see how Nora would act since Alexis had dropped the bomb on me that she and Andrew seemed to be in contact. We had decided that for now, we'd just sit back and watch, and wait for her to reveal anything to us. We assumed Andrew had already told her that he had run into Alexis at the gym, but she hadn't brought it up yet. I wondered if she was waiting for Alexis to mention it. Either way, nobody was budging yet. It was odd for someone in our group to have a secret from the rest of us. But Leon always tells me that you never know what people are going through, no matter how well you know them.

When we pulled up, I could already hear the music coming from the backyard. We walked around the side of the house to the back per Chloe's instruction. Brett and Chloe had a beautiful backyard with old, large oak trees and beautiful landscaping. She had the most beautiful patio lights strung from all the trees and a Restoration Hardware table that sat twelve with more relaxed patio seating around it. It was the perfect evening for a barbecue. Evenings can be extremely hot in Texas, but we hadn't gotten around to the outrageously high temperatures just yet. The tiki torches were lit, as well as some citronella candles to keep the mosquitos away. Alexis and her date hadn't arrived yet. It looked like Leon, Cyrus, and I were the first ones there. As soon as we got to the deck, Chloe came out in a beautiful, summery, white cotton dress. She looked so innocently lovely in it. She was balancing a tray with margaritas.

"Brett just made this batch, and we've also got beer and seltzers in the fridge, if you'd rather. Just let me know and I'll grab whatever you'd like. Oh, and you know I've always got wine," she said.

I grabbed a margarita and kissed her cheek. Leon did the same. Brady and Cooper came running outside and Cyrus was happy to be reunited with them. They immediately took off running in the large backyard, chasing each other.

I heard a car door shut, and soon after, Johnathan, Brett's colleague, and his husband, Blake, rounded the corner.

"Ziah, my love!" Johnathan shouted. "How can you look more fabulous every time I see you? It's like, the more you do for humanity, the more fab you become."

I laughed and gave him a big hug. "Johnathan, you're crazy! But thank you. I've been wanting to talk to you and Blake and get an update on your adoption journey! How is it going?" I asked him.

Blake chimed in, "Girl, don't even get us started."

"Less than perfect," Johnathan said.

"Well, I hate to hear that. You two will make excellent parents. You just have to wait until the universe says it's time." I tried to encourage them. "Y'all go grab a margarita. Brett made them, so they're extra stout."

They went inside to greet Chloe and Brett, and I thought about how unfair it was that they couldn't have a child right now. *The system is so broken*, I thought.

"Hi, guys," I heard Kyle say. He and Nora had arrived. She seemed to be tuned in to her phone. I wondered if she was on-call tonight. It was also likely that another nurse or a doctor could be texting her with a question, given how good she is at her job.

"Hey, Kyle! It's so good to see you. How is everything?" I asked. It was hard to ask Kyle specific questions because I didn't know how to talk about the things that he liked, and accounting isn't the most fun subject to discuss.

"Pretty good. I've been staying pretty busy at work. Nora's been picking up extra shifts lately, so I've been taking on more work than normal, so I'm not home alone. I mean, I've got the cats and Punkin', but you know what I mean," he finished.

I hadn't realized that Nora had been working extra, and I wondered if they were short-handed, or if she was avoiding home, or if something else was going on. I hated to pry, so again, I'd wait until she brought it up.

Nora looked up from her phone and slid it into her crossbody. She smiled and gave me a hug. "I want whatever I smell on your breath!" she said.

"That would be one of Brett's famous margaritas. Go get you one!" Right then Chloe came back outside with more margaritas and a bottle of wine. Johnathan and Blake followed her, carrying the meat for the grill. Brett was behind them with a tacky apron on that read, "Kiss the Cook."

Nora and I sat down in some chairs while the men stood around the grill. Chloe was in and out, bringing out more supplies and ingredients. I hoped that Nora would use this one-on one-time to confide in me and let me know what was going on with her lately.

"How are you holding up without Tommy?" she asked.

"We're good. I know that must have been hard on you. It wasn't lost on me that Tommy was the same age that the baby would have been, Nora. I hope you know that I will never forget what you've been through and what you continue to go through. And I'm always here for you. No matter what. I hope you always think of me as one of your best friends—or better yet, one of your best bras."

"You're so sweet, Z. I've actually been doing better over these last few months than I have been in a long time. Time heals a broken heart, I suppose," she replied.

"Do you think you'll try again?" I asked. I felt a little like I was imposing, but this was one of my absolute best friends.

"Hopefully, eventually," she said as she looked off at the boys running around in the backyard. She seemed to have gone somewhere else in her mind. I didn't want to push the subject, so I let it go.

Kyle approached us and asked Nora if she needed anything. Her response was a little short, and it seemed as though he walked away with his tail between his legs. I felt bad for Kyle.

He was odd, but Nora was the one who had married him.

Steph and Mark came around back and Mark made a joke about how they weren't the last to arrive for once. Steph flirtatiously socked his arm, and Benjamin, Ava, and Logan joined the others in their game of tag at the back of the yard.

"Hey, hey, hey!" I heard Alexis call out. I turned around to see her and a handsome young guy with a beard. Alexis wore a short blue romper that accentuated her eyes but didn't show off too much of her long legs. It was short, but not too short. Her date wore a chambray pearl-snap shirt with the sleeves rolled up and khaki shorts. He looked effortlessly handsome. He didn't look like anybody Alexis had ever dated before, but somehow, he looked exactly like her type. I didn't know how to explain it—Maybe it's just that they complemented each other very well.

She introduced everybody to him. His name was Dean, and he had a great handshake, and nodded his head as he met us all. It was a sign of respect that I appreciated. He seemed to know a little tidbit about each of us from his conversations with Alexis, and it showed that he'd put effort into remembering it all. To say that I was impressed would be an understatement. Not to be left out, Gibbs came bounding around the house and ran straight up to all of us, as if to say hello, and then ran off with the kids. Gibbs was a funny dog. He had a lot of personality and good manners. I always imagined that if somebody was going to voice Gibbs in a movie, it would be Liam Neeson. Alexis found this thought hilarious, and every now and then we'd imitate what he was thinking in Liam's voice. I have no clue why I imagine him with an Irish accent. Maybe it's the manners part.

Dean seemed to fit right in with Leon, Mark, Johnathan and Blake. Even Kyle was smiling. Brett hadn't come back outside yet for his introduction. But I could tell by Alexis's beaming smile that she was pleased with how the introductions were going.

Brett walked out and Dean made a face at him like he was trying to place him. Brett stuck his hand out almost too quickly and said, "Hey, buddy. I'm Brett. My wife, Chloe, and I have heard wonderful things about you. Let us know if you need anything."

Dean looked a little confused, and I studied the body language between the two. He finally said, "Nice to meet you. Thank you for allowing me to come to your beautiful home. You and your wife are extremely gracious hosts, and I'm looking forward to some delicious food!" He clapped his hands together as he said the word food and the guys laughed. I'm fairly sure that all the men there had a man crush on Dean.

My phone vibrated in my pocket, breaking my gaze. Shit. It was Lizzie. I walked inside and went to the guest bedroom to answer it.

"Hello?" I said.

"Ziah! It's about time you answered your damn phone," she said.

"I beg your pardon?" I replied.

"Well, not your phone, I guess. But I've been calling Leon for thirty minutes."

"We're out, Lizzie. What's going on? Is everything okay?"

"No. It's actually not. I was looking over the custody agreement, and your time with Cy doesn't start until this coming Monday," she said in a sassy tone.

"What? We've all known it started this past Monday for months," I replied in an extremely irritated voice. She know how to push my buttons and boy did she love to do it.

"Well, we were all wrong. I pulled out the custody agreement, and it starts this coming Monday. So you and Leon need to bring him to me right now. And because you've had him for these five days *that weren't yours*, I'll bring him back to you next Friday."

"Lizzie. Let Leon and I look over the paperwork, and we'll call you first thing in the morning. We are at a barbecue right now, and Cyrus is having fun, playing with his friends."

"Those aren't his friends, Ziah. They're *your* friends. And no. Bring him to me, and I'll show you the arrangement myself when you get here."

"I'll call you back," I said through a shaky voice, and I hung up. I ran past Steph, who said I looked sick, and I finally got to Leon. I relayed what Lizzie had said, and he was livid. He said that we needed to go home and look over everything and regroup in the morning. I told him that Lizzie wasn't standing for that, and we had to go over there right now with Cy, and we'd look it over with her.

How could he have ever been in love with this woman? I thought, as we pulled out of the circle drive. Luckily, we were first to arrive and didn't have to make everybody move their cars. It was already embarrassing enough to have to leave like we did.

Sure enough, Lizzie was right. Somehow, we had all gotten the dates mixed up, and nobody ever checked them because we were all on the same page. We dropped Cyrus off, and told him we'd bring all his stuff by the next day. When we left, I started crying.

"Now don't start with the Zi cry, baby. You know I can't handle that," Leon said.

"I'm just so pissed off at her, Leon! And you know this brought her even more joy because I'm a lawyer and I missed this. God, I hate her. I mean, I don't hate her, God," I said, looking toward the sky. "But dammit do I dislike her on a level that I can't explain! I just don't get it, Leon."

"I know. I know. How could I have ever loved her? You've asked me a million times. And the answer is that I don't know. Let's just focus on the good, and that is Cy. On the positive side of things, we'll have him for a week longer than we thought. Just relax, baby. It'll all be okay."

He was always good at talking me off the ledge when it came to Lizzie. Instead of going back to the barbecue, we decided to go on home. It was too much to go back and face everyone after that bitch had humiliated me.

STEPH

Alexis's date was very attractive. He didn't look like the typical men she dated. She's dated men of all ages, but they all have seemed too old or too young. This one actually seemed to be more her age. Even the previous ones who were thirty-five had seemed too immature. Mark hit it off with Dean immediately. Everybody did, really. He was confident, but not overbearing. And he was charismatic in an effortless way. Every time Gibbs ran past him, he'd bend down and scratch behind his ears. He put his arm around Alexis a few times, and I noticed that he wasn't too handsy with her, as some guys tend to be. When she'd approach, he'd open to her with his body language and welcome her into the conversation. He never talked over anybody, and he was very relatable.

After a bit of mingling, I pulled away from the group and went around to the front of the house where Nora was sitting in the porch swing. I sat down and asked her why she had wandered off. She said she needed a moment, and I totally understood. I have to leave group situations now and then because of my anxiety. Ever since Nora's miscarriage, she'd dismiss herself on occasion. I'm sure watching all the kids made her feel a little bit sad. I wasn't sure if she and Kyle were trying for another child, and I didn't want to impose. Motherhood was the single most important thing in my life, and I couldn't fathom not being a mother. Nora knew this without me ever having to say it. Mark was the love of my life. And, of course, the GBs were important to me, too. But here's how I know what's most important. Would I lay my life down for Mark without hesitation? No. Yes, I would probably die for him, but I'd hesitate because I would worry about my kids not having me. Would I die for the girls? Same answer. I wouldn't want my kids to be without me. Would I die for the kids? Absolutely, without question.

Nora closed her eyes and took in a deep breath. She looked really beautiful sitting on that swing. Something in her had changed. I asked her how she was doing, and she said she was great. We talked about Dean, and both of us felt the same about him. We felt hopeful and optimistic for Alexis. After a few minutes, I told Nora that I was going back to the backyard to join everybody, and that she should, too, when she felt like it.

When I got to the back, the song playing was loud and obnoxious. I didn't like the bass in it. It seemed to shake my insides and it made my head hurt. I started feeling hot, and as I looked out at the kids, my vision darkened slightly.

Shit, I thought. My hands started tingling and then they locked up. I looked at Mark, and he must have felt it, because he met my eyes immediately, and I could tell by the look on his face that he knew what was going on. He ran over to me and whisked me inside. By the time I sat in the club chair in the formal living room, I was in the middle of a full-blown panic attack. Alexis realized what was happening and ran inside, asking what she could do. Mark told her to please keep everybody outside, especially the kids. He knelt in front of me and started massaging my hands. When they lock up like that, I can't move them at all. Mark has dealt with these attacks enough to know the best methods to help me through them. I could barely talk because my mouth had locked up. I spoke through the small opening that my lips allowed and asked him to get me cold water. He ran to the kitchen and returned quickly. I held onto the bottle. Something about the coldness of it helps to bring my hands back. When I could finally move my hands again, I took a sip. I ended up downing the whole bottle without taking a breath. I then let out a big sigh and looked at Mark with apologetic eyes. He helped me up and said, "Come on, baby. Let's get the kids and go home."

"I'm sorry," I said. "I'll meet you in the car. Please don't let anybody make a fuss over this."

When I went out the front door, Nora was still sitting in the porch swing. I had forgotten that she was there. She was smiling and looked to be texting somebody. I wondered who would make her smile like that, when all of us were here. It wasn't the type of smile that she'd have if she were talking to family. She was surprised to see me, and she fumbled to put her phone down.

"What are you doing?" she asked innocently.

"We're leaving. I had a damn panic attack. I don't want to talk about it tonight. I'll text tomorrow," I replied.

"Oh, Steph," she said. She stood up and walked me to the minivan. She knew I didn't want to talk, so she helped me in and told me she loved me.

When we got home that evening, I felt one hundred percent better. Mark suggested that we go to bed and watch whatever I wanted to watch on Netflix. I chose a true classic— "Bridget Jones's Diary." I love that movie. Mark puts up with it because he knows I love it. He also likes it because I call him "Mark Darcy" in a British accent for a few days after I watch it. Watching the way Bridget acted around Daniel and her facial expressions as she and Daniel emailed back in forth at work reminded me of Nora's face when I had caught her off guard on the porch. I wondered what in the world she was up to. She's never been one to do anything bad, so surely, I was reading into something that was really nothing.

When the movie was over, Mark was already asleep. I sent the girls a quick text, because I knew they'd be worried about me.

"Goodnight, ladies! Sorry about tonight. That one came out of nowhere. I'm fine now. (Z, another damn panic attack.) Chloe, everything was perfect. Ziah, I hope Lizzie wasn't too much of a bitch. Nora, thank you for helping me to the van. Alexis, I like Dean! Can't wait to hear more details! Love y'all!" I hit send, turned my phone on Do Not Disturb, snuggled up to Mark, and went to sleep.

NORA

When I pulled into the Target parking lot, my hands were shaking, and my heart was pounding. I couldn't believe that I was really meeting up with Andrew. I found a spot towards the back, just like we had planned, and parked my car. I popped in a piece of gum, which made me feel even more scandalous. Why was I chewing gum? Did I think we'd kiss? I justified it by telling myself that we would be in close proximity, and it was the polite thing to do. I sent him a message that I was there. Just after I hit send, I looked up and realized he was pulling up right next to me.

Oh, my God, I thought.

He smiled at me and removed his sunglasses. His dimple seemed even more prominent than I had remembered. My cheeks went hot thinking about the pictures we'd traded. He put his truck in park and motioned for me to get in.

"Here we go," I said out loud, clenching my jaw, as I opened my door. I pulled myself onto the passenger seat of his truck and giggled. He stared at me and smiled for what felt like eternity. I felt completely awkward and simultaneously comfortable. He reached across the console and grabbed my hand. His hand was as shaky as mine was.

"What are we doing, Nori?" he asked, hypnotizing me with that killer smile.

"Just two friends catching up?" I heard my shaky voice reply in an innocent tone.

"That's right. We are two friends catching up."

How many times had Claire sat in the exact seat I was in? Where had they gone together in their married life? How many times were her feet up in the dashboard as they traveled together, listening to music? Does she like the same kind of music that Andrew and I listened to together? Did she know that "Who I Am" by Wade Bowen was our song? Did she know much about me at all?

Just holding his hand felt like home.

"I'm nervous," he said. "You look beautiful, by the way."

"Thank you. You're not bad yourself, you know. Turns out, you're like a fine wine," I joked back.

He laughed, and the dimple that I used to be so familiar with got me again. His hand lightly stroked my hand, and I stared at our hands for a moment. They looked older. More wrinkled. A lot of time had passed since I'd last studied his hand. He reached over with his other hand and touched my chin, making me look back up at him. And in that moment, everything went black, time froze, and the magnetic force completely took over my body. I leaned across, feeling as though I couldn't get close enough to him. Our lips touched and it was the most amazing kiss I've ever experienced. I had always known that he was the best kisser, but this was even better than past experiences with him. My hands stroked the back of his head. It felt like a scene straight out of a movie. My throat had traveled to my stomach, just as it had tended to do in the past when I'd been with him. When we finally stopped, we both smiled at each other.

"God, I've missed that," he said.

"Me, too," I said back.

We held hands again and we studied each other's faces. We looked so deeply into each other's eyes that it felt as if we could see each other's souls. We were re-familiarizing ourselves with something that we'd never forgotten, but that had changed over time.

"Do you think that other people have ever had the pleasure of feeling what we feel when we kiss? I mean, I've kissed my fair share of women, but there's something about when you and I kiss that is just... I don't know," he said.

"Magical?" I asked.

"Exactly," he replied.

"No. Nobody else has gotten to feel that, because nobody else is Nora and Andrew."

"Nordrew," he laughed. That was a nickname our friends had given us in college.

We both laughed and then found ourselves kissing again. And again, I couldn't get close enough to him.

"Do you ever wonder, if we were in a movie, would the audience be rooting for us to end up together? Or would they hate us?" I asked through a wondering smile, as we managed to take a break from our intense make-out session.

"I've never thought about it like that. I'd like to think that they'd root for us. We aren't bad people. What about you?"

"I don't know. I hope they wouldn't hate me for doing this

to Kyle," I looked down and fumbled with my wedding ring as I felt a pang of guilt.

"No, that's not what I meant," he said as he squeezed my hand, "Are you rooting for us to end up together?"

I honestly hadn't thought that deeply into what was occurring between us. Would I really leave Kyle? Would he leave Claire? My head started to spin.

"I don't know, Andrew. This is the craziest thing I've ever done. I can't even believe it's happening. It took me so long to get over you, and then here you are. I missed you every hour of every day for years. And then one day, I pushed the feeling down deep and stopped allowing it to surface. It never left; it just got pushed deep enough to allow me to finally move on," I said.

"I should have never taken that job offer in Austin. I thought we could handle the distance, and when we found out that we couldn't, I should have come home," he said, as he continued to look deep into my eyes. "It's that damned magnetic force between us, Nori. We couldn't stand the distance because of that. And then I tried to ignore it by staying. I'm sorry that I caused you pain for so long. You know, when you completely cut me out of your life, I ended up going to therapy for a while. The therapist told me that I needed to focus on who I was as Andrew, as opposed to who I was as Nordrew. I was finally able to start dating again, and that's when I met Claire." He looked out the window.

"You don't have to explain it to me. It is what it is. We can't go back in time," I replied. Really, I just wanted him to stop because hearing her name stung.

"I know I don't. But we are just two friends catching up,

so that's what I'm doing—catching you up. You know," he paused, "she cheated on me once. Well, technically twice."

I was shocked. I didn't know Claire, which was a good thing. But this revelation made me dislike her.

"No, I didn't know that. What's the story there? Bitch…" I said back to him, ignoring the fact that I was cheating on Kyle in this very moment.

"Ha! Well, it was about a year into our marriage. She'd been acting a little different, but I never suspected she'd cheat. Finally, the guilt got the best of her, I guess, and she confessed to me one day, out of the blue. The guy was a friend of a friend. One of those things. She said it didn't mean anything. She didn't have any feelings for him or anything. But she actually slept with the dude—twice."

My jaw dropped, as my distaste for her grew.

"We moved past it, and I honestly haven't thought about it in the last several years until you and I reconnected. I know that what you and I have going on here isn't the same thing. We aren't bad people. I guess I can see how you thought up that weird movie scenario. I think that Claire and her dude would probably have been viewed as villains in their movie. But I don't see us like that. We don't have some cheap, meaningless hookup situation occurring here. We're us." In that moment, without even hesitating, I leaned into his chest, closed my eyes, and said, "I love you."

He held me tight and said, "I never stopped."

As I drove away from him, my heart pounded, and my stomach tied into knots. I had just told the love of my life that I loved him, yet I was a married woman. And he had told me that he had never stopped loving me. And he was married!

This was uncharted territory for me. The whole situation was exonerating, but also tore me up with guilt. I thought back to mine and Kyle's wedding. I had said vows to him that I intended to follow. Maybe I was a villain in my movie. I knew I was in Kyle's life movie in that moment.

That night when I went to bed, Kyle pulled me close. I fell asleep with my head on his chest and it took everything in me to hold myself together.

As the days went on, Andrew and I continued to talk. We hadn't met up again, and we knew that we couldn't risk getting caught. I knew that he had already run into Alexis at the Y, and I was surprised she hadn't mentioned it to me. I assumed she was trying to protect me, but I kept waiting for her to bring it up when she had been drinking. Still, Andrew and I always talked as though we would see each other again soon. The Friday after our meet up was Brett and Chloe's barbecue. I snuck away a few times to sneak in a few messages with Andrew. One time, Steph almost caught me, but I don't think she noticed much of anything. She ended up having a panic attack, and I helped her to her van and then told myself I needed to be more careful. When Kyle and I got home that evening, I wondered if I had turned into a full-blown cheater. Of course, I had. I knew that answer, but I was constantly trying to justify my actions. But I knew that not one iota of this would be justifiable to Kyle. We made love that night, and when I pictured Andrew instead of Kyle, I knew I was in far, far deeper than I could have ever imagined.

ALEXIS

I felt like I was on cloud nine. I had taken a guy I was dating to meet all my friends and all their husbands, and for once, it went perfectly. I grinned over at Dean in the passenger's seat. Handsome, friendly, good manners— he was everything a great date should be. It was evident that the girls and their spouses were fans of him, as well. Even Johnathan and Blake snuck me a wink and a high five when Dean wasn't looking. I felt proud to have him with me. So many times before, I knew the girls' husbands didn't like my dates. They just didn't mesh well. But something was different about Dean.

Meeting him for the first time had been beyond exciting. We met at Hillstone, which is a nice restaurant in Preston Hollow. It's not ritzy, make-you-feel-unworthy-if-you're-underdressed nice, but it's nicer than an average restaurant. It was the perfect place for a first date. Dean had gotten there first, and when he spotted me, he stood as I approached. I could tell instantly that he was a true gentleman. Neither of us could help but smile. He was even more attractive in person, and I knew that he could tell that I was pleased. In return, I could tell he liked what he saw. I only hoped that he would like me for me as we got to know each other over dinner. Sometimes I was a little too much for a man. I'm loud—I'll admit that. And I curse like a sailor. But I've never been one to compromise who I am for a guy. I'm an in-your-face type of person, and that's just the way it is. Sure, I had fake boobs, Botox, fillers, blonde hair, and a spray tan. But those things make me feel good, and I'm all about feeling good.

I sat down, and Dean started our conversation with, "So, Alexis. What's your story?"

"Oh, Lord," I responded. "We're only here for dinner. My 'story' would take thirty-five years to tell." He liked my sarcasm, I could tell.

"Well, if you could condense thirty-five years into a dinner conversation, where would you start?" he asked as he took a drink of his water.

Our waitress approached and asked for our drink order. He ordered a Vodka Tonic and I ordered a glass of Merlot. She handed us our menus, and I continued talking.

"Well, I was born and raised here, in Texas. I obviously live here in Dallas, and I have a dog named Gibbs, whom I adore. I have four best friends who are like sisters to me. I have one brother, and both of my parents are living. I know you don't know much about the whole online dating thing, but I've been doing it long enough to know that you don't give out too much information about yourself on a first date. After all, you could steal my identity, Dean. If that's even your real name." We both laughed. "What about you? What's your story, as you say?" I asked.

Our waitress sat our drinks down and scurried away.

"Well, I'm not familiar with the ins and outs of online dating, but I can tell that I can trust you, Alexis. So I'll go ahead and give you the whole spiel. I was born in Oklahoma. My parents divorced when I was four, and my mom and I moved to Houston. I spent summers in Oklahoma with Dad but grew up in Houston. Mom married my step-dad when I was eleven. Mom's a waitress, and Jim owns his own roofing company. Dad is an electrician. I currently don't have any pets. I had a Border Collie mix who was my best friend. His name was Bevo, but I lost him to cancer last year. My heart hasn't healed enough for me to get another dog yet. I, too, have some good buddies, but none that I consider to be like brothers. I do have a half-sister down in Houston, and a couple of stepbrothers in Oklahoma."

I liked that he didn't say "my mom" or "my dad." Instead, he referred to them as if I knew them already. It was endearing. I listened intently as Dean continued to tell me the details of his life. I felt privileged that he'd share so much with me so soon.

"I went to school at UNT, and when I graduated, I got a job working at the club as the course manager. I didn't necessarily think I'd make a career out of it, but it's got its perks. I love meeting all the people, and I thoroughly enjoy the relationships I've formed with the regulars out there. Some of my conversations with the eighty-year-old men are some of my most valued moments. They have a lot of insight on life. Even though this specific moment would tell you otherwise, I'm a pretty good listener. I don't generally talk about myself." He laughed.

The more he talked, the more I liked him. And he was hot

as hell. I took a drink of my wine. Dean paused and took a drink, too.

"I'm sorry, Alexis. I feel like I'm just going on and on. I want to know more about you. Just refrain from telling me your social security number." We both laughed.

Just then our waitress came to take our order.

"I'm apologize," Dean said. "We haven't even had a chance to look. Would you mind giving us another few moments?" She smiled and said of course.

We opened our menus and he said, "I know that some men order for the woman, but I'm not all about that. You are woman—I'll hear you roar your order. Is that okay?"

"Oh, thank God," I replied. "I hate when men order for me. So what are you thinking?"

"I'm thinking I like you, Alexis," he winked at me, and then said, "I'm thinking about getting the ribeye. What about you?"

"I'm gonna get the roasted chicken," I said. "You know what? Fuck it. I'll get the ribeye, too. YOLO, right?"

Dean laughed. I reminded him that I had a potty mouth, to which he replied, "I fucking love it."

Our dinner was perfect. If I could score it on a scale from one-to-ten for a first date, I would give it an eleven. We rode separately there, but I had Ubered. Dean asked if he could drive me home. I was always leery of letting any guy drive me home, especially on a first date. Being a sexual assault victim and a single woman living in today's fucked up world, I had to be cautious. But there was something very trusting about Dean.

"You know," I told him, "letting a guy drive me home is pretty high on my list of no-nos." He cocked his head, and his smile faded just a bit, like he was considering this with much thought. I couldn't stand him looking so grim, so I grinned. "But I think I'll allow it this one time."

"Well I feel so honored," he said.

We got in his truck and talked more about our pasts. He told me more about growing up in Houston, and his days at UNT. When we arrived at my apartment, he kept the truck running as he came around and opened my door.

"Listen, Alexis. I know you have a list of dating no-nos, but would you mind if I turned my truck off and came in for just one moment to do something?" he asked.

I felt aroused. Dean had been such a gentleman, and I was hopeful he'd kiss me at the truck. But if he wanted to come in and have sex, I was actually thinking that I'd break that rule and go for it.

"Oh, alright," I said, playing coy.

We walked to my door, and when I unlocked it and walked in, Dean barely stepped inside. Gibbs came running for me, and Dean knelt down.

"Come here, buddy," he said to him. He pet him on his ears, told him to shake, and then clenched his teeth together and talked baby talk to him.

"Nice to meet you, Gibbs," he said. Then, much to my surprise, he stood up and said, "Thank you for allowing me to come inside for that, Alexis. I had a wonderful evening with you. I'll definitely text you tomorrow. Goodnight."

Talk about sweeping me off my feet. The one thing that Dean had wanted was to meet Gibbs. I melted.

"Hold on a second, Dean. I allowed you to do something you wanted to do. Now will you return the favor and let me do something in return?"

He smiled, and I leaned in and kissed him. His lips were soft, and I could feel him smiling through the kiss. It was a romantic, genuine, chick-flick movie type of kiss. He was the gentleman I took him for, and he went home.

Deciding to take him to the barbecue had been an easy call. He just kept qualifying himself to stick around! I was blown away at his adoration for Gibbs that first time, and afterward, too. Of course, I made sure we went out a few other times before I even mentioned him to the girls, knowing that as soon as I did, they'd immediately find a way to get to meet him. And thus, the barbecue was born. I'd been glad to have him there with me, and of course, just as I suspected, everybody loved him. That night, we'd decided to head out before it got too late. I enjoyed sharing Dean with everybody, but I wanted some alone time with him, too.

On our drive back to my apartment, I reflected on the evening while I gazed out the window, when he dropped the fucking bomb on me.

"Alexis, listen," he started, "I don't want to start drama or anything, but I like you a lot, and I know how much your girlfriends mean to you," he began.

"Umm. Okaaaaaay?" I said. My heart rate picked up, and my stomach dropped. I had no clue where he was going with this. Had he slept with one of the girls a lifetime ago or something? What the hell was he talking about? My mind raced. I knew he was too good to be true, damnit.

"I know Brett," he said.

"What do you mean you know him?" I asked. That didn't even make sense.

"I know him, Alexis. He's a regular at the club," he replied.

"Well, why didn't either one of you say so? Why did y'all act like perfect strangers?" I asked as my voice got louder. In a split second, I was trying to convince myself that it was okay that the two of them knew each other. But then he continued.

"Alexis. I don't know how to say this. I realize that this could cost me my job, but I like you enough that that's a risk I'm willing to take. Brett is a regular at the club," he said. The inner corners of his eyebrows angled up. "... with his girlfriend," he finished.

"What the hell do you mean?" I realized I was screaming at him.

"I'm so sorry. I know how much you love Chloe. I don't know how to fucking handle this either. I just know that I have to be honest with you and tell the truth. And the truth is, Brett has a girlfriend. He's been coming to the club for months with her. I had no idea the scumbag was married."

"Maybe it's somebody else, Dean," I snapped. But I knew there was no way it was somebody else. I could tell that he wouldn't tell me such a thing if he wasn't one hundred percent sure. He knew how much it would hurt me, and he'd spare me that if he could. I could see that it was hurting him to tell me.

"It's not, Alexis. It's Brett... Brett and somebody else." he said.

And as much as I hated to because of my ugly-cry-face, the tears started streaming down my cheeks.

We got back to my apartment and Dean stayed over that night, though we didn't have sex. He got me some ice water and sat on the couch with me. I woke the next morning and found myself lying on his lap while he'd slept in an upright position. Gibbs was under his other arm. There was no way that he could have been comfortable, but he had stayed that way for me. Much like he'd told me about Brett.

CHLOE

I'd say that the barbecue was successful. There were a couple of kinks, but the evening ended on a positive note. Towards the end of the night, Brett and I got to sit around and visit with Johnathan and Blake, Nora and Kyle, and Alexis and Dean. Brett and I both really liked Dean. He passed the test with me, for sure. He seemed extremely attentive to Alexis, and I really appreciated that. Brett is like that with me, so it made me happy to see that Dean was the same in that aspect. He also liked Gibbs, which is especially important to Alexis. Not to mention, he's very attractive. I loved the thought that this guy might be the one for her. I knew they'd only been dating for a little bit, but I've always been an optimist.

The boys went back inside to play video games. Johnathan and Blake were the last to leave. Johnathan and Brett started talking business, so Blake helped me get everything cleaned up. I insisted that he not do anything, but he was persistent. The two of them are like family to us. They've seen Brett and I through most of our milestones. Blake and I formed a two-person assembly line while he rinsed dishes and I loaded the dishwasher. We chatted a little bit about their journey to have a family. Blake seemed discouraged about it, but I assured him that it would happen when the time was right. He asked me if I enjoyed Brett being home more lately and I laughed. "Oh, please! Brett and Johnathan are the busiest they've ever been. Lucky us, but it's a double-edged sword, isn't it?" I replied. "I miss him, but these big commissions have been nice. I know they make him feel good. The only time he isn't at the office or at a listing, it seems he's golfing with Johnathan and clients. The two of them spend so much time together; their menstrual cycles are probably the same!"

Blake and I laughed hard at that. I wouldn't make that joke with just anybody—probably only Blake, Johnathan, and the GBs.

We got some more quality time in as we relaxed on the couch, and finally our husbands joined us again. I instinctively hopped out of the chair and let Brett sit in his favorite spot, and I sat on his lap. In several ways, I still felt like we were the same as we'd been in high school.

When Johnathan and Blake left, I checked in on the boys and they were fast asleep. Brett and I went to bed, and again, I felt like we were in high school still.

The next morning I checked my phone. "T minus 24 hours, bitches!" Alexis had texted. I was so excited for our trip to San Antonio.

"Can. Not. Wait." Steph replied.

"Y'all don't even know how badly I need this," Ziah chimed in.

"Love you all and cannot wait to be floating in the lazy

river with all of you tomorrow!" Nora texted back.

"Aahhhh! So pumped! What are we doing other than staying at the pool all day? Do we have plans for the evenings? In other words, what are y'all packing?" I asked.

"I vote we eat at the resort tomorrow night, and then Uber out Saturday. I'm packing multiple bikini options, and a jumpsuit, a strappy dress, and shorts and a tank to wear down there. Oh, and sleepy clothes and all that jazz. I'll bring a hairdryer if somebody else wants to volunteer a curling iron. We shouldn't all pack everything if we are staying in one suite," Alexis said.

"I'll bring a curling iron and a lot of ibuprofen," Nora said.

"I'll bring a straightener, shampoo, and conditioner," Steph replied.

"I'll bring body wash, toothpaste, and lotion!" Ziah texted.

"Okay, don't forget to bring whatever you're gonna drink in the room! I'll also bring snacks," I said.

I really was so excited. I had plans to meet Nora and Steph again to work out. I wondered if Alexis wanted to join. She worked out regularly, but usually didn't do any classes unless they were yoga.

"Hey, girlie! I'm meeting Nora and Steph for Body Pump at 11. Do you want to join?" I hit send, and then followed it with a GIF of a weightlifter.

"I'll pass, but thank you for the invitation. I'm actually going to lunch with Dean, and I've already done yoga this morning and taken Gibbs on a run," she responded.

I wished she could join us, but we'd all be together the next day, anyway.

When I got to class, I was surprised that Nora wasn't there

yet. I went ahead and started setting up all our stations with our equipment. Setting up for Body Pump was exhausting enough, and the work out hadn't even started!

Steph came in right before the warm-up began, and I was in absolute shock to see her before Nora. Nora usually didn't run late, and I started worrying about her. Steph asked where she was, and I told her I hadn't seen her yet and hadn't heard from her since our texts earlier in the day about our trip. I hoped she hadn't been in a wreck. That's how unusual it was for her to be late.

"Wow. I don't know that I've ever arrived before Nora," Steph noted. "But that's kinda scary, actually. I hope she's okay."

Just then, the studio door opened. Looking down at her phone, smiling, in walked Nora.

"What the hell?" I whispered to myself, but Steph could hear.

"Who the hell is that? And what has she done with our friend?" she responded.

She looked up and waved at us, jogging over. She put her keys, wallet, and phone against the mirrored wall that we'd set up next to and acted like everything was totally normal.

"Thanks for setting me up, guys. I'm so pumped for tomorrow! But speaking of pumped, let's get through this damned class one last time before we are in swimsuits in public, shall we?"

Steph and I shot each other a look and continued with our workout.

After class was over, Steph suggested lunch. Her kids were at her mother-in-law's house. My boys had both stayed over at friends' houses the night before, and I wasn't due to pick them up until after two. Nora said she needed to go by Target to get some last-minute things for the trip. So Steph and I opted to go—just the two of us.

We decided on a sushi bar close to the Y. When we sat down, Steph said exactly what I had been thinking.

"What the hell is up with Nora? She's never late like that. And who the hell is she texting?" she asked.

"I don't know! It was so unlike her! Maybe she and Kyle are doing really well all the sudden, and she's texting him," I replied. But Steph and I both knew that the odds of that being true were low.

"I don't know, Chlo. The look on her face lately when she's been on her phone reminds me of a giddy teenager. It's so strange."

"I know exactly what you mean. I don't know what is going on, but hopefully we'll get it out of her over the next couple of days."

"Yeah. The GBs don't keep secrets," Steph said.

"Mmm hmmm," I replied. I took a sip of my drink and changed the subject.

STEPH

I was so excited for our trip. My anxiety had been starting to rear its ugly head more frequently, but there was no rhyme or reason why. Mark hadn't been playing as many gigs on the weekends, the kids were helping me out around the house, and I had been diligent about working out. I felt like a weekend away from home in the sun could either be a recipe for disaster or beneficial. I wasn't sure how to plan for the trip as far as medication. I didn't know if I should take one of my anxiety pills ahead of time each day, or just roll the dice and hope it didn't hit. If I took a pill, then I couldn't drink, and that would be a big bummer for a GB trip. The girls would be disappointed. So I planned to make the road trip medication free, and then see how I felt when we arrived. We chose our hotel because it was in the Hill Country instead of the city, so I was hopeful that I could relax.

The day before the trip, I met Nora and Chloe for one last workout class before the trip. It was unusual that I arrived before Nora. Both Chloe and I noted that unusual detail, and when

Nora walked in, she didn't even seem like herself. After class, Chloe and I grabbed lunch while the kids were at Gayle's, and we talked about Nora's behavior. Both of us had noticed that she'd been acting differently, but neither of us could figure out what exactly had been going on. I had a suspicion that she was doing something she shouldn't be doing, but I wanted Chloe to mention it first—I didn't want to assume the worst of our friend. But she never did. Instead, we only talked about how she was acting differently. Chloe seemed to think we might be able to get it out of her over the weekend, but I wasn't so sure. It was completely unusual for one of us to have a secret from the rest of the group, but it was clear that Nora did.

When I picked Ava, Logan, and Benjamin up from Gayle's, I took them to get ice cream. I wanted to spend some quality time with them before I left the next day. I always felt a little bit of mom guilt any time I left them. Though, I had to remind myself that Mark would sometimes leave for entire weekends at a time with his band. At the ice cream shop, the kids each ordered a different flavor, and I decided that I'd get one scoop, too. It would probably negate our entire hour spent working out, but it was worth it. I chose banana pudding flavor. It was one of my favorites, and they didn't always have it in stock, so I was sure to savor every bite. I didn't allow myself to indulge often, after all. The kids were well behaved and getting along wonderfully with each other. I sat back and watched them giggling and snapped a photo with my phone. I wanted to savor these moments. You hear all too often how one moment they're children, and the next they're grown. Plus, there are all those things floating around on social media about how many weekends you have until a child turns eighteen. Things like that make me feel guilty when I spend weekends away from them. I put a black and white filter on the photo and opened my Instagram to share it.

The first photo I saw when I opened my app was Nora. She looked beautiful. Her brown hair was intentionally loosely curled, and she had longer eyelashes than I recalled. Her makeup was gorgeous. It wasn't a look that she wore to the hospital, but we all hadn't been out together recently with her looking like this. I wondered where she had been, and why she had posted a selfie like that. I navigated to her account and saw that most of her recent photos were similar. Beyond that point, her photos were usually our group, the sunset, or the cityscape, except for a few photos of her alone, and a few of her with Kyle. I noticed there hadn't been any posted with Kyle for a long time. I felt badly for him. He was a good guy, but it hadn't fit that Nora ended up with him. I saw a photo of her sitting on Chloe's front porch in the porch swing. It was the evening of the barbecue, and it must have been either right before or right after I caught her off guard in that very position. I wondered if that's all she had been doing in that moment—posting a selfie on Instagram. That seemed more innocent than what my mind had tried to convince me she was doing. I clicked on the photo and it only had a few likes. I tried to like it, but instead I accidentally clicked to view everybody who had liked it.

"Oh shit," I said out loud.

"Mommy!" Benjamin yelled.

"Oh, uh, I'm sorry, baby. Mommy didn't mean to say that. Are y'all almost finished?" I stammered. I hated cursing in front of my kids. That one just slid right out.

"Mom! I can't believe you just said that!" Ava exclaimed.

That just added to my disappointment in myself for having let the word slip out. I looked at Logan who was trying not to laugh. I gathered up all our trash and chunked it as I rushed the kids and myself out of there. I couldn't wait to get in touch with Alexis. I had to talk to her before our trip.

"Can you talk?" I texted her.

"I'm with Dean right now. What's up?" she replied.

"Info on Nora. I think she knows Andrew is in town. We need to talk," I texted back.

"I'll call you in 5," she said.

It took me about fifteen minutes to get home. I hit the magical button underneath the rearview mirror in the van that slid the doors open automatically and told the kids to go inside. I didn't care if people made fun of minivans. They are the best invention in the world for families. Alexis hadn't called yet, which was odd for her, but if she was with Dean, I knew she didn't want to seem suspicious sneaking away to have an important chat with me. I opened Instagram again and did some more investigating. Andrew had liked several of Nora's photos. I clicked on his profile and saw that she had liked his in return. He looked extremely handsome. Even more so than I remembered. I was scrolling through his account, trying to find out if he was still married, when Alexis's face popped up on my screen as an incoming call.

"Hello?" I said.

"Tell me what you know." She got right down to business. I could tell that she didn't have much time. She must have told Dean she had to use the restroom or something.

"Chloe and I went to work out with her a little bit ago. She was late. She walked in looking down at her phone and smiling. It's a smile that I can't describe. I'm sure you've noticed it lately. I reminds me of a teenager in love. Or…"

Alexis cut me off: "Somebody cheating?"

"Exactly. I hate to jump to conclusions and even use that word. But I looked on her Instagram and they follow each other! And they like each other's photos! First of all, stupid move for cheaters. Second of all, he looks really good, Alexis!"

"I told you he did! Okay, listen. I did some investigating the day I ran into him at the gym, after you and I met up, and I saw that they follow each other. I didn't want to burden you with it since you had been dealing with anxiety. I didn't want to add to it. Ziah knows as much as you and I know. Does Chloe know?" she asked.

It stung a bit that she had confided in Ziah instead of me. Especially when I had been the one who met her for brunch after she ran into Andrew. I didn't know she'd shared any of it with Ziah.

"No. Chloe's noticed her odd behavior lately, but she hasn't put anything together. But then again, she has no clue that he's in town. I really should have put all of this together sooner," I said to her. "I wish you would have updated me," I admitted.

"Oh, Steph, I didn't want to upset your anxiety. Don't get sensitive about it. Listen, I've got to get back to Dean. He probably thinks I'm taking a major shit right now, and I can't have that! I'll see you tomorrow. Maybe she'll tell us over the weekend. You think?" she rambled off.

"No. I don't think. But I do want to talk more about it. Let's not tell Chlo for now. She's too optimistic and cheery for this. I don't want to pop her bubble of bliss right now."

"Deal. Hey, Steph? I'm sorry I didn't tell you. I love you. We'll get to the bottom of this. Secrets secrets are no fun. Secrets secrets hurt someone. Okay! Gotta go! Muah!" She hung up before I could respond.

ZIAH

I was still pissed off at Lizzie. In fact, I was always pissed off at Lizzie. She's a nightmare as an ex-wife to Leon and a nightmare as a co-parent. The only thing I like about her is that she loves Cyrus. She doesn't always know what's best for him, but she does love him. I hated to give her so much control over me, and I knew that she loved that part of it all. I had a big case I was working on, and I was trying to get as much work done as possible before our big weekend. I had put in a few long nights at the office, and the day before we left, I decided I'd leave work in a timely manner and get some quality time in with Leon and Cy. Lizzie was dropping him off that day, and then our summer custodial time with him would really begin. She had subtracted the days that we had him when we weren't supposed to, but it all evened out in the long run. I was just finishing up and giving one of our paralegals some files when Leon texted me.

"Baby, Sherry just called. There's a situation."

"Tell me more," I replied. The timing was far less than

perfect, but just about every time we got a call, we felt that way. But we always made it work.

"4 year old female named Layla. No dad in the picture. Mom is a meth head. Grandma is working on getting her, but she needs a placement until she passes. Thoughts?"

"You know my thoughts. All in."

"All in," he wrote back.

I raced out of there in my stilettos and pencil skirt. The elevator seemed to move in slow motion. I wanted to get home as soon as possible so I could be home when she arrived.

A text from Alexis buzzed in my Prada bag. "T Minus 16 hours exactly!"

"Wahoo! Two countdowns in one day! That means we're super close! Should I just go to sleep now and sleep for 15 hours?! It's like Christmas Eve!" Chloe responded.

"I'll see you ladies in the morning! I'm packing right now and then gonna have an early dinner with the fam. Apologies in advance if I don't text back much tonight. Love y'all! Can't wait!" Steph replied.

"Can't wait!" Nora said. It was a short response from her. I assumed she must be working.

I quickly sent, "Yay! I'm headed home now. We are getting a new arrival. I'll give y'all the deets tomorrow. And don't worry, I'm still coming! :)" I knew they'd think that I might back out, but I've never backed out of a Good Bra weekend, and I didn't plan to start now.

I pulled into our gated neighborhood, and the damned gate seemed to take its sweet time opening for me. Leon and Cyrus were playing catch out front, and I was relieved to see that Layla hadn't arrived yet. I got out of the Range Rover and kissed Leon. Then I knelt down and gave Cy a big hug and kissed his sweet head.

"Lizzie really should educate herself more on his hair, Leon," I said.

"I know. I try to tell her, delicately. Maybe we can convince her to let us get it done while we've got him," he said.

I rolled my eyes. "Riiiiiiiiiiight. And monkeys will fly out of my you-know-what," I joked with him.

I dropped my stuff inside, and when I came back out, a car was pulling up. We had been through this process enough times to know the routine. Sherry stepped out with some paperwork and walked around to the other side of the vehicle to unbuckle Layla. When she walked up, holding her hand, I said, "No luggage?"

"Not this time, Ziah. Baby girl doesn't have a thing. I hope y'all have pull-ups and some clothes for her," she responded.

We didn't. Every foster child that we had taken in before had come with a suitcase. I needed to go shopping ASAP, but I didn't have time. Our trip was getting closer, and I wanted to try to bond with Layla and spend time with Cy and Leon before I had to leave. This seemed to be the way my life went: always busy with rarely a moment to catch my breath.

We invited Sherry in, and she led the way to the formal dining room. She knew the routine with us, too. We went over everything that Sherry knew about Layla. Cyrus was only three years older than her, and Layla seemed to have connected with him right away. She smiled at him, even though she was reserved around the adults in the room. Her blonde hair was swept up in two messy pigtails. She wore a T-shirt that was at least three sizes too big for her and leggings that had holes worn in the knees. She wasn't even wearing shoes.

Situations like these ripped my heart apart. How could a mother care more about herself than her child? Sure, I didn't have any biological children. But I was maternal. I wouldn't dare let anything happen to Cyrus. I would put my life on the line for him in a heartbeat. Leon and I had based our choice not to have children yet on our careers and our passion for foster care. I was far too busy to take off work for maternity leave. And Leon's veterinary clinic was growing by the week. Were biological kids in the cards for us? Hopefully, eventually. God willing.

I sent Leon to the store to get the necessities that would get Layla through the weekend. I could shop for her more when I returned. I told him that if he thought of anything else she needed, just place an Amazon order. His shopping spree only lasted forty-five minutes from the time he left the driveway until the time he returned. I knew that sending a man would be a time saver. While he was gone, I tried to entertain Layla with some of Cyrus's old toys. She hadn't spoken a word since she'd been dropped off, and she wasn't easily entertained. The only time I had seen her smile was when she was paying attention to Cyrus.

Leon walked in with his arms loaded with sacks. He had gotten everything she needed: sippy cups, pull-ups, pajamas, a few outfits, a hairbrush, shampoo and conditioner that was better equipped for her hair than mine was. And shoes. He got to the last sack and pulled out a baby doll.

"Here you go, sweetie," he said to her. "You can name her whatever you want." I watched in awe as she gingerly reached out her arms to the baby and smiled.

"Mine," she said.

A tear rolled down my cheek as Leon said, "Yes, she is, sugar. She's all yours."

When Cyrus's bedtime rolled around, we put him in his room and Layla in the spare bedroom that we had all setup for the children who came in and out of our lives. There was a twin bed and a monitor. Leon and I both took Layla to bed. She got under the covers and smiled as she snuggled down into them. Something told me she had never had such a comfortable bed before—if she had even slept in a bed before at all. Leon pulled a book out of the closet and started reading *Goodnight Moon*. Before he even finished, Layla was fast asleep. I looked at him in awe. He really was the best man ever. Instead of going in our room and moving forward with the original plans that I had for the evening, which had involved Leon and a bubble bath, I asked Leon if he'd mind if I slept on the floor in Layla's room. He smiled at me and said, "Only if you let me crash the sleepover."

We got a couple of blankets and our pillows and fell asleep, cuddled up on the floor, almost instantly.

NORA

Before our GB trip, Andrew and I were able to sneak in one more meeting. Our texting had gotten hot and heavy, and I didn't know where our meeting up would lead. The thought of it made me feel reckless and excited. We decided to meet at Andrew's apartment, since nobody would see us there. I wore sunglasses and a hat like in the movies when characters are trying to be clandestine. I had a coworker cover my shift. Kyle would never know any differently. The company that Andrew was working for let him do some work from home, so we had covered all our bases.

As I walked in, my heart pounded in my ears. I felt like the universe was really bringing us together, just as I had hoped for all those years ago. I mean, what were the odds that he would get transferred up here? And then find me on Instagram. I had gotten a little bit nervous about our public Instagram behavior. We had both liked each other's photos, and he didn't know enough about it to realize that other people could see it. I didn't think much of it in the beginning, but I started realizing what a dumbass move it had been. Kyle wasn't on Instagram, but the girls were. None of them had mentioned anything to me, but that didn't necessarily mean anything. After all, Alexis knew he was in town and still hadn't mentioned *that* to me.

I arrived at the door to his apartment and looked around to make sure nobody was watching. I wore a tank top and blue jean shorts. It was nothing much, but Andrew always preferred me like that. I curled my hair a bit to give it some beach waves, and I put on some blueberry flavored Chapstick. I didn't love the flavor, but I liked the way it made my lips look. And I knew that Andrew loved blueberries.

When he opened the door, he grabbed my hands and pulled me inside. My stomach dropped. We were inside an actual room, where nobody could see us or hear us. I kept being haunted by the fact that I was married. But Andrew truly was the love of my life. I've never loved or been loved the way that Andrew and I had loved each other.

When his door closed, he kissed me. I pressed my body against his because I still couldn't get close enough to him. The kiss was everything that a kiss should be. When we came up for air, we looked at each other and smiled.

"God, I needed that," he said.

"What the hell are we doing?" I asked through a smile.

"I don't know, Nori. Still two friends catching up, I suppose," he replied. "Come on in. I haven't done much to the place. I apologize. It seems more like a bachelor pad than a home, but my spare time has been a little ... preoccupied, I guess." His dimple melted me again.

The walls were bare, but he had nice furniture. The place was clean. Andrew had always been tidy back in the day. I told him that the shape his apartment was in made no difference to me. We made our way to the couch and sat down.

"Listen, Nori. I don't want to make you feel uncomfortable. I don't want to push things," he said. He didn't touch me as he spoke. The magnetic force got the best of me, and I put my hand on his arm. I could feel his bicep through his shirt, and it turned me on. Andrew had always been strong, but he seemed even stronger and more masculine now.

"I'm a big girl, Andrew. I make my own decisions, okay?" I replied. I didn't let my eyes slip away from his gaze for a long time. He continued to smile at me and when I blinked, my blinks felt long, as if I were blinking in slow motion. He mesmerized me completely. Our connection mesmerized me wholly. *How could I have married Kyle?* I thought. *Why did I give up on us? Why didn't I fight for us? For this?* He could tell that I was in deep thought.

"What are you thinking about?" he asked.

"I just don't know how we ever let each other go. Why didn't we fight for us? Why did we think that we could have this with anybody else? I don't know if you and Claire had this in the beginning, but I've never felt this way about anybody. I mean it when I say that you're the love of my life. I should have followed you. I could have finished nursing school closer to you. We shouldn't have given up. And now look at what a fucking mess we've made." I started to cry. I wasn't sure if I was crying because I'd missed him so much over the years, or because I felt so bad for Kyle and Claire. It was probably a combination of both.

"Hey. Don't cry, Nori. We're here. I'm here. You're here. We can change our paths. I never expected to live a life without you. And when I was forced to, I just made the best of it. But the best of the life I made never even compared to the worst with you. You're the love of my life, too, Nora. I mean that. I would never, ever do something like this with anybody else. I'm not some slime ball. I've never cheated on anybody or with anybody before. When we parted ways, I was a mess. That's why I went to therapy—I had to learn to live without you. As much as I didn't want to, the therapist had been right. I had to figure out who I was alone, post Nordrew. And then I met Claire. I knew you didn't want anything to do with me, so I moved on. It's the only thing I could do. I should have waited, Nora. Or come back home. I should have followed my gut, but I didn't. I didn't want to cause you any more pain than I already had by leaving. So I let you go. But I don't ever want to let you go again." He held my face with his hand. I noticed then that he wasn't wearing his wedding band.

"God, Andrew. Why can't we just rewind time?" I asked.

"Well, you're all about the universe. What if we had stayed together, and something awful had happened to one of us? What if the only way we could be happy was to be apart for all this time? What if the universe saved us by separating us?" he asked. I liked that he was thinking that way.

"I've never thought about that. But maybe you're right. Do you think we are home wreckers? I mean it. If we were in the movie I keep referring to, would people think we are awful, home-wrecking antagonists? Or would they root for us? We aren't bad people. How did we end up here?"

"Stop worrying about what everyone else thinks, Nori. We only have one life, and we decide how we live it," he said.

"I don't know what to do about Kyle," I confessed. "He's

a good guy, Andrew. He doesn't deserve this. And what about Claire? I know she was bad to you a while ago, but surely she's a good person?" I said.

"She is, Nori. But she's not the one. And I'm sure Kyle is fine and dandy, but you said yourself, he's not the one. Do you want to live the rest of your life in mediocracy because you feel guilty being happy?"

"Did you know I had a miscarriage?" I said suddenly.

"Wait. What? When? Oh, my God. I'm so sorry." I could tell I had caught him off guard.

"Last year. It knocked me down for quite a while, emotionally. Mentally…" I trailed off.

"Oh man, Nora. It must have been devastating for y'all," he replied.

"Well, it was devastating for me. Kyle didn't ever seem phased by it. You hear about loss making people closer or driving them apart, and I certainly don't think it brought us any closer. He never really understood the grief I had. I was a mess, and he was just… quiet. He didn't hold me when I needed to be held. He started working more. When I needed him most, he became the most distant he had ever been. I just don't think he knew how to handle it. And I've heard that a lot of men don't, but I just think that as my husband, he could have done better."

"He should have done better, Nori. I want to kick his ass for that," he said. And I could tell that he really was mad. The vein on the left side of his forehead bulged a little when he got mad.

"No, no. Don't go talking like that. It's fine now. I threw myself into work and started working out more, and I pulled myself out of the dark hole I was in," I replied.

"Well I'm so, so sorry you had to go through that alone." He was still visibly upset.

"I wasn't completely alone. I had the girls." I smiled.

"Thank God for them," he replied. "I've actually missed them, too, Nori. It was hard enough to lose you, but to lose some of my closest friends that I had gained through you added to the pain, for sure."

"You're sweet. I know they're amazing. I'm sorry for you that I kept them, but I'm so damn happy for me that they're mine," I said. I smiled at the thought of them.

Andrew laughed, and then he kissed me again. The fireworks bursting in my brain sped up. We lay down on the couch while we made out. I wanted him so badly, but I wasn't going to go there. He never pushed for more than kissing, and I appreciated that. I wasn't sure how much of him I could resist, even if I was dead set in my mind not to do something. We talked some more and made out some more, and eventually our hourglass of bliss ran out.

He walked me to the door, and I felt a trembling as if I were about to cry. I didn't want to leave him. I had spent so much of my life without him, that I didn't want to spend another moment that way. But I had to. At least for now.

I drove away from his apartment, wondering what the hell I was going to do. Kyle was a good guy. And I did love him. But was I doing him a disservice by not loving him completely? Obviously, I was doing him a disservice by having an affair with my college boyfriend. But had I ever loved him enough? I knew the answer to that. And it made me sad. I was an awful wife.

A couple of days passed, and Andrew and I continued to message each other. I told him that we needed to stop liking each other's photos on Instagram, and he completely agreed. Just as I suspected, he hadn't realize how it all worked. He told me that the only reason he signed up for an Instagram account was because he hoped he could find me that way. He knew it was more discreet than other forms of social media.

I was about to walk into the gym to meet Chloe and Steph when I checked to see if he had sent anything. I had one new message.

"I love you. I always have, and I always will. I just wanted to remind you of that. Have fun at your workout."

"I love you, too," I wrote. I tried to sit in my car for a moment and let the blood that had rushed to my face subside. When I finally felt like I looked normal, I entered the gym.

PART TWO

CHLOE

The day finally arrived. I was so pumped for our trip that I couldn't stand it. Dean would come by my house with Alexis to pick me up and then take us to Steph's. Leon would drop Ziah off at Steph's, and Nora would drive herself and leave her car at Steph's for the weekend. Brett had already left for work, and the boys were staying with friends for the day.

When Dean and Alexis pulled up, I laughed when I saw Gibbs in the window. Dean honked the horn a couple of times and they both waved at me, smiling. I stood out front next to my rolling suitcase as if I was a kid waiting on the school bus. I excitedly waved back to them and raced to the truck.

"Pardon me, Gibbs," I said, as I hopped in the back seat. He licked my hand and then scooted over. I appreciated that Gibbs wasn't an in-your-face type of dog. He allowed you to make the first move of affection, and then he'd follow your lead. I didn't want to smell like dog, so I didn't touch him the rest of the way. And in true Gibbs form, he respected that. Dean and Alexis were so happy together. I knew that she hated to leave him, but she was equally excited for this getaway. When we arrived at Steph's, she had all the doors of her minivan opened for us. Her hair was completely untamed, and her toothbrush hung out of her mouth.

"Sorry! I'm running just a few minutes behind but go ahead and put your bags in the van. You can come in for a cup of coffee, or y'all can get in the van. I think 'Secret Life of Pets' is in the DVD player if you'd like to watch a movie," she joked.

Dean put our bags in the van for us.

I opted to go inside and take Steph up on that cup of coffee and leave Alexis and Dean alone for their goodbye. It was exhausting watching Steph run around the house. She'd come through the room with her shirt halfway on, and then disappear, only come back with a totally different shirt on. I could tell she hadn't finished packing ahead of time, and it totally stressed me out. I hate when people wait until the last minute.

Nora pulled up and I opened the front door and waved her in. She put her suitcase in the back of the van and locked her car. She and Alexis came in together. Dean had just pulled out. I hugged Nora tightly. "I can't wait!" I said with my happy hands. She laughed and I led her to the coffee in the kitchen. As she was adding creamer, Ziah and Leon pulled up. We all raced out to see her new addition she had mentioned. Ziah jumped out of the car and held her hand up as an indication for us to stop.

"I'm sorry, y'all, but she's a little nervous. I don't want to bombard her with more strangers in such a short time." Ziah was so smart about that kind of stuff. Leon put her bag in the van, and they kissed goodbye.

Soon after, the four of us sat in Steph's living room, drinking coffee, waiting on her. I usually don't get impatient, but I had looked forward to this trip so much that I didn't want to be cheated out of one second of it.

"Is there anything we can do to help you, Steph?" I asked, as she did another lap past us.

"No. I'm just trying to find my other earring, and then I'll be good to go," she said.

It was no surprise that she was missing something. When she finally found it, she screamed in celebration. Leave it to Steph to leave one earring in an upstairs bathroom, and the other on the soap dish on the kitchen sink. I shook my head, and we all headed to the van.

"Let's do the damn thing!" Ziah said.

"I wish I could close my eyes, and then open them, and we'd be there," Steph said.

"I'll drive if you'd rather sleep, Steph," I volunteered.

"No, no. Driving will keep me focused. It's best for me if I drive. Thank you, though, Chlo."

"So tell us all about the new addition, Z!" Nora brought up what we had all been thinking.

"Oh, man. She's so freaking cute, y'all. Her name is Layla. She's four years old, and she came to us with literally the clothes on her back and that's it. She didn't even have shoes! She doesn't have a father in the picture, and her mom is on meth. Eventually, her grandmother will likely get custody, but she's got to go through the whole process. So I imagine we'll have her for at least a month or two."

We were all horrified to hear that she didn't have anything, and even more horrified to hear that her mother cared more about drugs than her. But that seemed to be a common denominator with the kids Leon and Ziah fostered. She also told us about the whole Lizzie summer custody thing, and it made us hate her even more.

"And I know you guys don't know much about black hair, but that girl does not know how to take care of Cy's hair! She needs to educate herself. I wish she'd educate herself on more than just his hair, for that matter." She was always irritated that Lizzie treated Cyrus like he was white instead of mixed. Ziah wanted Cy to embrace his culture, but Lizzie did everything she could to squash that.

Nora told us a few stories from the hospital that made us laugh, and Alexis told us more about Dean.

"He's really too good to be true. I don't know how I got so lucky, but I feel like something is going to jinx it or I'll fuck it up somehow. He's staying at my apartment this weekend so that Gibbs doesn't have to be boarded. He said there's absolutely no reason for that, when he's right there. His love for Gibbs adds to his perfection. We like the same kind of music, the same movies—he is a huge fan of The Office, and we laugh non-stop."

"How's the sex?" Steph asked from the driver's seat.

"Y'all won't believe it, but we haven't had sex yet. He's just such a gentleman. He's stayed over several times, and I've stayed at his place once, but we've been taking it pretty slow. It's sexy in a way. It makes me want him even more. I think it'll be happening soon, though. And y'all will be the first four to know!" She laughed.

"Steph, how you doing up there?" Ziah asked. Nora was in the passenger seat.

"So far, so good! We'll be in San Antonio in no time!" she said.

"I made a playlist for the trip. I tried to add all of our old faves," I said. Steph set my phone up to her Bluetooth, and we sang Britney Spears at the top of our lungs.

As we finished belting out Wilson Phillips as loudly as we could, we arrived at our hotel. The car ride flew by. Every moment flies by with the GB.

When we got out and the bellman gathered our luggage, Steph handed the keys to the valet. Alexis started laughing and said, "Okay, Steph, don't shoot me."

"Oh, God. What, Alexis?" she said back to her.

"I didn't want to tell y'all this until we arrived safely, because I didn't want Steph to be a nervous wreck ... but I brought us a joint!" She laughed to herself.

"Oh, my God, Alexis! Do you realize I could have been arrested if we had gotten pulled over?" Steph replied.

"Calm the fuck down. No, you wouldn't have. I would have taken the blame. And Ziah would have kept all of us out of trouble in the long run."

"Oh, no you don't. Don't bring me into this matter. I'm glad you didn't tell us until now because I would have located the damn thing and gotten rid of it myself," Ziah said. "I could lose my license as a foster parent, Alexis. Don't be pulling shit like that anymore."

"Okay, okay. I'm sorry. But I won't be when we smoke it!" Alexis laughed.

I couldn't believe she brought a joint, but at the same time, I was surprised she'd never brought one on a prior GB trip. I wasn't that judgmental about weed, really. It's legal all over the place. But it isn't in Texas. And aside from Steph freaking out, Z had good reason to be upset.

"If you don't want to smoke it, don't partake. But I know I'll be smoking it on this trip fa shizzle. Especially if you hussies are going to throw it away if we have to ride back with it!" Alexis said.

"I gotta see this," Nora chimed in.

"I won't be partaking, but I'll definitely be watching," I said.

"Well, I know that Z and I won't be around for it," Steph huffed.

"Okay, let's drop it for now and go see our suite." Ziah was always good at changing the subject.

Our room was gorgeous. We had a living room area and two bedrooms. Each room had two beds in it and its own bathroom. It was exactly what we needed. We truly could have been happy in a regular guest room, but they only allow four people to a room. The double bathrooms would certainly help, though. Our immediate plan was to put on our suits and go to the lazy river. I poured us all glasses of rosé, then threw my suit on and checked my face in the mirror. I didn't care too much about what I looked like on these trips, but I knew that photos would be taken. When everybody came out looking like movie stars, I suggested we toast. We all grabbed our wine, and I asked if anybody had a specific toast for us.

"I do," Nora said. "Here's to being comfortable, supportive, lifting each other up, and making each other seem better than we are. May we always continue to be good bras."

"Here, here!" Steph said.

We touched our plastic cups together and downed the wine quicker than ever so we could hurry up and get outside.

When we opened the doors to exit the lobby and entered the outdoor resort area, Alexis said, "San Antonio, you don't know what the fuck you're in for."

ALEXIS

I was so pumped to arrive in San Antonio, but I hated to leave Dean and Gibbs, even though I liked the idea of my boys spending time together. Dean planned to work at the club while we were out of town but spend nights at my apartment so he could take care of Gibbs. The two of us had gotten close quickly. Everything was going exactly how one would hope a new relationship would go. He'd been so supportive, especially since I had the weight of Brett cheating on Chloe added to whatever Nora and Andrew were up to on my shoulders.

I told him about Nora and Andrew, and he suggested that I let whatever was happening happen, and that Nora would tell us when she was ready. Regarding Brett, Dean was super pissed. He felt like he knew Chloe well just from meeting her the one time, and from hearing so many stories about her from me. He knew she was like a sister to me. He told me more details about Brett and his girlfriend. She was young, he guessed in her twenties. He said they had been all over each other when they came to the club. She drove a Mercedes SUV.

We didn't know her name, but Dean said he'd find out by looking back at membership information. We hadn't figured out how to address the issue yet, but it was something I wasn't going to be quiet about for long. We both knew that Brett could potentially have Dean fired if he got pissed enough, so we had to tread lightly.

Dean had recently deleted his Bumble account, because he said he didn't need it anymore. I told him that he was silly, but really, I was completely flattered. I hoped I could delete all my dating apps, but I would give it more time before I made such a bold move. He and I still hadn't even slept together yet. But we were getting more intimate, more hands-on and turned on. We connected on a different level than I had connected with any man I had dated before. He was extremely genuine. When we were together, we'd listen to music or watch TV and snuggle on the couch. He was attentive to me—and he adored Gibbs.

Dean drove Chloe and me to Steph's house for our road trip. After he loaded our luggage into Steph's van, we had a moment to ourselves to say goodbye. He kissed me on the lips and then my forehead. I knew I was going to really miss him. I had grown accustomed to sleeping in his arms lately.

"I'll miss you," I said, leaning into him.

"Hey, in the words of the great poet Usher Raymond, 'You got it you got it bad, if you miss a day without your friend your whole life's off track.' I got it bad, Alexis. I'll have to throw myself into work while you're gone. Have fun but stay in touch. I want to know you're safe, at least."

He kissed me again, and I told Gibbs to be a good boy. I watched them pull away and for the first time in the history of our GB weekends, a part of me wanted to stay home.

Back at the resort, the lazy river was stunning, but we quickly made our way to the adults-only pool. It overlooked an expansive golf course, and the view was breathtaking. A waiter approached our group and took our order. We decided to start off with piña coladas all the way around. I kept thinking about the joint I'd packed and how the girls acted so uptight about it, but I knew the perfect time for it would come.

I complimented all the girls on their swimsuits. Often, I was surprised how a group of five very different women could be so stylish in separate ways. I would happily wear any of the suits each of the ladies wore. I particularly liked Steph's one piece—it was sexy and not a mom suit. She looked hot in it. We made small talk, and I kept wondering if Nora would give us any kind of hint that things had been less than ideal at home. She was always so good about diverting attention off herself, though. She loved to hear stories about everybody else and didn't talk about herself nearly as much as everybody else did.

Ziah never seemed to realize how much she talked about her life and didn't ask much about everyone else. I knew that when she did ask about the other girls, she had to make a conscious effort to do so. I didn't blame her, though. She was always being recognized for one thing or another, and she was very important in every role she played. She'd become accustomed to being the center of attention. I always knew this particular trait bothered the girls at various times, though. Chloe started talking about Brett and I had to turn away. I could barely hold my liquor down at the thought of him. *What a piece of shit*, I thought to myself. I knew I couldn't let myself get too drunk on the trip, or I'd end up having diarrhea of the mouth, and spewing everybody's secrets out. Don't get me wrong, I'm obviously good at keeping secrets. But these two issues were taking a toll on me, and if somebody hit the right chord with me, I wasn't quite sure I could withhold the information any longer. As the other girls ordered another drink, I got a water.

"What the hell is that about?" Ziah asked.

"Pacing myself, Z. If we're gonna be in the sun all day, I can't be drinking the whole time. I told y'all, I'm getting old. I can't hang like I used to," I said. That wasn't quite true—I could hang like a college kid, but the excuse sounded legit.

"Stop with the old talk! We've all got a few years on you! You're the baby!" Steph reminded me. I didn't like it when she referred to me as "baby," because when she said it, it always had a negative undertone.

I swam over to Nora, who was in a trance, looking at the beautiful view.

"What ya thinking, boo?" I asked innocently. I suspected that I knew.

"Oh. You scared me. I'm just taking in all of the beauty," she replied.

"You wanna go ride the slide with me?" When I said it, I actually felt quite young, like a kid asking another kid.

"You know it!" she exclaimed.

We told the girls we'd be back, and we walked over to the tube slides we had noticed when we found our way to our main perch. While we waited in line, I wondered if I should take the opportunity to ask Nora about Andrew. She had asked me about Dean and I told her more about how close we had gotten in such a short time. I explained the heat that I felt between us when all we were doing was kissing, and she said she completely knew what I was talking about. I wondered if she was referring to her and Kyle, her past with Andrew, or her present with Andrew. Had they kissed recently? I couldn't take it anymore.

"Nora. What the fuck is going on with you and Andrew?" I surprised myself as much as I surprised her.

"What? Nothing. What are you talking about?" She tried to play coy.

"I know he's in Dallas. And I know you know I know he's in Dallas. Nora. It's me here. I'm not stupid. And I'm not naive. I may not have some fancy pants job title, but I'm a smart woman. I can read people well, and you know that. I know something is up with you and Andrew." Just then, in the worst timing ever, Chloe approached us.

"I want to ride! Don't sneak off like that again! I turn my back for one second and you two take off for the fun. I thought y'all were just going to the restroom or something!" She had cut in line to join us.

Damnit, I thought as I shot Nora a look.

"Sorry, Chlo. We had the sudden urge to ride these slides. We should have asked everybody, but I knew another round of drinks was on its way," I said.

Nora looked at me with pleading eyes. She was busted, and she knew it. But she didn't dare want me to continue talking about it in front of Chloe.

"No problem. I just want to get in as much fun as possible!" Chloe responded. "I think we are gonna order a couple of appetizers to share at the pool to hold us over until dinner. They were talking about the different restaurants here. It sounds like they're craving Mexican food, but I bet that they'll be so drunk soon, they won't care where we eat."

"How does Steph seem to be holding up to you guys?" I asked.

"Exceptionally well!" Chloe exclaimed. "I'm proud of her. I don't want to mention it to her, because sometimes when she seems to think about the anxiety, it makes her feel anxious. But she seems to be doing really well. I think this is the perfect location."

"I was thinking the same thing," I said. "She's a trooper."

"Maybe she'll get so drunk that she'll forget all about it," Nora said.

"I don't think it works like that," I responded.

"I know. Wishful thinking." She winked at me.

ZIAH

We usually try not to use our phones much on our GB trips, but the girls knew that I'd have to make an exception on this one. I needed to make sure Layla was adapting well, and that there were no changes in her family's legal situation. Our road trip to San Antonio had gone really well. We laughed at how easily we could all belt out songs together in the minivan. We felt like young, college-age girls again, and here we were, all cruising in the minivan—we laughed at the irony of it. After being in the adults-only pool for a while, I found myself alone with Steph, which was nice. I loved Steph, and sometimes I felt like the two of us got a little out of sync.

"How shocked do you think they'd be if the two of us took a shot while they're gone?" I asked. It was totally out of character for the two of us to take shots without being prompted by one of the others.

"Oh, my gosh! They'd freak! Let's do it!" she exclaimed. I was surprised. But then again, I had also stunned myself for even suggesting it. But it would be a fun bonding moment for us. We found our waiter and flagged him down.

"Two shots of... whatever you want to bring us!" I said. Again, out of character for me.

We were talking about Layla when our waiter returned with two shots on a tray.

"Hope you ladies like fireball!" he said.

We laughed and grabbed them from him.

"They're not going to believe us!" Steph said.

"To us, Steph!" I said.

"To us, Z!" she said back. We clinked our glasses and downed the shot. We laughed and laughed afterward. I started feeling buzzed almost instantly. It wasn't like me to drink so quickly, and I could tell Steph felt the same way.

"Hey, listen, Z. While they're gone ... I know about Andrew and Nora. I mean, I don't know exactly what's going on, but I know something is," she said, unexpectedly.

I was caught off guard. It made me uncomfortable to talk behind any of the girls' backs, but this was a rare situation. I didn't want to talk about it and risk having Nora come back suddenly. I didn't want to look guilty. But I figured that we had a few more moments of alone time.

"I can't believe it, Steph. In fact, I don't want to believe it. There is no proof that anything is going on other than the fact that they follow each other on Instagram. That's pretty innocent. The only thing that makes me think it could be more is the fact that she hasn't told us anything about him. I don't like it. I don't like any part of it. And you know that I adore Andrew. But I don't approve of this sneakiness. Whatever it is," I finished.

"I feel the exact same way. Honestly, I knew Kyle wasn't

right for her, but he doesn't deserve to be cheated on."

"Well, we don't know if there is any cheating going on. I don't want to think the worst of any of our girls. We don't keep secrets. But... apparently, we do," I trailed off and felt a pang of sadness at the reality of it.

"Okay, well I just wanted you to know that I'm in the loop. We can change the subject now. I don't want to get busted. We'll just have to take note of her behavior this weekend. We'll have to see how often she checks her phone and what not," Steph said.

It seemed as though Steph's intention of bringing up Nora and Andrew was to let me know that she knew rather than to discuss it. She tended to feel left out at times. I'd say that Steph is the most sensitive of the group. This was neither a good nor bad trait, but it caused us to have innocent misunderstandings throughout the duration of our friendship, because I tend to not be very sympathetic. It's something I try to work on within myself, but it's a work in progress. Steph's mentioning of Nora checking her phone reminded me that I should probably check mine before I got too drunk. I waded over to our chairs and left Steph to look out at the beautiful scenery alone. I got out of the water and fumbled through my bag until I found my phone. I was already tipsy, no doubt about it. I had five text messages and two voicemails.

"Ugh." I said out loud. I opened the texts.

"Hey, baby. Just wanted to let you know that things are going okay with Layla and Cy and me. Hope you're having a great time. Tell the girls hello for me."

"Hey, baby. Big news. Check your voicemail. Text me when you can! You're a superstar!"

"Call me! I'm too excited!"

And the last two were photos of Cy and Layla.

I wondered what could be going on. Maybe something with his job? The numbers from which I had missed calls weren't familiar. So it wouldn't be anything with the vet clinic. I plugged my left ear and put the phone up to my right ear while I strained to hear the voicemails.

"This call is for Ziah Mathis. My name is Penny Newman, and I'm with *O Magazine*. Please return my call at your earliest convenience." She left her number and hung up.

Weird. I thought. *I wonder what the hell O Magazine is calling about.* I clicked on the next message.

"Hey, Ziah. This is Penny Newman again. I confirmed this is your number with your office. We'd like to run a piece on you and what you've done to raise awareness about foster care. Please call me back as soon as you can. I look forward to hearing from you."

I couldn't believe it. *O Magazine* thought I was important enough to interview! This would be a great platform to raise more awareness. I was ecstatic. But... I was buzzed. I couldn't call Penny back now. Could I? I called Leon first.

"Baby, I got the messages! This could be huge! This could do wonders for the children and for the entire system!" I said as soon as he answered.

"Have you called her back yet?" he asked.

"Well... I've already had a glass of wine, two piña coladas, and a shot of fireball," I replied in a sheepish voice.

"I'm sorry. Who is this? Can you put my wife back on the phone, please?" he joked.

"Leon! We are just having fun!" I said.

"I know, baby. I'm just giving you a hard time. I find it hilarious. But you don't sound drunk. How do you feel? Do you think you can have a short conversation with her and then let her know you'll call her later or something? I mean, obviously not today. You seem to be headed down a path that wouldn't make for a professional conversation later." He laughed.

"Yes, I think I can call her now. I was hoping you'd tell me I didn't sound drunk. I'm so excited. I love you. Take care of those babies for me, okay?"

"You know I will. Good luck, Ziah. I love you, too. I'm proud of you," he said as we hung up.

I called Penny back and she answered on the first ring. I introduced myself and she sounded exuberant to hear from me. We went through the usual introductions and she summed up what it was they were wanting to publish.

"I'm actually away on a girls' weekend right now, so I can't talk much. But I'm definitely interested in doing the piece. Can you email me all of the details, and I'll call you back Monday morning?"

"You bet," she said.

I gave her my email address and we hung up. I texted Leon back and updated him.

When I got back in the water, all the girls were together. I couldn't wait to tell them. This was huge.

"Ziah! You were right! They don't believe us!" Steph laughed.

"About what?" I asked.

"I told you y'all didn't take a damn shot!" Nora said.

"Oh! Yes, we did! We took a shot of Fireball!" I said back.

I could tell Steph was disappointed that I didn't immediately jump into the conversation. But she didn't realize what had just happened to me.

"Y'all aren't going to believe this. I checked my phone and *O Magazine* wants to do a piece on me and our work for the foster care community!"

"Oh my gosh, Ziah! That's phenomenal!" Chloe said.

"What in the world? What a huge platform for you, Z!" Nora responded.

"Holy hell! Are you going to be on the freaking cover with Oprah?" Alexis asked.

"Haha, I don't know about that. But just to get my voice out there on a level like that is an unbelievable opportunity."

Steph was quiet. She didn't say congratulations or anything. I knew I must have hurt her feelings with the whole shot thing. We had a plan to have fun with it and tell the girls about it, but my news had taken precedence. This was a major moment that could do wonders for kids in foster care. But Steph didn't see things like that. I decided to move on. Another drink was exactly what I needed.

"Sir! When you get a chance, I'd like a Bloody Mary, please," I yelled across the pool.

Chloe started telling a story about something that Cooper had done recently, but I wasn't paying much attention. I couldn't stop thinking about the *O* article. When the waiter brought me my Bloody Mary, I realized I needed to get back in tune with the girls. The *O Magazine* piece could wait until Monday. That's when I told Penny I'd call her back, and that's when I should focus on it—not all weekend. I had to remind myself that these get-togethers happen fewer and farther between the older we get.

I playfully splashed Steph to break the unspoken tension between us. She laughed, and then Alexis suggested we have a handstand contest, and get everybody else in the pool to vote for the winner. It was humorous to think of five grown ass adult women having a handstand contest, but we were all game. Alexis said the winner should choose what we did for the evening. We all agreed that sounded fair, and we rounded up everybody in the pool who was willing to be a judge, and down we went. When I popped back up for air, Alexis and Chloe were still holding their handstands and going strong. Alexis's long legs looked like a ballerina. She was doing some fancy moves, too. Chloe popped up, and it seemed like another minute before Alexis came up. It was no surprise that she won. But what was surprising was what she planned for the evening.

STEPH

I was proud of myself for not getting anxious on the car ride down to San Antonio. Driving certainly helped with that. I decided that I would go ahead and drink. I had a big breakfast, and I'd done everything in my power to feel well, so I figured I'd go ahead and proceed with the weekend as I had hoped.

Ziah and I shared a nice moment together in the pool. I told her that I knew about Nora and Andrew. I could tell I'd caught her off guard, but she'd opened up to me about her feelings regarding the whole situation. We both seemed to want to give Nora the benefit of the doubt, but it sure was hard with all the evidence in front of us.

Ziah had the wild idea for the two of us to take a shot while the other three were riding a slide, and I thought it was hysterical. The thought of the two of us taking a shot without Nora, Chloe, and Alexis would be unbelievable to them. The waiter brought us Fireball, and it went down a little too smooth. Ziah needed to check in on Layla, so she got out of the pool. I looked out on the golf course and the beautiful hills and drew in a deep breath. It was truly lovely. I started thinking about how lucky we all are to have such a tight group of friends. My mind drifted off to home, and I hoped that Mark was having a good time with the kids. I was hopeful that they were cleaning the house and getting caught up on laundry while I was gone.

Laughter interrupted my daydream, and I turned around to Chloe, Nora, and Alexis approaching. Their hair was soaking wet and they were being loud. I was excited to tell them about Ziah and me taking a shot, but Ziah wasn't back in the pool yet. They said the slide was a lot of fun, and that we'd all have to go do it in a bit. I looked over at Ziah, who was sitting on a lawn chair talking on the phone. I went ahead and told them about the shot we took because I didn't know how long she'd be.

"You're so full of shit!" Alexis yelled.

"Shh! No, I'm not! We did! We knew y'all wouldn't believe us." I laughed.

"What in the world enticed y'all to do that?" Nora asked.

"It was Ziah's idea! I just followed her lead," I said.

"Well I guess we're gonna have to catch up, ladies," Chloe said to the two of them.

Finally, Ziah headed back to us in the pool.

She didn't even realize we were talking about the shot when she first got in. It was like she had already forgotten, and it made me feel stupid. Naturally, she had some big news to share, which diverted all attention away from our shot surprise. *O Magazine* wanted to run a piece on her. Everybody oohed and aahed. I was excited for her. She deserved it—she truly did a lot of good for the foster care community. But I was irritated that she had forgotten so quickly about our plan to shock the girls in taking a shot. And I was equally irritated that the entire conversation was about her again. Talking about other people's lives had never been Ziah's strong suit.

Somehow, we got involved in a handstand contest, and Alexis won. We decided that whoever won would get to choose what we did for dinner that evening. When Alexis won, I got a little nervous. She could be a loose cannon now and then, and there was no telling what she would get us into. I only hoped that her plans wouldn't involve the joint she'd snuck in. She told us that she'd have to do a little bit of research before she informed us of the plans, but of course, she was elated to have won.

We spent the rest of the day in that same pool, laughing, splashing, and drinking. I lost track of how many drinks I'd had, and when it was time for us to get ready for the evening, I don't think any of us were walking straight.

The shower made me feel a little less drunk. We were all dying to know what Alexis had in store for us, but she wouldn't tell us anything other than we'd have dinner at the resort and then Uber out from there. Everybody looked gorgeous when we were ready to head down to dinner. We spent about twenty minutes trying to prop Nora's phone up at just the right angle and use the self-timer to get a good photo of all five of us. When we finally all approved of one, we went to dinner.

Alexis took her role as evening event planner a little too seriously and had plans that exceeded where we went. She also had plans for what we did while we were there.

"Okay, ladies. We are going to order our drinks, and then put our phones on silent and play a little game," she said.

Just as she had started to explain the rules of what she had planned, our waitress brought over a bottle of wine and five glasses.

"Good evening, ladies. This bottle of Chardonnay is courtesy of a gentleman by the name of Gibbs," she said.

"Oh, my God!" Alexis squealed. "Dean!"

"Could he be any more perfect, Alexis?" I asked.

"How the hell did he pull that off?" Ziah inquired.

"When I talked to him in the room earlier, I told him what we were doing tonight. Ugh. He's such a fucking dream boat," she said.

"So a man gets to know, but we don't even get to know? No fair!" Chloe laughed.

"Oh, you'll know soon enough, Chlo," Alexis said.

We clinked our glasses as Ziah said, "To being a good bra and to needing a good bra!"

"Okay, back to the rules of the night ..." Alexis began, "No phones. I brought this joint to pass around," we all screamed in shock.

"Chill out! I'm kidding! I wouldn't do that!" She laughed. "Really, I brought this condom to pass around. And the holder of the condom can ask anybody at the table a yes or no question. Once that person answers, they can pass the condom to whomever they want to ask next, and so on and so forth. Make sense?"

"Alexis! We can't pass a condom around the table in front of everyone eating here with their families!" I said. I was appalled. It was typical Alexis to be so careless.

"Lighten up, Steph. It's in a freaking wrapper. Just hold it in your hand where nobody can see it. It'll be fun," she said.

She was right. I needed to chill out and appreciate the

evening. I still had a good buzz kicking, and I needed to embrace it, instead of being an uptight party pooper.

"Okay. You're right. I'm in," I said. And I felt a weight lift off my shoulders. Ziah laughed and high-fived me across the table.

"Yes, queen!" Chloe said. "Who goes first?"

I looked over at Nora, and she looked a bit uneasy. I wondered if she was worried somebody would bring up Andrew. In fact, I wondered the same thing. Would we find out any dirt on them? It was still unbelievable to me.

"I'll start," Alexis said. She handed the condom to me.

"Oh, shit," I laughed.

"Steph. Is Mark well-endowed?" she asked. Everybody laughed, including me.

"Do you want details? Or just a yes or no?" I asked. They squealed in delight.

"I mean, yes or no was the original game, but if you want to give details ... by all means!" Alexis replied.

"Just say yes or no," Nora quickly responded. I could tell she was nervous.

"Yes," I said. And we all laughed some more.

I passed the condom to Chloe. "Do you have any secrets from the group?"

She hesitated a moment and then said, "Yes."

"Whaaaaaaaa?" Ziah said.

"The rules of the game are yes or no," Chloe smiled. She then handed the condom to Nora.

"Do you?" she asked.

Oh, shit, I thought. Chloe had no idea about anything regarding Andrew as far as I knew. She was just innocently asking her. Four of us at that table knew the answer was yes.

Nora looked around and confidently said, "Yes."

"Y'all must not be nearly as open as I am," Alexis said.

"Well, that's a given with anybody!" I said, as I took another swig of my wine.

Nora passed the condom to Alexis and said, "Do you ever wish you were married with children?"

"Yes and no," Alexis said. It was a fair enough answer. None of us contested.

Our waitress approached to take our orders. Alexis didn't hide the condom while she ordered her taco salad. It was embarrassing but also comical. When the waitress walked away, we continued.

"Is Leon the best lover you've ever been with?" Alexis asked Ziah.

"Hell to the yes," she said as she raised her hand up and closed her eyes as if she was in church.

"Have you ever imagined what your life would be like if you didn't end up with Brett?" Z asked Chloe.

"Yes," she said to my surprise. But then again, I'm sure everybody has wondered what their life would be like had they taken a different road. I knew Nora did, at least.

"Do you ever wish that Mark didn't leave so often on the weekends?" Chloe asked me as she handed me the condom.

"Yes," I said. That was a given. But it was extra money for our family, and Mark loved playing with the band. It was no different than having a husband who traveled for business. It was the same thing. He traveled, and it was business. It just wasn't his main source of income. I wanted to explain this to them, but that wasn't part of the rules.

"Have you been with more than twenty partners?" I asked Alexis.

"Yes," she said as she snatched the condom from me. We laughed again, and our food arrived.

"Okay," Alexis began, "We may or may not pick up where that left off later. But for now, let's enjoy our meal. Don't get too full. We've got a lot of night ahead of us!" She giggled.

We all started throwing around guesses of what could be in store for us. Ziah mentioned a psychic coming to our suite, and Alexis said that was a phenomenal idea and that she wished Ziah had won the handstand contest. I guessed dancing, Chloe said she was stumped, and Nora guessed a BINGO hall.

"Oh my gosh, y'all! You're outdoing me with your ideas! BINGO would have been amazing! And it surely would have made us feel young!" Alexis laughed.

We finished dinner and Alexis arranged for our Uber to pick us up out front. She gave us permission to check our phones, and I noticed that Nora immediately went to the restroom. I wondered if she was communicating with Andrew. When we regrouped out front, Alexis said, "I hope you ladies have a full battery on your phones. You'll definitely be wanting to take lots of photos and videos!" She got in the front seat of the Ford Flex that had picked us up. She made us wait while she gave the driver the address. I was feeling more than buzzed. The wine at dinner had tipped me beyond that point. We all piled into the car, and off we went.

After about fifteen minutes, we arrived at a bar.

"Okay. What's so special about this place, Alexis?" Nora said.

"We could have stayed at the resort if we wanted to sit at a bar," Chloe threw out there.

"Obviously y'all didn't read the marquis," Alexis said. "It's karaoke, bitches!"

"Oh for fuck's sake," I said. And we all giggled as we stumbled in, leaning on each other.

NORA

During our dinner game, I was terrified that somebody might ask if I've ever cheated. Guilty conscience for sure. I didn't like lying to them, and I didn't like keeping secrets. I had always been pretty open with them. Lucky for me, I escaped the game without having to divulge any major information. Earlier in the day, Alexis had already confronted me about Andrew out of left field. I knew she'd bring him up at some point, since they had run into each other at the gym. But I didn't expect her to bring it up in an accusatory way. I already felt eaten up with guilt about the whole thing. I hated what I was doing to Kyle, and I hated not being up front with the girls.

Before dinner, I told Andrew what Alexis had said, and I asked him how I should handle it. He wasn't much help because he didn't care if they knew or not. He made it clear that he wanted to be with me. His certainty made me blush with excitement. But it didn't help me at all. I told him that I missed him and that I'd figure it out and cross the bridge when it arrived. I also texted Kyle to let him know everything was going fine. As I hit send, I felt like such a liar. I was playing the role of the innocent wife, while I was excitedly messaging my ex-boyfriend on the side. What had I turned into? In the shower, I thought about all the numerous ways this could play out, and none of them were perfect. Any way I twisted it, Kyle would be hurt. The thought of it all was killing my buzz, so I did my best not to think about it.

Then came the second part of our evening.

In all our years together, we had never done karaoke as a group. I couldn't imagine Steph doing karaoke, and I wasn't even sure if I could imagine myself doing it. But if I knew Alexis, we'd all be singing by the night's end.

When we walked in, arm in arm, everybody stared at us. I could tell it was a bar full of regulars. The clientele probably came every weekend, and they probably sang the same song each time.

"Okay, ladies. I have different genres of music written on five scraps of lovely hotel stationary," our ringleader of the evening said. "The rules are that starting oldest to youngest, we will grab one of them, open it, and pass that genre on to the GB of our choosing, until we've all been chosen. Got it?"

It sounded more complicated than I thought it should have been, but we went with it. My head was a bit fuzzy from all the drinks. Steph drew, then Ziah, me, Chloe, and then Alexis.

"Okay, show us what you got, Steph!" Alexis said.

Steph unfolded her paper and it said, "90s Country."

"Oh my gosh!" Steph laughed. "Okay, so do I hand off the genre to somebody else and they choose the song? Or do I choose a song for them?"

"You hand off the genre, and they choose the song," Alexis

clarified.

"Oh my word! Okay, I designate 90s country to Chloe." We all squealed. This was a pretty good idea that Alexis had. None of us would have ever come up with something like this. It was a true Alexis move.

Ziah unfolded hers and it said, "2000s Rap."

"Can I give it to myself?" she pleaded.

"No, but I know somebody in this group who will absolutely slay that genre!" Alexis answered. She pointed to herself as we continued to laugh at the whole thing.

"Mmmm. I think I'll give it to Steph," she said.

Steph got beat red and the thought of her rapping cracked us all up. Alexis pretended to pout, and then it was my turn. I unfolded my paper, which read, "80s pop." We all knew that any of us could do a good job at this, but I chose Ziah. She fist bumped me, and then Chloe showed us her paper.

"Anything by Britney Spears" it read.

"Well that's a fun one!" she exclaimed. She passed it to Alexis, and Alexis did a celebration dance.

"Well all that's left is mine, and I guess it goes to Nora," Alexis said. She unfolded it and it read, "Singer's choice."

"Yessss!" I said. I had no clue what I'd choose, but I was relieved I didn't have to rap.

I asked the girls what they wanted to drink, and Steph went with me to order from the bar.

"What are you going to choose?" I asked her.

She laughed and said she had something up her sleeve that would knock all our socks off. I loved this looser version of Steph. She was drunk, but she wasn't too drunk. She was certainly letting her curly hair down, though.

"What about you?" she asked me.

"I have no earthly idea," I responded. There were so many songs I loved to sing in my shower or the car, but I'd never sung in front of people before. I loved Americana music and Texas country, but I didn't know if I wanted to sing something from that genre. I at least had a little while to think about it.

When we brought the drinks back to the table, we asked Alexis if we had to sign up in the order in which we had been handed our papers. She said it didn't matter. Once we knew what song, we could go sign up. She said that she had already signed up, and the guy running it said she should be up in about 3 songs. I got excited for what a fun night it was going to be.

"Maybe we should do a shot first?" I suggested. I needed to loosen up, too. "I'll be right back," I said.

I made my way back to the bar and ordered a round of Patrón for the five of us. I looked back at our table, and nobody was looking at me. I used the opportunity to message Andrew. I was feeling pretty drunk, and I missed him. He hadn't messaged me since our last conversation, but I sent him a quick one just to let him know I was thinking about him.

"I love you. Don't ever doubt that. I never stopped and I never will." I hit send. The message immediately said "read" underneath it. I waited a moment for him to respond.

"I love you, too. I know you know where I stand with this. But I want you to have fun tonight. Don't get caught messaging me if it'll stress you out. Have fun with the girls, Nori. I'll never stop, either."

My stomach did a quick flip, and I smiled. The bartender put the shots on a tray, and I carried them back to the table.

"To an evening spent like never before!" I said, as we raised the glasses. We tipped them back and all of us winced at the flavor. Just then, the DJ called Alexis to the stage.

"Oh, shit!" Steph yelled. Chloe got her happy hands. Ziah pulled out her phone as Alexis walked up to the stage as if she owned it. "I'm a Slave 4 U" started playing, and Alexis sang every word right on beat and danced like she was Britney. At one point, she pretended to have a snake draped over her arms. We were dying laughing, and we also admired what a badass she was. Everything she did up on stage was exactly what karaoke should be.

When she finished, we gave her a standing ovation, and a group of men approached her as she stepped off the stage. They were a little forceful, and Alexis shoved her way through them. She never put up with bullshit. She'd been a victim before, and she didn't play games when it came to standing her ground with men who acted in ways that made her uncomfortable.

The handsy men realized she wasn't going to fawn over them like they were fawning over her, so they sat their asses back down. We all high-fived her for her singing, dancing, and for her shutting the slime-balls down. One by one, the girls signed up for songs. I still hadn't decided what I'd sing. We were all making small talk at the table when Chloe's name was called. When the music started, we screamed. She had just enough of a twang in her voice to belt out Reba McEntire's "Fancy," and she did it perfectly. She was completely out of her element, but she loved every second of it. We gave another standing ovation, and then the man called out Ziah's name.

Ziah glided up there with no hesitation. She was used to being the center of attention, and her confidence was evident.

The song she chose was "I Wanna Dance With Somebody" by Whitney Houston. She did a great job, too. The four of us stood up the whole time she was singing and sang with her. It was one of the songs we had belted out in Steph's van on the drive down. When she finished, I decided to get one more shot. The girls were doing great. They were having fun, but they were also damn good at it. The only two left were Steph and me. When I approached the bar, I realized that I was taking the shot alone, but I was taking it for Steph as much as I was for me. I was completely nervous for her. Rapping was so not her. I checked my phone again since I was alone. Nobody was looking at me. I was beyond drunk at this point. I had lost track of how many drinks I had even had since we'd arrived in San Antonio. With butterflies in my stomach, I sent a quick text to Andrew, and then put my phone away. I walked over to sign up for the song I had finally chosen, and when I went back to the table, the girls were all laughing hysterically. They were showing each other photos and videos from the performances thus far.

"Oh shit!" I said. "I don't want a video floating around on social media of me singing. Please promise me you guys won't post it," I pleaded.

We all agreed that we would only post photos or videos that we all gave the green light to post. Steph's name was called, and we all looked at her, completely shocked. What the hell was she going to rap?

She walked up on stage, snatched the microphone off the stand, and said, "This goes out to all of my GB girls! Hit it, Doc." We had no clue why she'd called the man running the music Doc, but it cracked us up. She winked at us and then blew a kiss just as "Forgot About Dre" started.

"Ooooooooh snap!" Ziah yelled.

Alexis scurried to pull her phone out and started recording. We knew this moment would go down in GB history as one of the best. And we all knew we were too drunk to remember every detail of it in the morning, and we wanted to hold onto it forever.

Steph rapped Eminem's part *and* Dr. Dre's part without even taking a breath, it seemed. To call it amazing would be an understatement. We never saw it coming, and she knocked it out of the park. I hated to have to follow her. Anybody would have hated to follow her. When she finished, she literally dropped the mic and walked off the stage with her arms up. The entire bar erupted in cheers and everybody she passed high-fived her. We were laughing so hard, tears rolled down our faces. She had handled it so hilariously. She continued with the confidence she'd had on stage. I think she would have stage dived if she could have. We told her how proud of her we were, and how she had been the best one of the night. I told her how much I dreaded following her act. And as I was feeling sorry for myself for having to go next, they called my name.

"Shit!" I screamed. "I really don't want to do this. But anything for my girls!" I walked up on the stage and suddenly felt a rush of confidence come over me. I don't know if it was the alcohol or the adrenaline, but I wasn't nervous anymore. The music started, and I closed my eyes. The room was quiet. I knew the song by heart. I didn't need to read the monitor. I never pulled the microphone from the stand. I held onto the stand and felt like I was in a dramatic spotlight. I started, and could actually feel the words I was singing. Suddenly, the spotlight feeling disappeared, and I felt as though I was alone in the room. My confidence grew, and my voice got louder. Before I knew it, the song was over.

I opened my eyes to see everybody looking at me silently. A wave of nerves washed over me again. Then suddenly, everybody stood up and clapped. I looked at the girls, and they had tears in their eyes as they clapped reverently. I said, "Thank you" in the microphone and then hurried back to our table. It was as if I'd had an out-of-body experience up there.

"Holy shit, Nora! I had no idea you could sing so well! I mean, I've heard you sing in the car, but not like that!" Chloe shouted enthusiastically.

"That was amazing. Adele, right?" Steph asked.

"Well, The Cure originally recorded it, but you probably remember it from 311 back in our day. But yeah. That was the Adele version," I said.

"You literally moved us to tears," Ziah said.

"I love you so much, Nora," Alexis said, as she hugged me. I knew that she had read between the lines; she knew what the song meant. But I was so drunk that I didn't care in the moment. I loved Andrew, and I knew that in that instant she knew it, too.

"I love you, too, Alexis. Thank you for planning the perfect evening for us." I squeezed her tightly.

We hung around a little bit longer and laughed our asses off some more. I don't even remember the Uber back to our hotel. I just remember us getting in our pajamas and completely crashing. Alexis passed out ibuprofen like it was candy, and Chloe reminded us all to drink a glass of water, but I think we were all too drunk to listen.

ALEXIS

The first evening of our weekend will go down in history as one of the most memorable GB nights of all time. At karaoke, there was no doubt that the song Nora sang was about Andrew. When she sang, I felt like I finally understood. She sang the song with such emotion, and I could see on her face, with her closed eyes, how much feeling was behind it. I decided to back off and not push it with her. She knew that I knew, and now I'd just let her approach me about it when she was ready.

When we woke up Saturday morning, everybody was hungover. Everybody but me, that is. I had been up for about an hour texting Dean and drinking coffee when Nora emerged. Everybody else was still in hibernation.

"Oh, my God! No! No! No No No No No!" Nora screamed.

"What?" I screamed back. I was worried something bad had happened back home.

"Oh, my God. What the hell have I done?" Tears started streaming down her face.

"What is it, Nora?" She plopped herself down on the couch with her head in her hands, so I got up and sat next to her, rubbing her arm.

"I'm such a fucking horrible person, Alexis. How did I get here?" she asked through tears. She smelled like alcohol. I wondered if it was possible for tears to contain alcohol.

"What is going on? Just tell me," I said. It wasn't like her to be so frantic and out of control.

"Apparently I texted Kyle last night." She wouldn't look up at me.

"Okay? Is this going where I think it is?" I asked.

"It was a message meant for Andrew, Alexis. There's no denying it, either. I can't cover this up. What the hell am I going to do?" she sobbed.

"Okay. We can figure this out. What did the text say?" I tried to be encouraging.

"Ugh. Shoot me now," she said as she handed me her phone.

I read the text: "I want to be with you. We'll make it work. I just have to figure out how. Don't give up on me. We'll put together a plan when I get back. I want you so bad. I love you."

"Oh. Fuck. That's bad."

"Exactly! What in the world am I going to do, Alexis?" She finally looked up at me.

"Okay, let's take a deep breath and think it through. What did Kyle say back? I didn't scroll down." I tried to remain calm for her sake, but this was really the worst-case scenario. I also tried not to show how shocked I was at how serious this thing with her and Andrew had become.

She handed me the phone again.

"Yikes," I said, as I read his messages.

"I'm assuming this wasn't for me. So, the question is who was it meant for, Nora? I'm also assuming you're drunk."

He'd kept texting after the first: "Still waiting on any form of an explanation. Who do you want to be with? And want so bad? And love??? Call me."

"Nora. You can't avoid this. Tell me what the hell is going on," read the third one. He'd stopped texting after that, but she also had five missed calls from him.

"You haven't responded or called at all?" I asked.

"No. I don't know what to do, Alexis. I never wanted to hurt him. And my drunk ass sent the worst of the worst. Ugh," she said.

"Have you told Andrew yet?" I inquired. I was relieved that Nora and I were the only two awake.

"Yes. He doesn't have much input because he wants to be with me. And I want to be with him, Alexis. God, I've got so much to tell you. To tell all of you, really. But the last thing I wanted to do was hurt Kyle in all of this. I need to deal with this head-on with Kyle and then I'll tell all the girls tonight. I have to face the music. I made my bed, and now I have to lie in it." Nora was still crying. It was evident that she felt deeply ashamed.

"Go call him, Nora. Call him before everybody else starts waking. I know that Andrew is the love of your life, and now that I feel this intense connection with Dean, I understand it more than I ever had before. But Kyle shouldn't be left hanging like this," I said. I patted her leg as a form of encouragement, and she walked onto the balcony.

I texted Dean what was going on. He had been up to date thus far, so I went ahead and let him in on the latest development. He was concerned about me. He said he felt like I was taking on too much stress from the girls' drama. I assured him I was tough and could handle it. But he knew that the knowledge of Brett cheating on Chloe was really weighing on me. I loved that he cared so much about me. It was such a nice change. He told me that he was heading into work and he'd reach out later.

"Remember to have fun! I miss you like crazy. So does Gibbs. We can't wait for tomorrow evening, but we want you to enjoy every moment with the girls! And don't worry about us. Even though we miss you, we are relying on each other to get the other through. Lots of snuggles happening without you. Don't be jealous," his text read. I was pouring myself another cup of coffee when Nora walked back in. Her face was splotchy and red, and I could tell she had been crying pretty hard.

"Come here," I said. "Have this cup. I'll make another." I handed her my coffee cup and pulled her into me. "What happened?"

"Oh, Alexis. It's awful. He was crying. I was crying. I told him I'm sorry he had to find out like this, and I had been planning on telling him soon. He immediately knew it was Andrew. He said we need to talk more when I get home. Said he'd noticed a difference in me lately," she sobbed.

"Well … that doesn't sound … completely horrible." I tried to be optimistic. Suddenly I wished that Chloe was there and aware of the situation. We could've used her optimism.

"He ended the conversation by telling me to have fun and not to worry about him. How can somebody tell their cheating wife to have fun and not to worry about them, Alexis? He doesn't deserve all of this." She was still crying. I handed her a hotel tissue to wipe her nose and her tears.

"You're right. He doesn't. But he's right, too. You still need to have fun this weekend. Try to keep your mind off it. And if being with Andrew is what you want, then you're one step closer. But for now, dry it up and pull it together. The other girls will be up soon. And just so you know, Steph and Ziah know you're communicating with Andrew. Chloe doesn't have a clue."

"What? How? Did you tell them?" she said accusingly, which kind of pissed me off.

"Nora. You weren't exactly secretive about it. You both follow each other on Instagram and like each other's photos. First time cheaters, for sure." I laughed.

She actually giggled back and said, "Yeah. I figured out a little too late that that was dumb. Well, like I said, I'll tell everybody tonight and get it all out there. Meanwhile, where's the ibuprofen?"

I handed it to her, and she went to take a shower.

I sat down on the chair that looked out the window and thought about all that had happened—and all that was to come. Who would have ever thought this is where we'd all be right now? Ziah's upcoming interview with *O Magazine*, Steph rapping Eminen and Dr. Dre, me with a serious boyfriend, Chloe's husband cheating on her, and Nora cheating on Kyle with Andrew.

When Nora came out from showering, she looked much better. She had pulled herself together. She said she'd called Andrew and told him about her conversation with Kyle. He was relieved to be one step closer to being with Nora. He still hadn't told his wife, but he and Nora were going to sort everything out when she got back into town. I felt sorry for her. They had been our own Brad and Jen. Anybody who knows her, and who had known her and Andrew together, knows that they were meant to be. But none of us had stopped her from dating Kyle—or marrying him for that matter—because Andrew got married. We thought that door had been closed. But sometimes the universe will bust down doors when we least expect it, I suppose.

Pretty soon after Nora's shower, the others emerged from their alcohol-induced deep sleep. Steph's hair stood straight up. She still had her eye makeup on, but it had smeared below her eyes. She came out of the room leaning on Chloe, who looked pretty damn good for first thing in the morning after a late night like the one we'd had. Finally, Ziah joined us. But she didn't come out of a room—she came into our room with a key.

"What the hell? Where in the world were you?" I asked.

"I've been up since 6. I was swimming reverse laps in the lazy river while nobody was down there," she said. "It's so nice! One of the best, most refreshing workouts." Of course, she was. Here I was thinking I was the first up, and Ziah had beat me by two hours!

"Damn, early bird!" I said.

We sat around, discussing our plans for the day. We all agreed that we'd stay at the resort the entire day and night and not have another adventure like the previous night. Not that it had been bad—everybody was in agreement that it had been the best. But none of us felt great, so we wanted to keep it lower key.

"I feel like ass," Steph said.

"Same," Chloe said. Even though she looked great.

"Let me get my magic pills and all will be well," Steph said, as she fidgeted around in her purse.

"What are your magic pills, Steph? You aren't about to pass around Xanax, are you?" Nora laughed.

"Oh, y'all are gonna die when I tell you. But I promise you that they work for almost any ailment," she replied. "Other than my anxiety, that is."

"What are they? Flintstone vitamins or some shit?" I asked.

"Y'all just take one, and then I'll tell you. Come on. Do it for the sake of the GBs," she said.

We all put out a hand, and she gave us a dark capsule. Even though Ziah and I were in better shape than the others when it came to being hungover, we still weren't one hundred percent.

Ziah grabbed two glasses of water and we passed them around as we each took a mystery pill.

"Well, now we are closer than ever, ladies. You just swallowed some of my placenta!" Steph laughed.

"Oh my gosh! Are you kidding me?" I screamed. "I'm not about all of that, Steph!" I started gagging.

Ziah laughed, and Chloe didn't seem phased at all. Nora looked a little disgusted but said, "So tell us how this helps again?"

"I swear, y'all. It's like a cure-all. You watch. We will all feel better within the hour," Steph responded.

After the shock of swallowing Steph's placenta had dissipated, we decided to get our swimsuits on and go down to the pool. I went into the restroom to change and checked my phone.

"Brett is here with her!" Dean had texted. He sent me a zoomed-in blurry photo, and I couldn't make out a face. I couldn't even tell that it was Brett.

"Oh no! Keep an eye on them! Let me know what he says to you! Be safe, James Bond. Don't lose your job! I can't support us forever. ;)"

He immediately responded, "Forever, huh? ;)"

"Oh, you know what I mean. Just watch him! We are heading to the pool."

All the girls came out wearing different suits from the previous day. And per usual, everyone looked great. Ziah had a headwrap around her braids and looked like she had walked straight off the cover of Vogue. Chloe wore a sporty bikini that had a lot of coverage but was super chic, too. Nora wore a one-strapped one piece that was gorgeous, and Steph wore a strapless black tankini with gold ties on the side. My white bikini made me feel confident. The girls were surprised that I wasn't worried about it being see-through, but I had never had issues with it before.

As soon as we got in the pool, I ordered a round of Bloody Marys for the old hair-of-the-dog. About halfway through our drinks, Nora said, "Well, I never thought I'd hear myself say this, but Steph, I think your placenta cured me. Be sure to save some for tomorrow."

CHLOE

This GB trip was turning out to be the best one ever. We
started our second day in the adults only pool with a round
of Bloody Marys. Steph had given us some placenta pills to
cure our hangovers, and everybody was disgustingly shocked.
I didn't mind so much, but everybody else's reactions cracked
me up. To everybody's surprise, they really worked. Steph said
that they were a cure-all for basically anything except for her
anxiety. And Lord knows she had tried everything to help with
that. I was happy for her that it seemed to be in-check on the
trip so far. Even I feel a little anxious when I leave Brett and
the boys home. Though I know that my homesick nerves are
nothing compared to what Steph battles.

I called and checked in on the boys before we went down
to the pool. Brett didn't answer, so I texted Brady's iPad. He
wrote me back and said they were at Johnathan and Blake's
house and about to go swimming, while Daddy was running
errands. Since Brett didn't answer, I called Johnathan. I asked
him how everything was going, and if the boys were behaving

themselves. Blake spoke over him loudly in the background, "Don't worry, Chlo! We won't let them drown! You can trust us!" I laughed, and Johnathan said that they were very well-behaved and using their manners. They had just ordered pizza and were about to get in the pool. I asked him where Brett was, and he said he was meeting a client at the golf course. Johnathan golfed, too, but he usually left the main client schmoozing to Brett. He said after he went to the course, he had a meeting with their real estate photographer at one of the new listings. Johnathan had volunteered to go, but Brett wanted him and Blake to have some time with the boys, since he knew how important children were to them. Brett was thoughtful like that. We wanted Johnathan and Blake to be able to adopt so badly, and since everything had been less than smooth in that department, we had been letting the boys go over there more frequently to hopefully help fill a void. I told them to be careful and that I loved all four of them, and I got off the phone to join the girls. I sent Brett a quick text in the elevator.

"I love you. Text me when you can. Have fun on the course."

I checked my phone one last time before we got in the pool, and he still hadn't responded.

Oh, well, I thought. He probably didn't have good service on the course.

We made our way over to the spot we liked the most—the infinity part of the pool. The water poured over the edge, looking out onto the golf course. My mind went back to Brett golfing. He sure worked hard to seal the deal. I wondered if he was golfing well. There was no doubt that he was charming the client. And I also had no doubt he'd get the listing. Dallas real estate had gotten crazy lately. He told me that agents were doing all kinds of things to go above and beyond to get the listing. I was happy that he was smart enough to stay ahead of the curve, since it seemed like it was ever-changing now that social media existed. Having any kind of job in sales, you had to be a marketing genius to stay ahead.

"Cannonball!" Alexis sprinted and jumped into the pool in one of her famous cannonballs. It was comical for such a site to take place in an adults-only pool by a woman who looked like a swimsuit model in a white bikini. Everybody clapped when she popped up. She bowed and then swam over to us. I didn't even know where she had come from since I had been daydreaming.

Ziah caught us up with what was happening back home with Layla. Leon said she had a good night. He'd slept on the floor in her room, and she never woke in the night. He said that he and Cy wanted to take her for ice cream since he wasn't sure if she'd ever had any before. Ziah's love for Leon seemed to grow even more every time they had a foster child. He was an incredible father. Nora asked if there had been any drama with Lizzie in the last twenty-four hours, and Ziah told us about an ignorant Facebook post Lizzie had made that Leon had to confront her about. Ziah explained to us more about white privilege and the Black Lives Matter movement. Any time that she could educate us on that subject, all of us listened intently. We all wanted to better ourselves, and we wanted to empathize. Ziah once told us that if somebody doesn't have the ability to empathize, then they don't have the ability to love greatly. She said when your mind is closed, your heart can't be open. We loved our learning sessions with her. She enlightened us and made us better.

"And *that*, my dear, is why you are famous," I said.

"Oh, please! I am so not famous, Chloe," she replied.

"Well, you know what I mean. You're always getting recognized for being a great human being."

"Well, thank you. But I don't know about all that," she blushed. "Let's get another drink and talk about something less serious."

"Wait! Before we do that, is anybody up for a slide ride?" Steph said.

"I don't even know how you're able to think of riding a slide after how much you drank last night!" Nora said.

"I'm telling you guys. It's the placenta pills!" she responded.

"So what exactly is it?" Alexis asked.

"It's my dehydrated placenta put into capsules," Steph laughed.

"Oh, Lord," Ziah said.

"Well, I'm a placenta capsule believer, because I do feel good. And honestly, I lost track of how many drinks I had yesterday," Nora replied.

"Oh, girl. You outdrank us all," Steph said back to her.

"I know. I know. Let's not talk about it," Nora went under water.

When she popped up, Ziah said, "Okay, we won't talk about it again, but damn, girl. You slayed that song. I had no idea you could sing that well. I need to hear more of that voice you've been hiding from us."

"Deal," Nora said. "Now how about those slides? Who's game?"

We all decided to go, and we crossed our fingers that our

spot in the pool wouldn't be taken over when we returned. We could either ride single or ride double. Ziah and I decided to ride together, and everybody else went solo. That was the only downside to us being an odd number—if there were ever partners, somebody would be left out. We tried to avoid it when possible, just like we did on the slides. We knew we'd ride them multiple times and have other chances to ride with each other or solo. But this way, at least it didn't leave one person out.

The line moved pretty quickly. The slides weren't marvelously tall, but they were big enough to be fun. There was an adorable little girl behind us in line, and I asked her mom if I could feel her hair. It looked so cute and I wanted to see what it felt like. The mom looked at Ziah, and then me, and then said okay. I wondered what that exchange was about as I patted her puffed buns.

"She is absolutely precious," I doted on her.

"Thank you," she said as she looked off.

I looked at Ziah wondering what in the world I did wrong, and Ziah winked at me and said she'd tell me in a bit.

When it was our turn on the slide, we screamed in delight as we took turns and dips, and then, in no time, we reached the bottom.

"Okay. What the hell was that all about?" I asked Ziah.

"Girl. You cannot touch our hair. I mean, you can touch my hair because you're like my sister and I know your heart. But you cannot just touch hair that doesn't look like yours because you're curious about it."

"Why not? It looked like it felt neat. And she was adorable," I said.

"Exactly, Chlo. You're fascinated by it because you don't see it like that often. For us, it goes back to slavery. It goes back to white people doing whatever they want with us just because they want to. It's like she was your little toy for a second. Just because you think something is pretty or neat, doesn't mean you get to touch it. Or ask to touch it. It also reminds us that our natural hair isn't in the spotlight often, and that's demeaning to us as black women. Look, Chlo. I know this is way deeper than you thought. But I just want to explain it to you, so you don't make the same mistake twice. I know you meant well, girl."

She put her arm around me. I was almost in tears. I had no idea that could be so offensive, but I was so happy to have a friend like Ziah to inform me of such.

"I love you, Z. Thank you for being you," I said, as we walked back towards the pool with our arms around each other.

When we got back, I checked my phone before getting in. No messages from Brett. Blake had texted me photos of the boys in the pool and a selfie of all four of them. I laughed and texted them back a selfie of me with the pool in the background. I really did love Blake and Johnathan like family. I counted myself blessed that Brett had a business partner like him. The other girls arrived back from the other slide, and we made our way back to our spot. There were two couples there, but we crowded them out of the way—there's power in numbers, after all. Nora ordered us all piña coladas, and we started a game of charades of movie titles. We weren't keeping score, and there weren't real teams. It was just a fun way to pass the time.

Alexis was acting out "Sex and the City," as I heard my

phone ringing in the distance.

"Crap!" I said. I swam over to the steps as quickly as I could without looking ridiculous, climbed out, and pulled my phone out of my bag.

"Damnit," I said. I had missed Brett's call.

I tried to call him back immediately, but he didn't answer. A voicemail popped up.

"Hey, babe. We're just about to hit the back nine, and I wanted to check in. The service isn't great out here. Hope you're having fun. Love ya!"

I tried calling him back in hopes that I'd get through. No answer. Alexis came toward me.

"What's up, buttercup?" she teased.

"I just missed a call from Brett. He's at the golf course today and has bad service. I haven't been able to reach him," I replied to her.

"Bummer. Where are the boys?" she asked.

"Blake and Johnathan's," I smiled. We all adored them.

"Awww, cute," Alexis said.

"Well, don't worry about Brett. He's fine. Let's go have fun," she encouraged.

"I wasn't worried about him. Should I be?" I joked.

"You know what I mean," Alexis said, as we swam back to the group.

ZIAH

I kept wondering when Nora would inform us that she and Andrew had reconnected on social media. Our weekend had been so much fun so far. Day two started with a nice meditation session for me in the lazy river. Swimming against the current was a workout but also felt amazing. The only other people down there at the time were employees getting ready for the day. I had the entire waterpark area to myself. Breathing in the morning air in the beautiful hill country felt great.

When everyone woke and got ready, we had another amazing day at the pool. We all told Steph what a badass she was, and she loved the attention. She seemed to be having the time of her life on this trip, and I hoped that nothing would change that. We decided to ride the tube slides and waited in line with all the children and families. I loved that when were all together, we revert to our childlike selves, yet at times, we seemed wise beyond our years. Having a group of girlfriends like ours was unusual, and that was never lost on me. We were very lucky and blessed. Throughout all our changes in life, we knew that we always had each other's backs.

When we returned to the pool, Steph suggested that we play "Never Have I Ever." The rules are that somebody says, "Never have I ever _____," and if you have done it, you take a drink. If you haven't, you don't drink. You didn't have to explain anything unless you wanted to. It was like the game Alexis had us play the night before, but this one applied to everybody at the same time. This wasn't the first time we had played this game together. We'd been playing it for as long as I remember, but we hadn't visited it in a few years. It had a tendency to get dirty, but it was always funny. You'd think that we'd have answered everything by now, but the game never ceased to surprise us with answers we didn't expect.

"I'll go first!" Steph exclaimed. "Never have I ever had sex in a moving car."

Everybody but Chloe drank. Alexis went into detail of her having sex while the guy was driving, and we all laughed. Alexis was a great storyteller and an even better impressionist. Hearing her rehash details and act out every part of a story always made it that much more enjoyable to hear.

"Never have I ever had sex on a golf course," I said, as I took a drink of my piña colada. Only Alexis drank with me.

"Never have I ever passed gas out loud in yoga class," Alexis laughed. Nora and Alexis both drank, which made them reminisce about the first time they'd met.

"Never have I ever cheated," Chloe threw out, unexpectedly.

Shit, I thought. I knew that Nora had been communicating with Andrew, but I didn't want to think it had gone as far as actual cheating. But many would consider an emotional affair cheating. I hated that Chloe had said that, but she had no clue what was going on with Andrew and Nora. I realized that the question could cover any relationship we've ever been in, so I was hopeful that other people would drink, too.

Alexis and I made quick eye contact, and then I glanced at Steph. She winked at me without anybody else noticing.

Steph and Nora both drank.

"Oh, my gosh! Spill the beans!" Chloe said.

"Hey, we are talking high school and college, too," Steph covered for them. I was pretty sure that she had never cheated on anybody but was protecting Nora.

"Of course! We're talking in our whole lives," Nora agreed.

"Okay, fine. Y'all won't spill it. Dare I say, party poopers?" Chloe conceded.

"Never have I ever been a member of the mile high club," Steph laughed. I looked around and nobody drank. I took a small sip of my drink and tried to be discreet. But they all took notice and screamed in an uproar, demanding the details. I laughed and decided to give them the information they so desperately wanted. After all, it was a GB weekend.

"It wasn't with Leon," I began. They squealed. "I was flying from New York to DFW when I was modeling. There was a male model on the flight with me. We'd done a few gigs together before, and this dude was fire hot, y'all. Some of our shoots were kind of sexy, and we already had that sort of attraction and sexual tension built up. Anyway, we were flying back into town and we both got up to go to the restroom at the same time. When he went in, he pulled my hand and I joined him. The rest is, as they say, history!" I laughed.

"No, no, no. You don't get to tell us something like that and then just stop. You have to give us more details than that,"

Nora said.

I laughed. "Okay, well I obviously knew why he'd pulled me in there with him. There's only one reason two people go into an airplane restroom together. It turned me on immediately. The bathroom was obviously tiny. And you guys know I'm no short woman. And this dude was buff. I think every square inch of that space was occupied by us. There wasn't a lot of time or space for any type of foreplay, so we got right to it. And to be honest, we were both so turned on by the whole thing that there was no need for foreplay. It was quick. But it was steamy and hot. It was some of the hottest sex I've ever had. He was no Leon, but it was an experience I will never forget. When we finished and returned to our seats, nobody had a clue. Nobody was waiting in line to use the restroom or anything. I couldn't believe we had done it, and I couldn't believe that nobody had an inkling about what had just gone down. I didn't tell anybody after it happened because one-night stands were so out of my element. Y'all don't even know how long I've been waiting for you to ask this question in this game." I laughed. "I guess we all have more secrets than I thought." I looked over at Nora instinctively, and she dipped under water to wet her hair.

"Do you still know the guy?" Chloe inquired.

"Hell no. We did a couple of modeling gigs together before that, but I haven't seen him since. I don't even remember his last name." I laughed again.

"Z! I never took you for a one-night stander! Or a one-*flight* stander! I'm assuming you stood," Steph quipped.

"Of course, we stood! I'm telling y'all. Next time you get in an airplane, go to the bathroom and think about your girl! You'll give me mad props," I bragged. "One-flight stander.

That's a good one, Steph," I laughed.

"Okay, let's move on!" I suggested. "You haven't gone yet, Nora," I noted.

"Okay. Never have I ever flirted with a cop to get out of a ticket," she said. Only Alexis drank.

"Never have I ever slept with somebody another GB has slept with," Alexis giggled.

"Oh, man. This is getting juicy!" Chloe said. We were already feeling buzzed. Luckily, nobody drank. But we all cut eyes at each other, looking back and forth.

"Thank God," Alexis said. "If any of y'all told me you knew Dean in the past, I would die!"

"Oh my goodness! Like we wouldn't have told you by now!" Steph said.

"Well, shit! Nobody would have known that Z had a one-flight stand without that question!" We laughed again.

"Move on, y'all!" I reminded them.

"Let's take a break and order something to munch on," suggested Nora. I think the game made her nervous. She had already dodged one major question. Who knew how long her luck would last if we played all day? Curiosity was still getting the best of me, but I knew in time we'd find out. It just wasn't like us to keep secrets from each other.

"Sounds good to me!" I happily agreed.

"Do y'all want to get an order of nachos and an order of quesadillas and pick at both?" Nora asked.

"Perfecto, my lady!" Steph said. She was still having a great time, and we were eating it up.

"I'll eat just about anything other than your placenta again," I joked to Steph.

"Ugh! Don't even remind me!" Alexis yelled. "But I will say, it seems to have worked. I didn't feel that hungover to begin with, but I know that Nora and you would have been. Good old placenta to the rescue!" More laughter ensued.

"So how long does a placenta stay good in capsule form?" Chloe inquired. "I mean, Benjamin isn't exactly a newborn."

"Hell, I don't know. I'm sure they're expired by now. But I'll keep taking them as long as they keep working!" Steph laughed again.

"Great. Expired placenta. Ugh. Hey, will y'all go ahead and order? I'm gonna send Dean a quick text," Alexis asked as she started wading away from the group.

"Do y'all mind if I check in with Leon, too?" I asked.

"Y'all go ahead. I'll order and when y'all come back, I'll go check my phone," Chloe volunteered. "Go check in on your fam, Steph. You, too, Nora. I'll fight anyone who tries to overtake our spot. Don't worry."

We all followed directions, hopping out of the pool for our two lawn chairs that held our bags and pulled out our phones. I laughed inwardly at the image of innocent Chloe fighting someone.

Leon had texted me that Cyrus and Layla were still getting along. He said that they were both playing together with the tea set, but neither had ever had a tea party before. The next text was a photo of the three of them holding their teacups. I sent him a typical "I love you" and put my phone back in the bag. I looked at the others. Steph was laughing at her phone. Alexis walked off with hers. I assumed she was calling Dean instead of texting him. Nora looked worried. I wasn't sure what was going on with her, but I wasn't about to ask.

STEPH

The weekend was everything I had hoped. We were all getting along, and my anxiety was in check. Of course, there was no guarantee it wouldn't sneak up at any given moment, but so far, all was beyond well. As open as we all tended to be, we were still learning more about each other. I loved that about us. I had no clue that Ziah was a member of the mile-high club, and I didn't think I could ever fly again without thinking about it. Our karaoke evening had been one for the books. I loved surprising the girls with my "Forgot About Dre" rendition. They didn't know that Mark enjoyed all kinds of music, so I knew my fair share of rap songs. But that one was my favorite, and I knew I could nail it. Nora sang a beautiful version of "Lovesong" that was clearly about Andrew. It moved us all. And after all these years, none of us had a clue she could sing so well. But there was obviously more to Nora than what we thought we knew.

During our game Saturday, somebody mentioned cheating, and I drank. It was probably the first time that I had lied to the girls, but I was worried that Nora was going to drink, and I didn't want her to drink alone. I knew I could divert some of the attention if I played it off like it had been long ago. I wished that Nora knew that I had done that for her, but I couldn't let her know that I knew anything was up yet. I was still waiting for her to come clean to all of us with what was going on, though I wasn't quite sure what exactly that was.

When I texted to check in on things at home, Mark laughed at me. He said it seemed like I had a good time the previous night, and I laughed and asked him what he meant. I scrolled up to see all the texts that I had sent him. Several mentioned how much I missed him but also how much fun I was having. A few were photos of me trying to be seductive and failing miserably. And then there was a video of me doing karaoke. I laughed when I saw it but was a bit embarrassed that it existed. Mark would get nervous when I let loose, but that really only applied to fancy events. He didn't mind so much when we were on our GB weekends.

After my big scene at Ziah's award when I had gotten drunk out of my mind, we had a long talk about it. He was able to recognize that I don't get away much, and, of course, there was the whole aspect of me forgetting that I had taken an anxiety pill. He was much more supportive of me cutting loose now. He was relieved that I hadn't had to take any of my medication and optimistic that it would continue that way. And he appreciated my attempt at sexy selfies. He let me know that the kids were fine, and that he wanted me to continue to have fun. He was proud of me. He also told me the sweetest thing that he could have possibly told me—the laundry was almost all caught up and would be totally done by the time I returned.

"Hallelujah! You're the man of my dreams!" I sent back.

I was happy to hear that things were running smoothly with the kids. I didn't leave town often, so it was refreshing to know that Mark was having a good time and handling it well. Leon was always doing "Dad of the Year" things, and there's no doubt that Mark is a wonderful father. But it made me happy when everyone else could see what was always clear to me. His plans for the day included taking the kids to a movie and then out to dinner wherever they chose. Being away from him made me miss him. He was the best. I put my phone away and bragged about him to Ziah and Nora. At times, I worried that the girls thought he was boring. I knew they thought that he left me alone too often, but they just didn't get it. And I had to accept that they probably never would. Besides, Brett was beginning to leave Chloe home alone a lot lately too, and nobody made any mention of that.

Alexis returned from her phone call with Dean and was giddy. She said he was on a break at work and told her how much he missed her, and what he wanted to do to her when she got home. They still hadn't slept together, so I'm sure the anticipation was killing her. He let her know that Gibbs was perfectly fine, too. And obviously, that made her happy. She usually boarded him at a facility that had 24/7 access to surveillance cameras. It wasn't unusual for Alexis to be checking her phone for the sole purpose of watching Gibbs while we were on GB trips. But she liked having Dean watch him even more. Even though she couldn't check in on him via camera, she knew Dean was snuggling with him each night, and that meant more to her than any type of surveillance.

Nora was texting, but she looked worried. She didn't have the same excited look on her face that she'd had lately when we would see her on her phone. I wondered if things had changed with her and Andrew. I reminded myself that I was jumping to conclusions, and those conclusions were killing my buzz. So I got back in the pool. Chloe had ordered us some food to share and a pitcher of beer. I usually stuck to fruity drinks or wine, but a beer sounded refreshing. And Alexis brought her beer salt, which made it one hundred times better. Soon we were all back in our spot overlooking the beautiful golf course. Chloe had mentioned that Brett was golfing with a client, so Alexis asked her what course. She wondered if it was the same one that Dean managed.

"Oh, no, it's not. I asked Brett if he had been there before and he said it's not the typical type of course they take clients to. He's heard of it but hasn't been. But we should all try it out together sometime!" Chloe said.

I wondered if it hurt Alexis's feelings that Chloe had framed it in that way—it almost came out as if Brett was too good for Dean's course. I knew that Chloe didn't mean it that way, and she was repeating whatever Brett had said. She wouldn't hurt a fly's feelings even if she knew how. Chloe is as innocently sweet as they come in a thirty-nine-year-old package. I came across as innocent in this bunch, too, but Chloe had me beat for sure. Chloe was the type of friend everybody needed—all the women were. We were all so different, but put together, our traits all meshed together to make the perfect combination.

Chloe was the super sweet friend: she was optimistic and genuine, and when she was sorry about something, her apology was truly heartfelt. Alexis was the wild one: she brought life to any situation. She was vivacious and loud and, at times, a little too much, but she was genuine. She didn't have the type of personality that everybody appreciated, but she didn't care. We loved her because she was her true self one hundred percent of the time. She didn't change based on where she was or who she was around. As much as that killed me at times, I respected it. Ziah was our world traveler. She could always enlighten us, and we loved to learn from her. Even though I caught myself resenting her at times for often acting high and mighty, she was a wonderful person and an even better friend. She hurt my feelings now and then, but she tried hard to understand other people's situations, including my anxiety. Nora was the quietest of us: she listened a lot but didn't talk as much as the rest of us. She loved to laugh, and she loved to love. She was affectionate with us. She always hugged and kissed us. But then again, we all did that. Nora had gotten quieter after her miscarriage. That was a subject we didn't know how to handle as a group. We had flowers delivered to her immediately, and we brought her and Kyle dinner for a week. She didn't like talking about it, so she shut it out. When she started changing the subject whenever we tried to bring it up, we all decided that we wouldn't talk about it anymore unless she initiated it. And she never did.

Then there's me. I suppose I'm the sensitive one. I'm the stay-at-home mom who feels misunderstood and under-appreciated. I don't think the women respect my marriage as much as they respect each other's, and that kills me. Mark has never done anything bad to me or my kids or the girls. I wish they'd see him the way I do. I'm also the only one who battles anxiety, and I had some postpartum depression after Benjamin was born. The other girls can't relate to that, so conversation about it is difficult. Nora might be able to empathize with that, but I'd probably never know since, as I mentioned, she doesn't talk about the miscarriage.

When our food came, we devoured it so quickly that we ordered another order exactly like it. Nora dropped a piece of lettuce in the pool and we all tried to catch it before it hit the bottom, but then we gave up. We looked around to make sure nobody was watching. Shortly after, Alexis dropped a huge clump of sour cream and we were certain we were about to get kicked out. Instead of being high strung about it, we all laughed and kicked it away until it dissipated in the water.

"It's better than all of the urine in this pool!" Alexis said.

"No way! This is adults-only, Alexis. Surely people are getting out to go," Ziah replied.

"Umm. No. Do you see how many people are in here drinking? And how many times have you seen them get out?" Alexis said back.

"Oh, gosh. Don't even go any further. Enough," Nora gagged.

"On that thought, let's go do a lap in the lazy river, where at least the urine is moving!" Chloe laughed.

We were all on board, so we found a few tubes and got in. As we started going around, Chloe suggested we continue with our "Never Have I Ever" game.

"What if we play Truth or Dare instead?" Ziah asked.

"Oooh, Z. You must be feeling feisty!" I said.

None of us ever wanted to be the party pooper, though I had worn that hat more times than the others. We all agreed to go for it.

First up, Alexis chose dare, and Ziah dared her to tap a random guy on the shoulder and say, "There you are! I've been looking for you!"

She did it to a guy who was in front of us in the lazy river, and his wife didn't appreciate it nearly as much as all of us did, including the man. It was silly and immature, but so were we when we played games.

Alexis then asked Nora truth or dare, and she chose dare, as well. I'm sure she was terrified of choosing truth.

"I dare you to tell that lifeguard that you've been trying to get CPR-certified, but you've failed twice, then ask him if he'd mind if you practiced on him."

Nora screamed in a shocked laugh. Nora didn't like to feel defeated, so she went for it. The lifeguard was about twenty-one years old, at most. He laughed and then to all our surprise, he asked for her number.

"No, sir. I'm sorry. I'm just trying to get better at my CPR. But thank you," she replied.

She swam back to us mouthing, "Oh, my God!" and we screamed in delight.

"Well, you still got it!" Ziah said.

"Okay, Z. Truth or dare?" Nora asked her.

"Truth."

"Have you ever gotten so mad at Leon that you left?" she asked.

"Whoa, Nora. Going deep! No, I haven't. I have gotten so frustrated with Lizzie stuff that I've slept on the couch before, but I've never left. Leon and I probably wouldn't fight at all if it weren't for Lizzie, to be honest. But she knows how to push my buttons, and it always makes me get angry at Leon for having ever seen something in her to begin with. She's just the worst ex-wife to have to deal with. But luckily, there's Cy. He's the rainbow from that damn hurricane. Anyway, Steph, truth or dare?" Ziah asked me.

"Hmmm. Dare," I said. I knew they were surprised I'd choose dare, but I had been having so much fun outside of my comfort zone all weekend—I figured I might as well keep it going.

"I dare you to pop a nipple out and pretend like you don't know, and ask the next lifeguard where the restroom is. But do NOT do it in front of any children. Be discreet."

"Oh my gosh! You're on!" I said.

Since I was wearing a strapless suit, it wasn't that hard to pull one of my breasts out. It also wasn't that far-fetched that it could have happened without me knowing. I made sure that there were no children within sight, and I stood up straight, which made the water come up to about my belly button, and I said, "Excuse me? Where is the closest restroom?"

The lifeguard noticed right off the bat. He was cute—probably paying his way through college by working there for the summer.

"Umm, ma'am?" He said. I was mortified at the thought of him telling me. "Your swimsuit...umm.." and he motioned for me to pull it up.

"Oh my gosh! I am *so* sorry! How embarrassing! Thank you so much. Now then...The restroom?" I asked.

He gave me directions and as we floated away as we cracked up. Nora asked if we could go back to our spot in the pool and get another drink. Nobody argued with that idea.

NORA

Texting Kyle instead of Andrew had been mortifying. I had all kinds of emotions about it. I felt completely crushed for him. He certainly didn't deserve to find out about Andrew and me like that. And the fact that I had said "I want you" and "I love you" made it even worse. There was no getting out of it. When I talked to him, he said we would address it when I got back home. He still wanted me to have fun on our trip—and that killed me. Andrew was supportive, but he wasn't nearly as worried as I was, because Kyle knowing about us was one less hurdle for us to clear. However, it felt like I had run right into the hurdle full force instead of clearing it. I was living in two parallel worlds. On one hand, the love of my life, the person who made me happier than anybody else ever had or ever would, wanted to be with me. The person I thought I had lost forever. The person who loved everything about me. The one who understood me like nobody else. He was back, and the one thing he wanted most in the world was to be with me.

But on the other hand, I had hurt somebody I loved

very much. And I was continuing to hurt him. I had made a mistake by marrying him, and he had wasted his entire thirties on a relationship that was doomed. I told Alexis what had happened, and much to my surprise, she informed me that Ziah and Steph knew that I had been talking to Andrew. She said that nobody knew the extent of it, but they had suspicions. I promised her that I would fess up to the girls that evening. I checked my phone right around lunch time, and Andrew had sent me some sweet messages about missing me and how he couldn't wait for me to be in his arms. Kyle hadn't sent me anything. I don't know what I expected, really. When I pulled my phone out, I dreaded seeing any messages from Kyle, but then when there weren't any, it stung a bit.

I tried to keep it all off my mind as we played a couple of games in the pool and the lazy river. We ended our day at the pool, watching the sunset from our favorite spot in the adults-only pool. None of us drank as much as we had the night before, but we were all still inebriated. That evening, the plan was to stick around the resort. We ate dinner in the bar and grill area. We didn't dress fancy, but we fixed ourselves up enough for photos, at least. One thing our GB trips never lacked was an abundant amount of photos.

After dinner, I suggested that we sit around one of the fire pits set up outside. I had planned to tell them all about Andrew here. I was nervous but anxious to get it off my chest. I didn't like having secrets from anybody, especially the ones I love most. This was the biggest secret I had ever held, and not telling my best friends was major. Though, I knew they would be supportive of anything I did. Or, at least, I hoped they would be.

When we all got comfy, we started talking about home. Ziah said that everything was going well at her house. She told us she was having a great time with us, but she was also looking forward to going home to spend time with Layla. She felt she was missing out on some important moments in those first few days. Steph said Mark and the kids were doing great. He was happy she was letting loose, and he hoped she'd get drunk enough to FaceTime him naked later. We laughed in unison at the thought of that. Chloe said Brett had a meeting with his and Johnathan's real estate photographer after he golfed, so she assumed that's where he was. The boys were still at Johnathan and Blake's, and Brett hadn't called her back yet. Alexis was so giddy every time she talked about Dean, and it was so refreshing to see her so happy. He was back at her apartment after work and he had sent her a selfie of him and Gibbs watching "Parks and Recreation." It made her homesick, which she rarely ever felt. I was waiting for the right moment to tell the girls, and then Alexis whipped out the joint she had brought on the trip.

"Oh, my God! Alexis, put that away! This is a family-friendly resort!" Steph said.

"Chill out. Nobody is around. I can guarantee you nobody has a clue what is going on. All the families are clear across the other side of the resort roasting marshmallows. We're fine. And if we go down, I'll take the heat," Alexis said. "Now then, who wants some?" she asked as she lit it.

"Oh, man, Alexis. I don't even know if I should be around it. I don't have an issue with it, but it's still illegal," Ziah started to get up.

"Wait!" I startled her. "This might be a good time for me to talk to y'all."

Ziah sat back down slowly, and I could tell she was trying to read me. I knew she was wondering if I was about to spill the tea about Andrew.

"I've been keeping a secret from all of you, and I have to get it off my chest," I said. I could feel my heart beating quicker, and I tried to steady my voice.

"Oh, my God! You're pregnant!" Chloe said. "Wait. No. You've been drunk all weekend. Okay, sorry. Wishful thinking."

"It's okay, Chlo. But no, I'm not pregnant. Gosh, I don't even know where to begin. I'll just dive right in, I suppose. My only request is that y'all let me talk and get it all out there before you try to respond."

Alexis started smoking the joint, and the girls didn't even look her way.

I took a deep breath, hoping to inhale a little of the smoke. "Andrew is in Dallas. He's been transferred there for his job. He and his wife are separated, and she's still in Austin. He found me on Instagram, and we've been talking. Y'all know what a connection I have with him. And you know that I love Kyle. But it's no secret that what Kyle and I have is not anything close to what Andrew and I had.... or have," I shook my head a little as I searched for more words and started losing my confidence. I decided to focus on Alexis because I knew she'd be most supportive, though I hoped they'd all follow suit. "We've been talking, reminiscing, dreaming. I don't know. It's crazy. It sounds even crazier when I say it out loud. We've met up a couple of times. And it's gotten physical." The looks on their faces gave no indication how they were receiving this breaking news—only blank, shocked stares. I trudged on.

"We've only made out, but it's been so intense, y'all. It feels like the love we had all those years ago isn't just back—it's like it never left. I would say that I've never felt this way before, but I have. With him. He's the love of my life, and I never should have let him go. I didn't want to tell y'all because I feel like a piece of shit. I hate cheating on Kyle. I hate not having any control. I hate the whole lying part of it all. Last night when I sang, I was singing for Andrew. That song is exactly how I feel about him. He's the one. And y'all know that as much as I do. And it's not like he's some asshole who broke my heart, and we are all mad at him. Life just took him a different direction. And I told him back then that maybe the universe would bring us back together someday, and it has. Now."

"Well for fuck's sake, pass me the fucking joint," Steph said to all of our surprise.

Alexis passed it to her. I had never seen Steph smoke before, and I wasn't sure if the others had either.

I continued: "I hate this so badly for Kyle. I was planning on telling him, but I wasn't sure when or how. But then last night, it turns out I got too drunk and mistakenly texted Kyle a message meant for Andrew. Ugh. It was awful. I didn't even know about it until I woke up this morning. I called him and told him a little bit about what's going on. He said we'd talk about it when I get back home. He wasn't surprised it was Andrew, either. I've been so torn up over this whole thing. I love Kyle, but I know he isn't right for me. And Andrew is the love of my life. The timing is just awful. It makes me realize how many regrets I have, and so many things I should have done differently. I don't know how my conversation with Kyle will go when we get back."

Steph took another hit off the joint, and everyone else kept quiet, so I continued.

"I need you girls, though. I know it sounds like I'm a horrible person, but I promise I'm not. I'm still me. I never thought I would do something like this, but at the same time, I'm not surprised that Andrew and I are back to us. I don't know how to explain it." The girls continued to stare at me. They were clearly taking it all in. I don't think they expected it to go the exact way that it had. "Somebody say something, please," I begged.

Ziah finally broke the silence. "Well, I can't say that I am proud of your actions in this situation, but you know that I always have your back. I *know* that Andrew is the love of your life. I've known you longer than anybody here, and I know what love looks like on you, and I haven't seen it on you in a while. I just wish you had broken it off with Kyle before striking something up with Andrew."

"I know you love Andrew, Nora. I think this will have a happy ending. We will figure it all out," Alexis reached over and rubbed my leg. She was always so supportive.

"Well," Steph paused after taking another hit, "I just feel really good right now. If Andrew makes you feel anything like I feel in this moment, I say go for it, girl," Steph slurred.

"Oh, Lord, she's high," Ziah said.

We all busted out laughing. It was the icebreaker I yearned for. Steph's eyes were halfway open, and she had a smirk on her face. She was definitely high. She had taken several puffs off the joint in a small period of time.

"Chlo? You're being quiet. Do you hate me?" I sheepishly asked. Chloe was usually the most optimistic, so her silence surprised me. She hadn't said one word since the big revelation.

She stared at me intently. It wasn't a look I was used to. Then she finally spoke up: "What about his wife, Nora? You're so busy thinking about you and Andrew and Kyle. What about her? Does she know about this? Are you sure they're really even separated?"

"Yes, I have thought about her. A lot, actually. Claire is her name. They are definitely separated. I feel badly for her, just as I do for Kyle. But they don't have the perfect relationship, either. She has cheated on him in the past. And I know that doesn't make what we are doing okay. But they've had their troubles."

"Well, I've heard too many stories about people thinking that they're gonna run off into the sunset together, but when push comes to shove, it doesn't end up working out and every single person involved gets hurt, including the innocent bystanders." She was clearly offended by my actions, and I didn't blame her. I probably would have been, too. She had difficulty coming to terms with the fact that one of the GBs could be so inconsiderate. She was the only one of the group who hadn't been aware that he was in town. I knew everyone else had a little time to process their assumptions, at least. I didn't blame Chloe for processing it negatively right in front of me.

"Well, I feel much better now that I've told y'all. I will keep you in the loop after Kyle and I talk when we get home. And you know that I love y'all. And I need you," I said.

"We love you, too, Nora. Don't ever doubt that," Alexis said.

"I love aaaaaaaaallllll of you guys," Steph said, as she dramatically moved her arm around to point to each of us.

Alexis, Steph, and I finished off the joint. Ziah and Chloe

didn't partake, but at least they hung around for it. Steph ended up FaceTiming Mark right there and whispering very loudly, "I'm hiiiiiiigh!" Mark laughed so hard and asked to talk to one of us. When we looked at him, he had tears in his eyes from laughter.

"What in the world have y'all done to my wife?" he asked.

"Got her drunk and high. What do you expect?" Alexis replied. We all laughed, and Steph professed her love to Mark very loudly over and over. She finally let him off the phone, and then it was our turn. She professed her love to each one of us individually.

"Ziah. You are absolutely perfect. You're the most beautiful woman I've ever met. And your popularity and fame make me jealous. But I fucking love you, you beautiful queen, you."

We looked at each other with a worried look.

"Alexis. You are the bomb, man. I wish I had your legs and your ability to do a handstand in the water. You are a true gem, my lady."

We laughed.

"Chloe, Chloe Bo Bowie. I love how happy you are all the time. I wish I could always channel your optimism and be like that around my family. I mean, tonight you're being pessimistic, but I'm talking about the other times."

"Oh, shit," I said under my breath.

"And Nora who is not a bore-a! You are a good friend. Maybe not a good wife, but you sure are a good friend. I love you. Just like everybody else does! Exes and all!" Then she started laughing and closed her eyes while she slumped out of the chair onto the ground.

"We are going to have to carry her up, aren't we?" I asked.

"For. Sure." Alexis said.

"Let's call it a night. You get her arms, Alexis. Chloe, you make sure her head doesn't hit the ground. Try to cradle it if you can. Ziah, you and I can get her legs."

Chloe found a luggage cart, and we put Steph on it and wheeled her up to our suite. Even though the night had taken a serious turn, all of us could appreciate the fact that we were rolling our thirty-nine-year-old friend, who was stoned out of her mind, through a family-friendly resort lobby on a luggage cart.

ALEXIS

Day two was a doozy. On the surface, the day itself was fun. But the other girls didn't know that Dean was filling me in on all that Brett and his mistress were doing. Brett had approached him and stuck his hand out for a handshake. Dean said it was an extra firm grip this time, and he introduced him to Heather. Dean felt like the entire exchange was his way of threatening him and reminding him to keep his secret. When he introduced her to him, he used the word girlfriend. I told Dean that Chloe told us that Brett said he had not been to his course before. Dean scoffed at that. He kept a close eye on Brett and Heather and said they were very cozy together.

I felt so sorry for Chloe. She thought he was golfing with a potential client, and here he was cheating on her, with somebody he had evidently been seeing for a while. I thought about Nora and Andrew. Nora wasn't doing much different to Kyle than what Brett was doing to Chloe. I mean, there were obvious differences, but also major similarities. During our lunch time conversation, Dean told me that if Brett kept up his arrogant act, he would say something. I told Dean to cool it and let it rest for now. I hated the position this put him in. He said that the only reason he hated being in that position was because it put *me* in a bad position. I loved that our relationship was starting out with such honesty and trust. Every hour of each day, my fondness for Dean grew. He had become a confidante for me in such a short time.

We knew that it was just a matter of time before I told Chloe about Brett and Heather, but we had to figure out exactly how I would address it. Chloe tended to think that Brett could do no wrong, and it wouldn't surprise me if she shot the messenger.

Other than conversing with Dean any chance I could, the girls and I had a fun day together. Since Nora had promised me that she would tell everybody about her and Andrew that evening, I kept wondering when and where and how it would all go down. A couple of instances came up that would have allowed her to confess to us, but she seemed to really want to wait until the evening.

Before dinner, I was able to talk to Dean out on the balcony while everybody else was still getting ready. He said that Brett and Heather had left about two hours before he left work. He wasn't sure where they were going. I wondered if their day date was ending. Surely, he needed to pick up Brady and Cooper from Johnathan and Blake's. The thought of Johnathan and Blake brought another question to the forefront. Did they know about Brett's affair? No way. Johnathan and Blake were loyal to Chloe. They were loyal to all of us. They were like family. But then again, would Johnathan's loyalty to his asshole business partner override his loyalty to his girlfriends? I didn't like thinking about it.

Dean told me to stop dissecting everything and to just focus on our plan to blow his cover. I would have blown his cover the moment I found out about it if it weren't for Dean's job. I was so worried about him getting fired. Brett was powerful in Dallas. But Dean had worked there for years. I wondered if his boss would understand, or if losing a remarkably high-paying customer would piss him off. There's no doubt that Brett would try to take Dean down. He might even try to take the whole club down. Brett had become very savvy with social media, and I wouldn't put it past him to slander the business all over each platform to which he had access. I shared those fears with Dean, and he promised me that he would be fine either way. Dean had a good relationship with his boss, but he wasn't sure if Brett threatened his boss, whether Dean would be expendable. I hated every part of the scandal. We decided to sleep on it and talk more about it the next day. I told him I needed to go back into the suite and then head down to dinner with everyone. He told me that he missed me more than he knew he could, and that he and Gibbs were now best friends. I reminded him that I was Gibbs's best friend, and he said, "Well, that's debatable now, Alexis. Have fun. I can't wait to see you." I told him I hoped to be able to text him later. When we hung up, I had more butterflies in my stomach.

I was relieved that Nora had finally fessed up after dinner. And I was also relieved that the joint got smoked and I wouldn't have to throw it away or smoke it by myself. After the big confession and our pot smoking session, we went back to the room and put high Steph to bed. Chloe called Brett again and he finally answered. I could see the relief on her face as she stepped out on our balcony. I was surprised at how hard Chloe was on Nora during the big revelation. She was extremely defensive of Kyle and Claire. She certainly didn't cut Nora any slack. It killed me to watch her react that way, while I knew that her own husband was cheating on her. I realized that Dean and I needed to act fast. I didn't like keeping this from her one bit.

I texted Dean that Nora had come clean and summed up Chloe's unsupportive reaction to it all. He said that he couldn't stand it any longer, either. He decided that he would talk to his boss about the situation and see if he would be in any kind of trouble if he confronted Brett about the affair. I tried to talk him out of it, but he made me realize that having that conversation with his boss wouldn't cause him to lose his job. It would just allow him to see where he stood if he did confront him. I loved our alliance we had formed.

Ziah was on the phone in the other room with Leon, and Nora was in the restroom getting ready for bed, so I told Dean I'd call him instead of texting. When he answered, I felt a strong longing to be near him. His voice sounded extra sexy. Maybe it was because I was high. I told him that he sounded hot and he laughed at me. Then I told him I was high, and he laughed even harder. He must have told me twenty times that he missed me. I missed him, too. I was excited to get to see him the next afternoon, and I was sure to let him know. I told him that I planned to give him the goods, and he laughed at me again. He said that information was probably going to prevent him from being able to sleep. He was looking forward to it as much as I was. I told him I heard Nora finishing up, and that I better go. He told me to tell Gibbs goodnight, and he put the phone to his ear. I told my boy goodnight, and then told Dean goodnight. After we hung up, I deleted every dating app that I had.

Nora joined me in the living room area of the suite. I asked her how she was holding up, and she said she was okay. Part of her was over the moon with excitement, and the other half was sad for hurting Kyle. I felt badly for her, because one hundred percent of me was over the moon with excitement for Dean. I would hate if I was also having to deal with guilt at the same time. But then again, I *was* dealing with Brett's cheating stuff, and that was making me feel guilty. However, I refused to let Brett's stupid ass steal my joy. I talked to Nora more about Dean, and how much I liked him.

Ziah joined us shortly after. She said that Layla was still adapting. She had an outburst during dinner and became inconsolable. Leon didn't know what to do, so he talked to her calmly through her entire fit, and eventually she wore herself out. Ziah and Leon hated when that happened in front of Cyrus with any of the children they had. Leon said he put her to bed, and she went right to sleep. He planned to sleep in his and Ziah's bed instead of on the floor that night. I asked Nora if she had texted with Andrew, and she said yes. He was happy that she had told all of us, and she smiled as she told us that Andrew had missed us and was happy to get us back. Just then, Chloe walked back in.

"I wouldn't be so confident in getting all of us back," I said, as I looked towards Chloe. She didn't know what we were talking about, and she looked distracted.

"I'm gonna go ahead and crash. I'll see y'all in the morning," she said.

We looked at each other, wondering what her deal was. I wondered what her asshole of a husband had said to her.

"I think we should probably all go to bed on that note," Ziah suggested. Nora and I agreed, and we all headed to bed. I sent Dean one last text for the night.

"Tomorrow..." it read. And instantly, he wrote me back, "Tomorrow..."

CHLOE

I was having difficulty processing the bomb that Nora had dropped on us Saturday night. She had gone on and on about how much she loved Andrew and he loved her and how they were destined to be together. I couldn't believe it. It was as if I was in the Twilight Zone. I felt horrible for Kyle and for Andrew's wife, Claire. Luckily, Kyle had found out about it because Nora sent a text intended for Andrew to him instead. I was shocked at how innocent Nora was making herself come across. An affair is an affair. I had always had an immense amount of respect for Nora. She is one of my best friends in the entire world, and this revelation knocked the wind out of me. I was surprised that the other girls took it so well. They listened intently and seemed to fall into some sort of spell Nora seemed to be casting with her confession. I saw sympathy on their faces, and it floored me. It was utterly baffling.

Alexis had lit her joint and she and Nora and Steph smoked it. Normally, I would have excused myself, but my need to hear Nora's explanation felt as if I was magnetized to the seat. I will give it to her, we all knew that Andrew was the love of her life. However, there is *no* excuse for cheating. If she and Andrew are destined to be together, she should have split with Kyle, and he should have split with Claire before they ever started any sort of relationship. When she told us that it had gotten physical, I almost lost my dinner. That was so far from okay in my book. As the evening wound down, the four of us ended up having a moment of laughter together, but I was still pissed off at Nora.

I was finally able to reach Brett when we got in the room. He had been golfing all day, and there was a cell tower issue nearby, so his signal was hit or miss. After their game, they drank a few beers in the club, and then he had to meet the photographer who does all his listing shoots. He picked the boys up from Johnathan and Blake's pretty late, in my opinion. But he had been working so hard. I was pretty irritated that I couldn't get a hold of him all day, but the cell tower situation made sense, and then he had to rush to the listing to meet the photographer, and I knew how much he hated being late. He hadn't become the successful businessman that he was from being late to appointments—that was for sure. He'd sweet-talked me out of being mad, like he always does. He said that he and the boys were headed home to go straight to bed, and that he would text me when they were home safe. I talked to the boys briefly and they said they had a great time with Johnathan and Blake. I loved hearing that, and it made me long for the day that Johnathan and Blake could have a family. When I came back into our suite after getting off the phone, Ziah, Nora, and Alexis had been visiting. I wasn't sure what or who they were talking about, but all I wanted to do was crash. We had such a fun day, and then the evening took a dark turn that I hadn't been prepared for in the least. I was exhausted.

The next morning, I wasn't quite as pissed off at Nora. Clearly, she had never been on the receiving end of cheating, and the way she was acting... I could hardly stand to think of it. Especially on vacation. This was my time to get away from those kinds of worries, and I was so upset she was ruining that for me by acting selfishly—like cheaters did. But I wanted to at least enjoy our last half day with her without being a bitch. I could put on my big girl panties and get along with everybody. But the first thing I said was that I didn't want to hear about Andrew and her. And if she could grant me that wish, I was willing to have a great last day with everybody. We all agreed that would be doable, and we packed our bags, threw on our suits, and headed down to our favorite spot.

I was able to get in touch with Brett before we went to the pool, which made me happy. I was hopeful for a peaceful day with no drama. Brady and Cooper and Brett were going to be working in the yard all day. I had no objections to that! I loved our beautiful home and our amazing landscaping. I also appreciated when the boys learned how to do different things around the house. Brett knew this would make me happy when I got home, and he knew I had been pretty upset when I couldn't reach him all day the day before. It wouldn't have surprised me if I came home to flowers, too, honestly.

Everybody looked stunning on our last day. We all had gotten a good tan. The first thing we decided to have was a Bloody Mary, and then a couple more drinks for everybody but Steph. She would be driving in a little while, and she didn't want to overdo it. Steph remembered smoking the joint the night before, but she didn't recall all the things she had said about us. We laughed as we reminded her, and her face turned red. When she found out that she had FaceTimed Mark, she was worried. We assured her that he thought it was hilarious, and she blushed.

"I've never seen you smoke weed before, Steph," Alexis informed her.

"Me neither," Nora said.

"Yeah. Because I haven't in like twenty-two years. I don't know what the hell I was thinking," she laughed.

"Well, I do, but we are forbidden from speaking about it," Alexis said.

"Alexis. Follow the requests of every GB," Ziah supported me.

We decided to ride the slides one last time, and Nora asked me if I would ride with her. I knew it would be awkward, but I really did love her, and I longed to feel close to her again. The information I had been privy to the night before made it difficult for me to look at her, and caused a definite rift between us that was evident by all. But I agreed to ride with her. The others headed for the other slide to ride single.

While we were in line, she broke the rule.

"Listen, Chlo. I know I've hurt you. I want you to know that you can ask me anything about the situation, and I will answer you honestly. I don't want to keep secrets. You're one of my best friends. After all, you're comfortable, supportive, you always lift me up, and make me seem better than I am." She winked at me.

I had to smile at the Good Bra reference.

"I know, Nora. Just give me time. You know I love you, too. I just need time to process it."

When it was our turn to ride, we squealed and laughed the whole way. When we exited the slide area, I gave Nora a hug. I knew she needed it. No matter what was going on in any of our lives, we always had each other's backs. And when she used the Good Bra quote on me, it made me realize that I hadn't been one for her. The pain and agony she was causing Kyle and Claire didn't have anything to do with our friendship. I wasn't over it, by any means, but I knew I could handle it better moving forward.

We finished our last couple of drinks in the pool, and then went to the bellhop area to collect our bags the hotel was holding for us. The valet brought us Steph's minivan, and we hopped in.

"Goodbye, San Antonio! You were good to us! We'll never forget karaoke, Ziah's one-flight stand, Steph's luggage cart ride, or anything else that happened here. Thank you for the memories!" Alexis shouted as we pulled away.

On the ride home, we sang at the top of our lungs again. We made Nora sing another Adele song for us. She was embarrassed, but she did it for us. The ride went by quickly again, and soon, we were back at Steph's.

Dean picked Alexis and me up. Alexis ran and jumped into his arms, and it was like a scene out of a movie. Gibbs waited patiently in the truck. While Dean moved our luggage from the van to his truck, we hugged everybody goodbye. Mark came out to greet all of us, and he and Dean shook hands and laughed a little. I could tell that both were happy to have their ladies back. I was anxious to get back to my house and see my crew.

Leon pulled up for Ziah, and he got out to give us all hugs.

Ziah let us meet Layla, since a few days had passed. Leon said she had loosened up a little, so Ziah felt it was okay. She was a doll: little blonde pigtails and big blue eyes. She held on tightly to her baby doll that Leon had given her. Cyrus was in the car, too, and we all fawned over him. He's a really good kid. And for having a mother like Lizzie, he was an exceptional child. We all had a group hug and said our goodbyes. We knew we'd be texting soon, but it was still always hard to say goodbye on that last day of our trips. As soon as I got in the back of Dean's truck, Gibbs gave me a look that seemed to say hello. He knew I didn't want to pet him, so he didn't come any closer. It was written all over Dean's face how happy he was to see Alexis. I'd even say that he was happier than Gibbs was, and that is saying a lot. When we pulled into my circle drive, I gave Alexis and Dean both a hug, and I gave Gibbs a little pat on the head.

"I love you, Alexis! Thank you for doing so much of the planning! I guess I should thank you for winning the handstand contest!" We both laughed and I walked inside.

Brett was watching golf, and Brady and Cooper were out back, working in the yard.

"Hey, sweetie!" I said, as I parked my luggage.

"Hey, babe! How was it?" Brett asked without looking away from the television.

"It was good. We all had a nice time together," I said, walking between him and the TV.

"No drama? Steph didn't mix her pills with alcohol or anything? No secrets revealed? Nothing juicy?" He inquired.

"Nope. Just a lot of fun," I lied. I didn't want to get into it with him at the moment.

I walked out back and Brady and Cooper ran up to me.

"I missed you both so much!" I exclaimed.

"We missed you, too," Cooper said.

"We had fun with Johnathan and Blake, though!" Brady joined in.

"What about with Dad?" I asked.

"We weren't with him much, and today he's just had us working out here pulling weeds and stuff. But yeah, I guess it was fine," Cooper disclosed.

"Well, Mommy is home now!" I shouted as I pulled both into a big hug with me.

Brett walked outside and put his arm around me, and something inside me instinctively pulled away.

PART 3

ZIAH

Coming back from our weekend was bittersweet. I wanted to bond with Layla while it was still the beginning of her stay. I told the firm that I'd be staying home from work Monday to do just that. Plus, I needed to get back in contact with *O Magazine*. Leon had a busy week at work because one of his associate veterinarians was on vacation. Cyrus was still with us, and I loved to have an extra day off with him, too.

When I got both kids fed and settled in front of the television watching Disney Junior, I stepped into the office to call Penny with *O Magazine*. I was excited to get more details about the piece they wanted to run. I had thought about it a lot since she originally called and was over the moon with excitement. However, I tried not to let it consume my thoughts on our GB trip. Penny answered immediately and seemed to be very thrilled to hear from me. She asked me several interview questions about the foster care system, and specifically why it had become my passion. She explained to me the next step would be sending a photographer to my home to take some photos of Leon and Cyrus and me. We weren't allowed to have photos of children who are currently in foster care posted on any public platform, so photographing

Layla was out of the question. I spoke about several of our past children who had come in and out of our home. I told Penny about the photo album that we kept containing memories of each child we'd been blessed to have, if even for a short while. The interview was going well, but midway through, Sherry called. I hated to ever miss a call from Sherry, in case there was a situation we needed to know about, or if there was a break in a case with a current foster. I asked Penny if I could place her on a quick hold, giving her a brief rundown of who Sherry was. I knew that this was even more information for the piece she was writing on me. She completely understood.

"Hey, Sherry," I answered.

"Ziah. It's Little Tommy," she said in a frantic voice.

"What? What's going on? Is he okay?" I asked. I couldn't seem to get the words out fast enough.

"He's okay. But he's got a fractured collarbone," she replied.

"What in the world, Sherry?" I started to cry. "He can't ever go back to them. You know that, right? We have to protect him," I said.

"I know, Ziah. But you know how all this works. Their rights are currently in the process of being terminated. In the meantime, can you and Leon take him?"

"Without a doubt. Bring him as soon as you can. And bring any medical information you've got," I said through tears.

"We'll be there this evening," she said as she hung up.

I switched back to the other line. "Penny? I'm sorry. Forgive me. One of my previous babies is going to be coming back tonight and things aren't good for him. I'm sorry. I'm a complete mess now. But go ahead. I'm focused on this interview now."

"Ziah, you have given me exactly what we need. I'll be in touch via email to get more info regarding your different awards and to schedule that photographer. It was a true pleasure speaking with you. I am in awe of everything you do and everything you stand for. Thank you so much for taking time out of your busy day to visit with me," she politely concluded.

"Oh, Penny. The pleasure is all mine. I'm sorry we got interrupted. Thank you for everything, though. If this goes to print, it can do so much for the foster community," I informed her.

"Ziah. This is definitely going to print. I'll be in touch," she said as she hung up.

I had so many emotions. I was so proud of the *O Magazine* piece, but I was angry about Little Tommy's family. I couldn't wait to have him back with us and show him the love that he had always deserved. We'd never gotten a foster who truly didn't have anywhere to go, but it seemed that Tommy was now in that situation. I wondered if Leon and I would consider adopting him. We'd not talked about that before, but we also hadn't ever dealt with circumstances this dire. We also had never gotten a previous foster back. I needed to call Leon and fill him in. I also needed to let the girls know. I knew they wanted to know how the interview went, and they'd definitely want to know about Tommy.

Leon was on board with us getting Tommy back, of course, and he also wanted to beat Tommy's family's asses. I had to talk him off the ledge. His nurse interrupted us and told him he had an appointment waiting. I told him I'd see him after work. I knew I needed to call Lizzie, as we did any time we got a new foster. It was in our custodial agreement that she be informed.

"Hello?" she answered on the third ring.

"Hey, Lizzie. I just wanted to let you know that we are getting one of our previous foster kids back. The baby who had the broken ribs—he's coming back to us," I said.

"Mmm. Why? What's the story now?" she asked. She didn't even have one ounce of sympathy in her tone.

"Well, his home life isn't any better, and he needs a temporary placement while they find somewhere else for him to stay long-term."

"I mean ... I guess it's fine with me. I just don't like Cyrus being exposed to all that stuff. But as long as it isn't long-term for y'all, I'm fine with it for now," she'd responded with an attitude. She loved holding the power.

"Thank you for understanding, Lizzie," I forced out as I hung up.

She was such a bitch. Once again, I found myself wondering how Leon had ever loved her. Before I put my phone away, I texted the girls.

"Interview with the magazine went great!" I started.

"Yay! So happy to hear!" Chloe said.

"That's awesome, Z! I can't wait to hear details," Nora noted.

"So good to hear!" Steph chimed in.

"Oh, I'm so pumped for you! But even more so, I'm pumped for me! (Sorry, Z!) But I've got to tell y'all about my and Dean's night! OMG! Ugh. I'm getting hot just texting about it. Let's meet up soon. I was thinking about having a Botox party this Friday. I know you and Steph aren't all about that, Chlo, but would y'all at least come for some wine? Z, Nora, and I can all get injected. I'll also invite Johnathan and Blake.

My girl says she has some new filler she wants to try under my eyes, and I told her to sign me up! And I know we all need some smoothing out. No offense!" Alexis followed her lengthy text with a funny Botox GIF from The Real Housewives of Orange County, one of her favorite shows.

"I'm game!" I said. "But I need to tell y'all that Little Tommy is coming back to us. I don't know what will end up happening with him. He doesn't have anybody in his family worth a shit to take care of him," I informed them.

"Whoa," Steph said.

"I need to hear about all of this. Can we do dinner sooner than then? I need to fill y'all in on my conversation with Kyle, too," Nora said.

"I want to hear about it, too, but I can't meet up this week until Friday. I'll be at the Botox party, though," Chloe said.

"OMG, Z and A! I will be there. Nora, please give us the summary in text form! Or call me!" Steph said.

I was excited to hear all about Alexis's night with Dean, and of course, I wanted to know about Nora and Kyle, but I simply had a lot more on my plate. I could wait until Friday at the Botox party. We all agreed we'd be there.

STEPH

I was so glad that I was able to let my hair down and fully enjoy our GB trip without having an anxiety attack. I had actually felt more anxiety since returning home than on the trip. I had knots in my stomach for Nora. I was anxious to hear about her and Kyle's conversation that we knew would be happening. I was equally interested in hearing from Alexis about her evening with Dean, as she'd informed us that they'd planned to sleep together. We all lived a little vicariously through Alexis now and then, since she was single and always in the exciting, early stages of relationships. But I think she also lived vicariously through us at times, too. We knew she'd end up settling down someday. Hopefully, eventually, at least. Things seemed to be on the right track for a long-term relationship, if nothing else. We were all hopeful he was the one, but it was still early.

After Ziah told us about Little Tommy, I needed to talk to her. I wanted to call Alexis and Nora, too. But those stories could wait. I needed to know about Little Tommy.

"Z, what is going on with Tommy? Why is he back? Nobody

wants him?" I rattled off before she could even say a word.

"He has a fractured collarbone, Steph. They're awful people. And there's nobody else in his family that wants him or is qualified to have him," she replied.

"I can't handle that, Z. What can I do? This shouldn't happen." I felt panicked. I hated the thought of an infant having broken bones, and then having nobody who wanted him permanently.

"Well he'll get to us this evening, and you know we will give him all the love. And we will go from there. We just have to see how things go with the family's rights being terminated. Taking it one step at a time," she said back to me. She was very calm.

"I really admire you, Ziah. I know that sometimes I don't always show it, but I really do think you are amazing," I said.

"Oh, you told me all about it when you were stoned, Steph," she laughed. I embarrassingly giggled along with her.

"Well, seriously, Z. I want to help in any way that I can. I want to get involved." I knew this surprised her. I even surprised myself, but I couldn't stand the thought of Little Tommy being hurt by his family. I didn't know how I would make a difference, but I knew I had to try. She told me that we could talk more about it in person Friday.

When we hung up, I called Nora. I knew she was at work, but I took the chance that hopefully she'd be on a break. Her job was demanding, and she worked her ass off. Some days, they had to deliver babies in closets because there were no rooms available, and other days, it seemed nobody was having babies. I hoped this day was one of the slower days. I lucked out as she answered instantly.

"Hey. You okay?" I asked.

"Hey, Steph. Yeah, I'm okay." She sounded somber and a bit defeated.

"So how did it go? I've been thinking about you." I got right to the point.

"It was interesting. It was hard. It was informative. And it was surprising," she said back.

"Surprising? How so? Are you guys separating? Has Andrew talked to Claire yet?" I had a million questions.

"Can you meet me for lunch at noon?" she asked.

"Absolutely," I said.

"Let's grab sandwiches at the Starbucks near the hospital. Just come pick me up," she said.

"See you at noon."

My curiosity was killing me, but I knew she'd inform me of it all soon. I put my phone down and went out back to play with Ava, Logan, and Benjamin. They were all getting along well, which was nice. I asked them if I could join their game of keep away, and they agreed, if I started in the middle. Sweet moments like that were not lost on me, and I soaked in every second of it. I arranged for Gayle to come by the house while I met Nora, and I hated leaving the kids while we were all having such a wonderful time. But I knew Nora needed me. I could hear it in her voice. As much as I wanted to know about what was going on with her and Andrew and Kyle, I knew that she needed an ear and a shoulder, no matter what.

When I picked Nora up, she looked worn out. I had gotten used to a fresher, livelier version of her lately. She asked me how I was, and told her I was fine, but I was more worried about how she was. She said she'd give me the full rundown when we sat down to eat. To fill in the awkward lack of conversation, I told her about how I had left my debit card in San Antonio. She laughed and said she wasn't surprised. I knew she wouldn't be. But things are always just so hectic when it's time to pack up and leave. And I had been making sure everybody else got everything they needed, that I simply forgot the one small detail. I wasn't even sure where I'd left it. Instead of messing with calling the hotel, Mark immediately cancelled it. It wasn't the first time we'd had to do that. We pulled up to Starbucks in no time, as it was only a few blocks away. We both ordered wraps and tea, and we sat down.

"Are you able to do Body Pump this week?" She tried to keep from having the inevitable conversation.

"Of course, I am, Nora. But cut the bull. What the hell happened?" I asked.

She let out a long sigh and rubbed her temples before she started. "Steph. It's so much more than we even thought. Obviously, Kyle had time to process the whole Andrew thing before I got home. He did some soul searching and reflecting on himself. And threw darts at a photograph of me, I'm sure."

"He didn't!" I said.

"No, silly. Of course, he didn't. You know Kyle better than that. Well, actually, you don't know him quite as well as you thought," she continued, raising an eyebrow.

"I beg your pardon? Nora, cut to the chase. The suspense is killing me. Are you and Kyle splitting? Are you and Andrew going to get married? Does Claire know? Your lunch break is only an hour and I need to know everything."

"I want to tell all of you the full story after I talk to Kyle a little bit more about our plans moving forward. I hate leaving you hanging, but I promise I will answer your questions. Yes, Kyle and I are separating. No, Andrew and I aren't getting married. Claire will know by the end of today. Does that help?" she asked.

"Wow," I let it all sink in. "Yes, it does. But I want to know more, of course. I'm worried about you. You don't look like yourself." I reached across and touched her arm.

"I know. It's obviously been a rough time. And I'll give y'all the full rundown Friday. I just don't want to have to say it all more than once. You know?"

"Absolutely. I'll wait. I don't know what to say, honestly. I don't know if I should say I'm sorry, or congratulations, or what," I responded.

"Just say you love me, Steph. All I need right now is to know that I've still got y'all in my corner."

"Always," I said.

NORA

When I got home Sunday evening, Kyle was sitting on the couch with his elbows on his knees, his hands clasped, and his head hung. It killed me to see him like that. I hated knowing that I had caused him so much pain. The guilt of what I had done to him was brutal. I sat down in the chair and waited for him to look up. I had to face this head-on. When he finally raised his head, he didn't even look like himself. He had dark bags under his eyes. It was evident he hadn't slept much, and it looked like he had been crying. I said hey, and he gave me a half smile. He really was an attractive man. I knew that he could make somebody incredibly happy. And he had made me happy for so long. But neither of us were as happy as we should have been. And nobody could make me happier than Andrew.

"How was the weekend?" I asked awkwardly, then immediately felt stupid. I was looking for anything to break the ice, and that was all I could come up with.

"Umm. I've had better." He forced a small laugh.

"I'm sorry. I know. I don't even know where to begin,

Kyle," I said.

"Look, Nora. Before you start explaining, I want to say a few things." He caught me off guard.

"Of course," I nodded. At that point, I would have let him do or say whatever he wanted. Guilt was eating me alive.

"I've had a couple of days to think about all of this. And I have so many feelings about it all. I know exactly when we grew apart." I was surprised by this revelation. Kyle didn't express himself much, and his not only taking the reins of the conversation, but also letting me know that he'd reflected enough to pinpoint where he thought things had gone wrong baffled me.

"It was the miscarriage," he continued. "I internalized all of my grief, and you needed me to be more present for you. I didn't know how to deal with it, so it was easier for me to not deal with it at all. I wasn't there for you to lean on, and in turn, I didn't lean on you. It was a horrible thing we went through together, but we didn't go through it *together* at all."

My jaw must have hung open as he continued. His words were so truthful, and they opened something deep within me. "We've always been an opposites-attract type couple, but I never cared what others thought about us. I never expected that you would cheat on me, but I also know enough about your past to know how important Andrew was to you. Or—is to you, I guess I should say."

"Look, Kyle," I started, and he cut me off.

"Hold on. Please let me finish." I nodded again.

"After the miscarriage, I just didn't know what to do. I started throwing myself even more into work, trying to do more things that I find fun—the things you find nerdy. I went to more expos and conventions, trying to find my smile again. It turns out that a few people from work like the same types of stuff, so you know I would sometimes go with them."

I knew he had been to several conventions with coworkers, and it honestly made me happy because that kept me from having to go.

"Well, one of our clerks, Danielle ... she and I really bonded over our mutual appreciation for Star Wars ... "

"Oh, my God." My hands started shaking as I began putting things together.

"No, Nora. Nothing happened. I mean, nothing physical. We just have a lot in common, so talking to her came naturally. It was very organic how our friendship blossomed. And I mean that when I use the word *friendship*."

"Kyle. Is she who you went to the last function with when I was supposed to go with you? And you said that your coworker would go if I didn't want to go?" I felt a little sick.

"Yes. But I knew you didn't want to go, Nora. I knew you wanted to be there for Ziah, and Danielle really does love Star Wars as much as I do."

"Did you confide in her about the miscarriage?" I asked as a tear ran down my cheek. He was silent.

"Kyle! Did you talk to *her* about your grief instead of me?" I yelled.

"Yes," he said, somberly and hung his head again.

I felt like the wind had been kicked out of me. I sat in silence while my brain tried to make sense of everything. I wondered how in the world everything had come to this. Then I thought about Andrew. And I knew that everything I had been doing with him was worse than anything Kyle had done or was continuing to do.

"Do you have feelings for her?" I asked.

"I don't know, Nora. No. Yes. I think so. I mean, you and I are not in sync anymore. And you know that or else you wouldn't have turned to what's his name." He knew his name.

"How did we get here?" I asked through tears.

"It's just life, I suppose. Or the universe, as you like to say. It's pulled us in different directions. To quote one of my least favorite Star Wars movies, The Phantom Menace, 'You can't stop change any more than you can stop the suns from setting.'"

I laughed. And he laughed. I got up and sat next to him on the couch. He held my hand in his.

"I still owe you an explanation," I said. "I honestly never expected anything like this to happen with Andrew. Well, I guess I shouldn't say that. When he and I split up, there was a piece of me that wondered if our paths would ever cross again. But I always did everything possible to shut those feelings of wonder out. When I married you, and I said those vows, I meant them. I loved you. And I still *do* love you. But it's just different. I don't know how to explain it. I never stopped loving Andrew. I just started ignoring my love for him. And then we had the miscarriage, and I was in a dark place. You and I grew apart. I needed you, and you weren't there. Don't get me wrong. I'm not blaming you for any of this. But then out of nowhere, Andrew popped up. He contacted me on social media, and I didn't know it would lead to where it did. And to be clear, I know that my text message may make you think otherwise, but I have not slept with him, Kyle. But we have met up."

"Okay, stop. I don't know if I want to hear anymore," he

said, as he pulled his hand away from mine.

"No. I need to be able to get it all off of my chest," I continued. "He reached out to me and we started communicating. He is married but separated."

"Oh, lovely," he interrupted me. "Sounds like a standup guy."

"Kyle, please," I said.

"Okay, sorry. Go on," he replied.

"Anyway, we started communicating and reminiscing. And the next thing I knew, every feeling I ever had for him surfaced again."

"Nora, I appreciate your honesty, but you really can spare me some of the details. I don't want to know how madly in love with him you are. Really," he said. And as I looked at him, I saw the man I had married. Even through his hurt, smart-ass comment, I could see the sweet man that I'd stood at the altar with. And suddenly, I felt the room spinning. But I had to finish telling him everything. He deserved to know it all.

"I'm sorry. I know. It's just so not like me to do something like this, so I'm trying to get everything off my chest. But I guess the summed-up version is that I do love him, Kyle. You and I grew apart. The miscarriage probably had a lot to do with that, like you said, but there were other things, as well. We were never the perfect match. I don't think we were long for this world with or without a miscarriage. And with or without Andrew ... or Danielle," I looked down and my chin started quivering. He reached for my hand again and he squeezed it.

"I know. I'm sorry," he said.

"Oh God, Kyle. I'm the one who's sorry. I can't believe how badly I've hurt you and what I've put you through. Reading that text message must have been awful. And the fact that you couldn't reach me afterward … I can't even imagine," I said.

"Yeah. It was rough. But you're right, Nora. We weren't long for this world. And having the weekend to think about it all by myself helped me realize that. I love you. And I know you love me. We will be okay. We will be. I will always love you. But the road goes ever on and on." I recognized the quote from Lord of the Rings. We sat in silence holding hands for what felt like an entire hour and just a second at the same time.

"What happens now?" I asked.

"I think we take time apart. Isn't that what people do? See how things go with a separation? I'm sure you'll be with Andrew, and I'll figure things out on my own for a while," he forced a smile.

"I want you to be happy, Kyle. Maybe Danielle will give you something I never could," I replied. I looked at our wedding photo on the mantle. We had both been so naive. Those two smiling people never could have imagined this conversation would have taken place. Or at least I don't think we could.

"I'll be happy, eventually." He smiled at me.

I kissed his cheek and he hugged me tight. It felt nice. But it felt like goodbye.

We slept in separate bedrooms and when I woke in the morning, he was gone. I was too exhausted that evening to update Andrew, so when Monday morning came, I sent him a message.

"I talked with Kyle. It turns out, he's sort of been hanging out with a girl from work. Nothing too terribly inappropriate, but not necessarily innocent. But that's unimportant. We are separating. I don't know the logistics of it all, but at least it's done. I feel awful for him. Have you talked to Claire?" I texted him.

"Good morning, beautiful. I missed you last night. I know that must have been hard on you to have to tell him everything. If you need some time to yourself, just let me know. I've already told you that I'll wait forever. I am calling Claire at lunch today and letting her know that I'm going to file for divorce. We haven't spoken in several weeks, so I don't think it should come as any surprise to her. She'll be relieved that I file instead of her, I'm sure," he said back.

"I am exhausted. I need to fill the girls in, but I don't want to replay the scenario over and over. I'll wait until one of them brings it up and I'll ask if we can all meet or something," I told him.

"I'm sorry, Nori. I never would have imagined this. But then again, I would have," he said.

"Just let me know when you talk to Claire. I love you. And I miss you. Have a good day, and text me later."

"I love you, too" he responded.

I needed to get ready for work, but first, I pulled up my Yelp app and looked up therapists in the Dallas area.

ALEXIS

I was ecstatic to be in Dean's arms. I hadn't felt so strongly about anybody ever. Being apart from him for the weekend was confirmation that absence does indeed make the heart grow fonder. When we got back to my place, we couldn't keep our hands off each other. We both knew what was coming, because we had been talking about it and anticipating it. I put Gibbs in my bathroom, because I never liked the thought of him witnessing me participating in such acts. He was much too cute and innocent to know his mommy had such a nasty side.

I couldn't get Dean's shirt off quick enough. I smiled at his body and rubbed my hands all over his six pack and his pecs. His body was a ten. I grabbed his shoulders and squeezed them. His shoulders were broad, and his skin was smooth. He asked if he could do the same with my shirt. He pulled it over my head and unfastened my bra with one hand. When he kissed my neck, I felt like we were living out a scene in a movie. He was so strong but delicate with me. I didn't want to rush this moment, but it was hard to slow down. We made our way to my bed, only knocking down a few things in our path, and when we lay down, we kissed more passionately than I have ever kissed anybody in my entire thirty-five years. And believe me, I've had a lot of kisses. He started kissing down my neck and then to my chest. He raised his head back up and smiled at me. Damn he was hot.

"What is it?" I said between breaths.

"I'm just soaking in this moment, Alexis," he kissed my forehead, and then came back to my lips. I pulled him as close to me as I could, and I could feel that he wanted me as badly as I wanted him. I took his belt off and then went for his pants. He stopped my hands.

"Are you sure you want to do this? I know that I do, but I want to be respectful of you, and I don't want to make you feel pressured."

"I've never been more sure of anything in my life," I whispered in his ear just before I bit it. I got his pants off, and then I took it upon myself to take off my own. I grabbed a condom out of my nightstand and put it on him myself. He watched as I rolled it down and then threw the wrapper across the room. I wasn't disappointed in what I felt. He got on top of me and our kissing became even more heated. His body was amazing, and his biceps turned me on even more as he held himself up over me. He bit my lip, and when he did, I grabbed his ass and pulled him into me. I wrapped my long legs around his waist and an involuntary noise escaped my mouth. It was a combination of a gasp and a squeal. I had waited for this moment with Dean for a long time, and he felt perfect inside me. We were in the same rhythm with each other on an insane level. We continued, and every time I felt the urge to have an orgasm, I fought it so that I could continue to enjoy every second. I knew that Dean was doing the same. Every now and then, he'd pull away from my face and smile at me. Never had a man made me feel so wanted. I could feel his rhythm change a bit and his ass tightened. I knew he was about to go, so I completely gave into the feeling and allowed myself to go, as well. Magical doesn't begin to describe it. I don't even think Mr. Webster has a word for what we experienced. He kissed me again and rolled off me but pulled me in close to him. His arms around me felt so good.

"That was amazing," he said, as he breathed heavy.

"On a scale of one to ten, that was a one hundred," I said back.

"Come here," he said as he pulled my face towards him. He started to kiss me again, and I felt like I might explode from all the butterflies swarming my insides. Soon, we were both on our sides facing each other. He propped himself up on his elbow and said, "Alexis, I don't know that I've ever felt this way before."

It wasn't like me to not play some sort of cat and mouse game with men, but with Dean it was different. I didn't want to play any games. I wanted to shout from the rooftops how I felt about him.

"Dean. Would you think I was crazy if I said I love you?" I asked. I had never been the first in any relationship to say I love you. Not to mention it hadn't even been that long since we'd first met. This was a total non-Alexis move.

"Yes," he said, as he smiled. "I'd say you're crazy for loving me. But I'd say I love you right back."

We kissed again. "I have this safety feeling with you. I don't ever want to be out of your arms," I said.

"Good. Because I don't ever want you to be," he replied, squeezing me tight.

"Alexis?" he said as he sat up a bit more.

"Yes?" I blushed.

"I really do mean that. I do love you. I've never had this kind of connection before. I feel like I'd risk it all for you. Like you and I could take on the world, and as long as we had each other and Gibbs, we'd be fine no matter what. We really are crazy." He laughed. I loved that he'd mentioned Gibbs.

"Speaking of Gibbs," I said.

"Oh, I'll let my boy join us," he quipped.

"Ha! Your boy!" I laughed.

"What? We got close while you were gone. We did manly stuff. You don't even know," he laughed back.

He slipped on his boxer briefs, tossed me my shirt, opened the bathroom door, and Gibbs jumped in the bed with us while we watched "Tommy Boy" on TV.

The next morning, I woke up in his arms. He had to go to work, but we were sure to savor every moment we had together. While he showered, I made him eggs and toast. He kissed me and asked what he did to deserve me.

"You put the right lyrics on your Bumble profile, I suppose," I laughed. "Speaking of which, I deleted all of my dating apps. I just thought you should know," I looked down, a little embarrassed.

"Wow, Alexis. You really do love me." I loved it when he said my name. It made me blush a little each time.

"You better get going, mister," I said, squeezing his ass.

"Should I come here after work? Or do you and Gibbs want to come to my place?" he asked.

"Just come here. Gibbs is better here," I replied.

"Okay. Have a good day. And Alexis?"

"Yes?" I smiled, sitting there in my T-shirt.

"I love you." He grinned widely and closed the door before I could say it back. I quickly texted him, "I love you, too."

I couldn't wait to tell the girls all about it. Dean really was my perfect man. Though, I felt bad bringing it up because I knew Nora had been having her talk with Kyle the night before. I planned to wait until somebody else started the text thread. I took Gibbs on our morning jog and when I returned, the nurse practitioner who had done my Botox asked if I was interested in having a party on Friday. She had some new filler she wanted to inject under my eyes, and I was always up for it. I figured I'd invite the girls and Johnathan and Blake. They got Botox as often as we did, and they looked just as fab, too. I told her to count me in, and we could have the crew over to my apartment. The group texts started shortly after.

I would be able to invite them to the party, tell them I'd slept with Dean, and empathize with what they all had going on in one text message. There was a lot going on. I wanted to know what had happened with Nora and Kyle, but I knew she'd tell us Friday at the Botox party, or she'd text us details when she felt like it. I didn't want to press the issue like Steph seemed to be doing.

I decided to get my nails done, and while I was sitting in the pedicure chair, I reached out to Johnathan and Blake about the party Friday. All the girls had said they were in.

"Yasss, Queen!" Blake replied. He was always so funny.

"We are definitely in, Alexis! Our foreheads are looking like a shar-pei lately. No offense, honey," Johnathan texted back.

"OMG! Don't call me a shar-pei!" Blake replied.

"Okay, okay. So I'm counting y'all in," I said.

"For sure. Is it just you fab five and us?" Blake inquired.

"I think so. Is that okay?" I asked back.

"That's perfect," Johnathan said.

I sat back, enjoying my pedicure and manicure and thinking about my night with Dean. Just as I was thinking about him, he texted me. I could barely slide open my phone to read the text with my nails wrapped in foil.

"You have to tell Chloe soon. I talked to my boss. He doesn't give a rat's ass if we lose him as a customer. He said he's constantly harassing the waitresses and the beer girls on the course. I had no idea, or I would have kicked his ass sooner. By the way, I can't stop thinking about you."

I was dying to text him back, but my nails wouldn't allow it. I pushed down the button to talk text and said, "Okay. I love you." But Siri jumbled up my words. So I tried again. It ended up typing out, "Ole, all of you." I attempted one last time and shouted, "Okay, period. I love you, exclamation point." It worked. And everybody in the salon stared at me.

I was anxious for my nails to dry so I could talk to him. I needed to figure out how to tell Chloe, when a genius idea hit me. I'd confront *his* ass instead. Or I'd at least go to him first. I didn't want Brett to have a chance to deny it to Chloe if she confronted him. I wanted to see his face as he knew he was busted. It took my nails forever to dry, and I usually savor every moment of a good manicure, but I needed to talk to Dean about my plan. As soon as I left, I called my ally.

"Listen, I want to confront Brett in person. What do you think about that?" I asked.

"I'm worried about you doing that, Alexis. I don't know what that jerk will do to you," he replied.

"Dean. He may be a cheater, but he's no woman beater. I'll be fine. I've held my own with men before. You know that," I reminded him.

"Fine. But keep your phone near you and call me as soon as the confrontation is over. Be careful, baby."

I smiled when he called me baby. "I will."

I texted Johnathan to see if Brett was at the office. He said they both were, at the moment. I told him to please make sure that he stuck around for at least fifteen minutes. That's how long it would take me to drive across the city to his building. Johnathan had no idea what I was up to, but he agreed to stall him if he attempted to leave. When I arrived, I valeted. Their office was on the eighteenth floor of a ritzy building in downtown. I didn't have time to park myself, and quite frankly, I didn't want to. When I got in the elevator, I didn't even know what I would say to him. Adrenaline coursed through me, and then the door opened. I stepped out and I could see him through the glass doors of his swanky office. I also saw Johnathan across the way. I told the receptionist that I was there to see Brett and that he was expecting me. She picked up the phone and I watched him look at me through the glass as he spoke to her. He waved me in.

"Hello, Alexis. To what do I owe the pleasure?" he said smugly as he thumbed through some paperwork on his desk.

"Cut the bullshit, asshole. I know what you're doing to Chloe. I know about Heather," I said sternly.

"Alexis, you don't know what you're talking about. Trust me," he asserted. He regarded me with an unfamiliar look.

"Yes, I do. I know Heather is your girlfriend. And that y'all have been together for at least a few months. Who is she, anyway? Does she know you're married?" I asked.

"Alexis. Trust me. You don't want to go there." His voice was still smug, but there was a clear warning in it.

"Go where, Brett? You don't want me to tell your high school sweetheart—who thinks you can do no wrong, mind you—that you're fucking somebody else?" I was nearly in tears, but I had to stay strong. "Fine. Either you tell her, or I will. And I'm not fucking around with you. I'm serious. You tell her or I will. You have until Friday." I couldn't believe how bold I sounded.

"Alexis, listen to me carefully. You don't want to do this. If you love Chloe, you won't do this to her. The last time nearly killed her," he said.

"What the hell are you talking about?" I asked. "Last time? You're talking out of your ass."

"No, I'm not. I'm telling you. You don't know what you're talking about. This isn't exactly foreign territory for Chloe and me, Alexis. Please don't tell her. She's so fragile. She puts on this happy go lucky front for everybody, but she's very fragile."

"What the fuck do you mean this isn't foreign territory for y'all?" I was shaking.

"As much as you'd like to think you do, you don't know everything about Chloe. Two years ago, we had an issue, and it almost broke her."

"What kind of *issue*?" My voice was getting even louder.

"I had an affair with a client. It lasted about six months.

Chloe caught me. I promised her I would never do it again, but it almost broke her, Alexis." By this point his voice had changed to a pleading tone.

I was speechless for a moment. Chloe wouldn't keep a secret like that from us. We always had each other's backs. How could she go through something like that alone?

"I don't believe you. You're bluffing," I said.

"I swear to God, Alexis. Chloe caught us texting but didn't tell me she was onto me. She ended up following me to meet her at her house and busted in on us," he said.

"Fucking?" I screamed.

"Shhhh! Alexis! Yes, we were making love," he said.

"Making love? Did you love the bitch?" I demanded answers.

"Alexis, you need to calm down. Chloe knows all about that. We worked through it. It's in the past. But if she finds out about Heather, I don't know what it'll do to her. I honestly don't."

"Don't you dare put this shit on me. If I tell Chloe about you and Heather, her reaction is on *you*! Not me. You fucking asshole," I said, tears welling up.

"You need to be a good friend to her, Alexis. Think about how hurt she will be, and you'll be the one inflicting the pain on her. Now won't you feel like the bitch then?"

Before I could even completely process the bullshit he had just said, I reared my freshly manicured fist back and punched him square in the left eye.

"Get the fuck out of here, you bitch!" he yelled.

"Gladly, you piece of shit. You have until Friday," I said as I picked up my Louis Vuitton and walked out like I owned the damn place. It wasn't until I reached the elevator that I realized how badly my hand hurt. Johnathan chased after me while I waited for it to arrive on my floor.

"Alexis, but what the hell just happened?" he asked.

"I can't tell you right now. But you'll find out soon enough. I'm sorry, J. Just know that your business partner is a piece of shit."

"Well, I'm completely aware of that already," he responded.

"Good. I'll see you Friday," I said, as I kissed his cheek and got in the elevator. When the door closed, I started bawling. My hand fucking hurt, and I felt so awful for Chloe. Why in the world had she not told us about Brett's first affair? I felt a little betrayed. But Chloe had always been the optimistic one of us all. She knew that if she told us, we would have voted him out immediately. And if she wanted to give him another chance, that was really her business. But you know the saying, fool me once, shame on you, fool me twice, shame on me. Hopefully Chloe would realize that Brett wasn't worth her time. He was clearly a repeat-offender. And I had meant what I said to him when I told him he had until Friday.

When I got in the car, I called Dean. He answered on the first ring. I knew he was worried about me. When I told him Brett had called me a bitch, I had to talk him out of driving to the office himself. I reminded him that I'd taken care of myself all these years and had never needed a man to fight my battles before. He respected that and said he'd chill out for now, but he couldn't make any promises for the next time he saw him. I told him I was going to run by the cleaners and get my clothes, grab a smoothie, and then home to ice my hand and lay on the couch. What had started out as an amazing morning had taken a dark turn.

When I walked into my apartment, I was shocked to see that Dean had beat me there. He stood up in my living room, holding a frozen bag of peas and a glass of wine.

"How the hell did I get so lucky?" I asked.

"Good taste in music, remember?" He smiled.

CHLOE

I wasn't exactly happy with the way that Brett had been acting when we got home from our GB weekend. He couldn't even be bothered to stand up when I walked in the house. It reminded me of when we'd had some marital troubles a couple of years prior. I never liked to address those times. In fact, I pretended as if they never happened. Even the girls didn't know. But when he acted disconnected and aloof upon my arrival, I couldn't help but think of it. Plus, I wasn't in the best of moods anyway since Nora's cheating revelation. I fully expected to walk into the house to a beautiful meal set on the table with fresh flowers. Instead, he had the boys out back working in the yard while he watched television. That night when we went to sleep, I didn't snuggle up to him as I usually did. I told him I was exhausted and just wanted to sleep. The disconnect was evident.

The next morning, I kept my focus on other things. I couldn't wait to read the *O Magazine* piece on Ziah when it came out. I was excited to get together with the girls again

Friday, even though we had just been together. I wanted to know about Little Tommy. And as much as I didn't want to admit it, I really wanted an update on Nora's situation.

I threw myself into housework for the week. Since Brett had been dealing with clients all weekend, the house was a wreck. There was laundry scattered throughout the entire house, and dishes piled two feet high. As I picked up dirty towels, I reminded myself that someday, the boys would be grown and gone, and there wouldn't be dirty towels to pick up anymore. I needed to soak in the moments. Then a part of me thought about the fact that Brett would probably still be leaving his laundry everywhere, and it irritated me all over again.

Brady and Cooper were playing video games in Brady's room when I broke up their boy time and asked them to empty the dishwasher. That was the simplest of the chores, after all. They reluctantly agreed, while I continued collecting laundry. As I got to my bathroom, I started separating Brett's dirty laundry into piles of darks and lights. I felt something odd in one of Brett's pants' pocket, and when I pulled it out, I saw that it was a golf tee. I didn't think much of it as I tossed it into the dish on our bathroom counter. But as it landed, I saw the calligraphed writing. It had the name of the course that Dean managed. I recalled Brett specifically telling me that he had never been there before. I picked it up and examined it closer.

"What the hell?" I said out loud. Thoughts began to flood my mind. *Why did Brett tell me he had never been there? Were Brett and Dean friends? Why was Brett lying to me again?*

I went through every pocket of the rest of his dirty pants

and even checked his shirt pockets. I immediately felt like I had when he'd lied to me before, and I wondered if there was any chance he could be having an affair. Any time that suspicion had arisen between that time and now, I shut it down. There are four ways that a scorned wife can react. The obvious is to divorce him. Another is to stay with him and completely forgive him and move on. One option that a lot of women do when they stay is to obsess over every single thing that he does and try to catch him in the act again. And option four is to pretend like it never happened at all. Numbers two and four sound similar but are not the same at all.

When I first caught Brett cheating on me, I obsessed about everything he did. I monitored his phone log, checked the mileage on his vehicle, and tracked his phone location. But when I realized that no matter what, I was going to stay with him, I pretended that it had never happened. I didn't forgive him, because I tricked myself into truly going on with life as if there was nothing to forgive. I did my best to erase it from my memories. I never even wrote about it in my journal, and I never told a soul that it had happened. I felt completely humiliated. Brett was my high school sweetheart, and on the outside, we'd had the perfect marriage and the perfect life. I couldn't stand for anybody to have any other perception of us than that. Not even Johnathan knew about it, and he was like family to both Brett *and* me. Brett had kept it top secret from everybody at the office, which was a relief. Humiliation wasn't something that I dealt with well.

I continued to study the golf tee and considered calling Johnathan. I wondered if he could give me any insight. Then I wondered if Dean and Brett knew each other. I knew that

Dean had worked that weekend, and I wondered if he'd told Alexis that he'd seen him. I sat on the edge of my bed with the tee in my hand and saw glimpses of my future. If Brett was cheating on me again, would I really leave him? What would that life be like? I hadn't been without Brett in twenty-two years. I had broken completely when he cheated on me before. But I felt stronger now. Suddenly, Brady walked in and broke my concentration.

"Mom. We unloaded the dishes. Are we supposed to load the dishwasher, too?" he asked.

"Yes, please. That would help me out, honey," I replied.

"What are you doing?" he asked. He could tell I was in a daze.

"Oh nothing. Taking a break from all of this laundry you guys left me to drown in!" We both laughed.

"Sorry about that. We weren't home much while you were gone," he said.

"I know, babe. No problem," I replied. He walked out.

I wondered if I was jumping to conclusions. Nothing necessarily pointed to him cheating on me. But one thing was for certain—he was lying to me. And I was going to get to the bottom of it.

ZIAH

When Little Tommy came back to us, he had a small sling pinned to his onesie. Since he was so young, his bones would heal quicker than an adults would have. He only had to wear the sling during certain hours of the day, so it wasn't as bad as I'd initially thought. Layla adapted to him right off the bat because he was a baby, and I'm sure the baby doll that Leon had given her helped with that. Cyrus was happy to see Tommy again. Tommy smiled at me when Sherry handed him over, and I nuzzled him delicately. I didn't want to hurt him anymore than he already had been.

Leon was reserved. I could tell that he was thinking about the monsters who'd done this to him. I had to remind him that our job as foster *parents* was to love them while they're with us and love them big. Our job as foster care *advocates* is to work on changing the procedures so that these children are not only protected but given the opportunity for a bright future. But in this moment, we were foster parents, not advocates. We needed to focus on loving him. And luckily, that job came easily to both of us. Before Sherry left, she informed us that a relative of Layla's was close to being approved as a temporary caregiver for her. This meant that our time with her would soon be over if all went as planned. This was always the bittersweet part. But again, we focused on loving her big while she was ours.

Throughout the week, I had been in touch with Penny from *O Magazine* on multiple occasions. We scheduled the photographer to come photograph Leon, Cyrus, and me on Wednesday. She said they'd be sending a stylist with different options for all of us, which reminded me of my modeling days. I had been in magazines for articles about foster care before, but nothing on this level.

When the photographer and stylist came, I felt like a celebrity. The girls were always teasing me about that, but this time I really felt like it. I had never been treated like such a star. The dresses they brought for me were stunning, but I chose white pants and a sleeveless fuchsia top. I'd had my hair done recently and I was rocking kinky curls. The girls all loved when I had my hair like that, and I loved that it embraced my culture, but was still ultra-chic. Leon looked like a million bucks in his slim fit jeans, Gucci shoes, and beige sports coat. And little Cy had on slim fit khaki pants and a chambray shirt. We looked great.

The photographer took photos of us on our couch and in our backyard by the pool. She got photos of me alone standing in our foyer, and then in our outdoor swinging chair. I felt confident the photos would turn out perfectly. My experience in modeling certainly helped. And Leon and Cyrus were naturals. While we were taking the photos, Tommy and Layla did great. Tommy was in his stroller near us, and Layla sat on the steps watching, while Nina watched the two of them.

When the photographer left, I checked my phone and saw a missed call from Sherry. I called her back immediately. She said they had sped up the process of getting Layla's grandmother certified, and she was scheduled to leave Friday morning. I told Leon and he was crushed. He had grown really fond of her, especially since he'd helped her come around to smiling and feeling comfortable. I had to remind him again that the goal in all of this is for a fit family member to get custody of her. He knew that. But it was hard not to feel selfish while doing selfless acts sometimes.

Nina made a fantastic salmon dinner that night, and I tried to act like everything was normal. I told Leon about the case I was working on at work, and he told me about a few of his appointments that had come in that day. One particularly interesting one was a dog who had been on a fishing boat with his owner, and when the owner casted out, the dog jumped in and chased it and swallowed the hook. Leon had to perform surgery to retrieve the hook. I loved hearing him tell lifesaving stories about the pets he treated. His job was draining, and veterinarians are high up on the suicide list. I was sure to always talk to him about his day, so he was able to release anything that built up inside of him. I told him about Alexis's Botox party Friday, and of course, he was fine with me going. I hated that I couldn't get a little Botox before the photoshoot, but I knew they'd smooth me out in editing.

After dinner, I helped Nina clear the table while Leon carried Tommy to his room. Layla was under my feet every step of the way as Nina and I cleaned. I finally asked her if she was ready for me to read to her, and she nodded.

I followed her to her room, and I read her *Wherever You Are My Love Will Find You*. I choked up but didn't want her to see me cry. I tucked her in and told her goodnight. When I walked out, I found Leon rocking Tommy. I reflected for a moment on what we did for these children. I hoped they could feel our love, and I prayed that they would be loved just as much by somebody else. I made my way down to Cyrus's room and told him a bedtime story. He had almost grown out of bedtime stories, but I knew Lizzie didn't have any kind of sweet routine with him at home, so I wanted to continue ours as long as possible. When each child was sound asleep, Leon and I crawled into bed. I cuddled up close to him and he wrapped his arms around me. We really did make a great team.

STEPH

When Friday arrived, I could hardly stand it. I wanted so desperately to know what the hell was going on with Kyle and Nora. Nora told me that she only wanted to say it once, so I respected her wishes and didn't ask any more questions about it. There was one part of our conversation that I kept thinking about, though. She had said something about me not knowing Kyle as well as I thought I did. I wondered what that meant. And, of course, I tried to dissect it all week. We hadn't been able to work out together in a while, or I would have probably gotten it out of her there.

I'd reached out to Ziah about what I could do to help children like Tommy, and she had said she'd get back to me. I was hoping that when we were all together, she'd be able to talk to me some more about it. I just couldn't stop thinking about it all. We all knew that Alexis had had steamy sex with Dean, but we wanted to hear all those details, as well. It seemed that everybody had a busy week, and the get-together at Alexis's would be just what we needed. And Blake and Johnathan were always a bonus.

I kissed Mark goodbye and thanked him for letting me have another girls' night so soon after our trip, and I ran out the door. Then I quickly ran back inside to grab my keys and kissed him again. He laughed at me.

When I arrived at Alexis's, I was the last one there. Alexis had several bottles of wine open and since it was just us and Johnathan and Blake, we served ourselves. Her Botox lady was there and had just finished injecting Ziah. It always freaked me out how the skin bulged up right after the injections. Ziah looked like a beautiful villain for about five minutes before her bulges went down. Alexis tried to talk me into getting some, and I stuck to my guns and said no. Chloe was firm, as well. Blake sat down and got some filler under his eyes. I was completely fascinated by it. It looked like it hurt so badly, but he didn't even move. When it was over, he said that it hurt less than Botox. Then it was Johnathan's turn. He got Botox in his crow's feet, forehead, and between his eyes. He winced with each injection.

"Where's my tough man?" Blake teased.

"He's not here at the moment. Leave a message at the tone. Beeeeeeeep," Johnathan replied. We all laughed.

Nora was in good spirits. Ziah seemed a bit low, and Chloe and Alexis were both unusually distant. The group had a completely weird vibe. If it hadn't been for Johnathan and Blake, it would have been extremely awkward. I decided to break the ice and just dive in.

"Nora, are you going to tell us about Kyle?" I asked.

"Yes. I really need to, but I'll wait until Marissa leaves. She doesn't need to hear all about my life." She laughed, talking about the Botox injector.

"Alright, well Alexis is my last one!" Marissa said. "Come on down, Alexis!"

I watched Alexis get all kinds of pokes in her face and it made my eyes water. When Marissa finally gathered up all of things and left, it was finally just the seven of us. We all sat down in the living room. Nora brought us a bottle of red wine and topped off everybody's glasses, saying, "You'll need this." Blake and Johnathan were posed on the edges of their seats.

"Okay," she started. "When I got home from our trip, Kyle looked so defeated. It killed me. But it turned out that he had done a lot of soul searching of his own after I'd sent him that damn text message. He agreed that we weren't a perfect match. The news about Andrew stung, of course. It was an awful conversation that was long overdue. We talked about our miscarriage and how we had both handled it so differently—and how that had seemed to drive us apart." Her voice quivered at the mention of her miscarriage. "We talked about the obvious things we didn't have in common, and how in the beginning, that hadn't bothered us much. I told him everything about Andrew. I hated having to tell him, but I knew he deserved the full truth."

"So he was just fine with it?" Alexis asked.

"No. He wasn't fine with it. Neither of us are fine with it. But it's a part of life. We aren't destined to be with each other, and both of us know that. In fact, he's been spending some time with a girl from his office. Her name is Danielle."

Our jaws fell to the floor. Kyle has never been the type of guy anybody would expect to carry on an inappropriate relationship. But again, we hadn't expected it from Nora either.

"He hasn't done anything physical with her. I mean, he did take her to that Star Wars convention that I was going to go to with him. But in his defense, he told me a coworker wanted to go. He just didn't tell me it was a woman. But I'm not mad at him for that. I can't blame him. She likes what he likes, and I don't. The only thing that hurt me about it all is that he confided in her about our miscarriage, and I couldn't ever get him to talk to me about it." She looked down.

"You have got to be shitting me," Alexis broke the silence in true Alexis form.

"No. I'm not. And while that was painful, I know that none of it holds a candle to what Andrew and I have done to him."

"So what happens now?" Ziah asked.

"He is staying with a friend in uptown. And no, not Danielle. We both know that divorce is inevitable, but we don't want to run out and file immediately. In fact, I think there's actually a timeline, isn't there, Z? Well, either way, we aren't in a rush. It's not like Andrew and I are going to run off and get married," she said.

"Speaking of Andrew, what's the deal with Claire?" Chloe asked pretty stone-faced. I was surprised that she'd even spoken up. But it made sense she'd ask about Claire—she had been so concerned about her when Nora confessed to all of this.

"He talked to her Monday, and he legally filed for divorce. He gave her a heads up. She didn't argue about it. In fact, she's seeing somebody, and was happy to inform him of that. So, it is what it is. It's devastating, but at the same time, I'm excited for a life with Andrew again. And I feel like such a bitch for saying that. But I love him so much; it's beyond my control. Also, y'all will be shocked to hear that I started seeing a therapist."

"That is amazing, Nora! I am so proud of you!" Ziah exclaimed.

"What happened to your hand, Alexis?" Chloe changed the subject unexpectedly, and it looked like she was shooting daggers at Alexis with her eyes. Her voice cool. She hardly sounded like herself.

"Oh, it's just a bruise," Alexis responded. She sounded nervous, which was strange. I wondered what the hell this had to do with anything, but Chloe continued looking at her intently with squinted eyes, as if trying to see through her. I glanced at Alexis's bruised hand and then around the room at everyone else. Johnathan and Blake were looking down, swirling their glasses. It was obvious they felt awkward.

"Well I'm dying to know about the Dean sex!" I said, trying to change the subject and break whatever weird dynamic was happening between Chloe and Alexis.

"Oh, my gosh, y'all. He is so amazing. The sex is everything. I can't even put it into words. And y'all are gonna die when I tell you this!" She was always so animated when she told stories. "I told him I love him!" We all squealed and kicked our legs. Johnathan and Blake were adorably delighted at the news.

"Alexis, can I talk to you on the balcony for a moment?" Chloe asked. There was no emotion or excitement in response to Alexis's news. It was like she had been possessed. And for her to interrupt this particularly huge moment was even more odd.

"Um, sure," Alexis said, as she stood up. I wondered if this was how Chloe summoned her kindergartners to the hallway if they got in trouble, though something told me she'd not talked to many people like this before.

They were outside for about ten minutes while we all continued visiting and tried not to look their way. Then Chloe opened the sliding glass door and summoned Johnathan to join them. The night kept getting more bizarre by the moment. I used this as an opportunity to talk to Ziah.

"Z, I want to do something. What the heck can I do to make a difference?" I asked her.

"There's so much you can do, Steph. Monetarily you can..." I cut her off.

"No. Not monetarily. I want to actually physically do something to help these kids," I said.

"Well, I know that you're drawn to Little Tommy and his situation, but you should research the older children, too. They break my heart, Steph. Lizzie won't let us foster anybody over the age of ten, but they're the ones who need a lot of help in their lives. Some of them are going to age out of the foster system and not have any idea what to do or where to go. This is how they end up on the streets. It's horrible. The state just turns them loose and they haven't the slightest clue what to do," she said.

"Damn. I had no idea. Okay, I'm going to talk to Mark, and we will figure something out," I said. My wheels started spinning, but I needed Mark to be on the same page.

NORA

I contacted a therapist when I got off work Monday and set up a meeting for the soonest she could get me in, which was Thursday. After having my conversation with Kyle, I realized that there were issues I needed help working through. I knew I hadn't taken the appropriate steps after Andrew and I had broken up all those years ago. I should have seen a therapist then. I had been depressed and broken. If I had spoken to somebody professionally, they would have told me that I needed closure. And my guess is that trying to get that closure would have brought Andrew and me back together again. I also needed to finally address my miscarriage. It seemed taboo to talk about the subject, and I'd been fairly quiet when it came to talking to the girls, so I never discussed it in depth. One moment, I was pregnant, and the next, I wasn't. For one week food was delivered to us, and then life went back to normal, and nobody spoke about it.

I told Andrew I felt that I needed to address my issues, and he was one hundred percent supportive. He said that therapy had helped him immensely when he and I broke up, and he'd recommend it to anybody struggling with anything.

When I sat down across from the therapist, I was nervous. I wasn't a big sharer. But she made me feel comfortable. I started off by telling her about my past with Andrew, and how he had recently come back into my life. I gave her a quick rundown of my issues with Kyle and informed her of the miscarriage and that Kyle and I had separated. We had only one hour allotted for our meeting, so I was only able to give her summaries. She took notes, and I felt good afterward. Even though she'd only listened, it felt good to tell somebody everything—somebody who wasn't one of the girls and who didn't know all parties involved. We scheduled our next meeting for one week later, and she informed me that she would listen but also advise me at that visit. This first one was more of a listening session.

I called Andrew when it was over, and he was proud of me. I was proud of myself, too. I went to his place and we watched "Lonesome Dove" in its entirety. I felt safe with him again. A weight had lifted off me since Kyle and I had separated. Andrew and I made out several times, because we couldn't resist each other. But we both agreed that we shouldn't sleep together while my separation was so fresh, and his filing for divorce was new. It was extremely hard on both of us, but we knew we owed it to our spouses to at least refrain from that. In the grand scheme of things, we had already hurt them deeply, but having sex now would feel like twisting the knife we'd already plunged into their backs.

Work on Friday was nuts. Mothers gave birth left and right, and it seemed like half of the babies needed to go to the NICU. My job was bittersweet. At times, I got to be with people on the greatest days of their lives, and other times, I was with them on the worst days of their lives. I was relieved when my shift was over. I was ready for wine and visiting with the girls. I wasn't necessarily looking forward to telling them all about Kyle and me, but I knew I'd have to eventually, and this would be the perfect place.

Shortly after arriving, I dove right into it. I was impressed that they didn't have more questions than they did. They were all supportive of me going to therapy. Chloe was still a little harder to crack than the rest of them. Then she had some weird exchange with Alexis, and the two went outside. I wasn't sure what was going on. It wasn't like any of us to separate from the others and have a conversation like they were having. While the two of them were outside, I visited with Blake and Johnathan. They said they had a great time with Chloe's boys while we were on our trip. Suddenly, Chloe called Johnathan to join Alexis and her outside and the rest of us were left a little stunned. I snuck away to text Andrew.

"I miss you," I said.

"I miss you, too. Come home," he replied.

"We don't have a 'home,' silly." I hit send.

"Home is wherever we are together. So come home." It made my heart flutter.

"I will soon." I put my phone away just as Alexis walked in with tears in her eyes.

ALEXIS

I'd told that son of a bitch he had until Friday to come clean with Chloe. I hadn't heard from him, so I knew he was being a coward. I called his office and his secretary told me he was unavailable. I didn't want to bring Johnathan into it, so I let it rest. But I knew I needed to follow through with my end of the deal. I'd dealt with assholes before, and Brett didn't scare me one bit. I didn't like the idea of Chloe hurt, but he'd done the damage whether she was aware of it or not. I wasn't sure how I would tell her, but I'd have to do it at my apartment. After all, I wanted to at least give him until the end of the day to confess.

Nora had thrown us a curve ball when she told us Kyle had been hanging out with a female coworker behind her back. He always had seemed like the most innocent dude in the world, and to think of him being anything but that was weird. I told the girls about how Dean was amazing in bed. I wanted to give them all the details, but Chloe blindsided me by asking what had happened to my hand. She caught me off guard, so I said it was a bruise. And it was. That wasn't a lie. But when she summoned me outside, I had no idea what I was in for.

We stepped out on the balcony and she stared out into the city. I stood by, quietly waiting for her to say something. The air was cool and still. It was an unusual Friday night in Dallas. Finally, Chloe spun around and looked me dead in the eyes. She looked different, though I couldn't pinpoint exactly what had changed.

"I want to know what happened to your hand," she said firmly.

"Listen, Chlo, I ..."

"Alexis. What happened to your fucking hand?" I wasn't used to her cursing at me.

"I punched somebody," I said. I looked away.

"Did you punch Brett?" she asked. Her voice hadn't changed. She was stern and to the point.

"Why are you asking me this, Chloe?" I asked.

"Brett came home with a black eye. You have a massive bruise on your right hand in the exact spot that would bruise if you punched somebody. Did you or did you not punch Brett?" she asked again.

"Yes," I confirmed.

"What the hell is going on, Alexis?" She finally broke. Tears jumped out of her eyes. I remembered Brett saying that if she found out about the affair, it would break her. He'd said that when she learned about the last one, it almost killed her. I wondered how she had figured out something was going on, and how she'd fit me into it so quickly.

"Chloe, Brett has a girlfriend," I just spit it out. I owed it to her to get it out there. I had given the asshole a chance, and he hadn't confessed.

"How do you know? And are he and Dean friends?" she asked.

"What? Hell no. Dean hates him. No offense." She raised her eyebrow like she didn't blame him. "After your barbecue, Dean told me that he knew him. He said he's a regular at the club."

"Why didn't you tell me?" she asked through tears. "You're supposed to be my best friend. Why would you keep something like that from me?"

"Because I didn't want to believe it. I made Dean do some investigating, and when we were sure it was happening, we had to figure out how to navigate through it while also protecting Dean's job," I said.

"Gee, thanks. Protecting his job is more important than protecting your best friend," she sobbed.

"No, Chloe. I was protecting you, too. I needed to get all my ducks in a row before I confronted anybody about it. I knew if I didn't have all the necessary information, you wouldn't believe me. And you can surely see why I would think that, right?"

"I guess. So who is this person?" she asked.

"Her name is Heather," I said. "Brett is a frequent flyer at Dean's club and he introduces her as his girlfriend. I guess he thinks that course is a safe zone, since he doesn't take any clients there or something. She's younger. Dean thinks she's in her twenties, and she drives a Mercedes SUV," I finished.

"Fucking Heather," she cried.

"Do you know her?" I asked.

"She's their fucking photographer!" she yelled.

"Oh, shit. So she knows you exist."

"Does Johnathan know anything? Was he there when you punched him? Please tell me he hasn't known about this, too." Her mascara was running, and she looked nothing like the Chloe that summoned me outside.

She immediately opened the door and called for Johnathan to join us. I felt sorry for him, having no clue what he was walking into.

"Johnathan, were you aware that my piece of shit husband is having an affair?" she asked blatantly.

"What? What are you talking about?" he seemed genuinely surprised.

"He's fucking around with Heather! He's been taking her to Dean's club and introduces her as his girlfriend," she screamed.

"You have got to be fucking kidding me," he said.

"No. Tell him, Alexis." She nudged me.

"Well, everything that Chloe just said is true. When I came up there the other day, I confronted him about it and told him he had until today to come clean, or I'd tell Chloe myself. He called me a bitch, so I punched his face in," I said.

"He did what?" Chloe was shocked.

"He called me a bitch," I repeated.

"What a fucking piece of shit. Good for you, Alexis. You should have knocked one of his fake ass teeth out while you were at it," she said to my surprise.

"Chloe, I promise I had no clue anything was going on. I mean, Brett is a jerk, and that's a given. And he always does most of the appointments at the listings with Heather, but I would have never guessed," Johnathan said.

"Well what y'all don't know is that this isn't the first time he's done this shit. And I'm not putting up with it anymore. Alexis, do you have another joint?" she asked.

"Fresh out," I managed to giggle through tears.

"Well, let's go back inside and tell the rest of the crew this monster of a fucking revelation," Chloe said. I had never heard her curse so much in such a short time period in our entire friendship. But she certainly had reason to.

We walked in to silence as the room stared at us. Chloe's mascara had run down her cheeks, I was visibly crying, and Johnathan looked terrified.

CHLOE

"Well, Brett's a fucking dickhead. He's got a girlfriend. And I'm leaving his ass. Pass the wine?" I announced as we walked inside.

Everybody sat in silence. Alexis and Johnathan simultaneously grabbed my hands.

Steph spoke first, "I'm lost. Are you okay, Chlo? I don't know what to say. I'm completely shocked."

"Oh, don't be. This isn't the first time," I said, as I downed my entire glass. And there it was.

That morning, I'd been looking forward to this party, but I hadn't decided if I would share my thoughts with the girls. I had never told them about the first affair, and in a way, it felt like I'd betrayed them by keeping it to myself. I also wanted to try to feel out Johnathan and see if he knew anything. I wasn't sure how any of it would be brought up, or if I would chicken out. But when I'd arrived and I saw the bruise on Alexis's hand, it looked exactly like a bruise that somebody would get if they punched somebody.

After finding the golf tee, I'd waited for any other sign from Brett that he was being unfaithful to me. I thought back to that night at Hotel Zaza and how aroused he'd been the last few months. That was exactly how he had been when he'd cheated before. I started piecing more of it together.

Then he came home from work with a black eye, and he said he had been texting a client while looking down and ran right into a pole. Ordinarily, I would have believed him. But I couldn't currently believe anything that came out of his mouth. I was a damn good wife. I did everything that he wanted and needed without him even having to ask. I was a good mother to our boys, and I kept our house clean and cooked dinner every night. I kept thinking back to Andrew's wife, Claire, and wondered if she was like me. Was Andrew like Brett? And was Nora a horrible mistress that Claire wanted to take down? I knew the answer to that. The situations were completely different, even if I wanted to make them seem similar. I still didn't support Nora's decision-making, but I knew it wasn't the same situation I was in.

I hadn't even wanted to look at Brett when he came home. I felt as if my life was a complete lie. Luckily, I'd started my period, which kept me from having to have sex with him for a few days.

On the balcony Friday night, Alexis had confirmed all my suspicions and fears. Brett had a girlfriend. We'd had Heather over for dinner before and gone on double dates with her. Heather had met my boys. It made me sick. I was so relieved to know that Johnathan didn't know anything about it. And I wanted to kick Brett's ass even more when Alexis said he'd called her a bitch.

After I declared that he was cheating on me, everyone at Alexis's stared at me. I was no longer sweet, little Chloe.

Ziah, clearly at a loss for words at the news that this wasn't the first time, asked, "What?"

"Yep. He cheated on me two years ago. Had a full-on affair much like this one. Fucked her and everything. I'm over it. I'm too good for this bullshit," I said.

"Forgive me for not knowing what to say," Ziah replied.

"Oh, y'all are all fine. I just wanted to get it off my chest. I probably need a ride home though. Actually, you know what? Alexis, can I just crash here?"

"You know it, Chlo," she said back to me.

And that's the last I remember of the evening.

ZIAH

Hearing Chloe's revelation felt like getting kicked in the gut. I would have never suspected Brett to be a cheater. He and Chloe seemed to have the perfect life. Or it appeared that way, at least. I was completely dumbfounded to find out that he had done this to her before. She was getting drunker by the minute, and boy was she pissed. She told us that she was leaving him, and I wondered if that would prove true or not. I couldn't even wrap my brain around all she'd revealed. I didn't have time to process the major bomb of it all before they told us that Alexis had known about it and had confronted him and given him a black eye.

That's my girl! I thought to myself. Then I wondered if I'd be representing her again in court. I wouldn't put it past Brett to file charges on her.

I'd been looking forward to the evening, but never thought it would play out anything like it had.

That morning, Sherry picked Layla up early, and Leon and I both cried. We were going to miss her a lot. But it was all part of it. I had an early meeting at the firm, so I dried it up and headed on to work. Leon had a commute, so we told Cy and Tommy goodbye and left them with Nina.

It seemed that every compartment of my brain was constantly occupied. I had work, foster care, family, and events to think about at all times. On my drive to the firm, I wondered what the *O Magazine* piece would end up looking like. I hoped that my voice would come through as I'd wanted it to, and that others would realize that they could help the system, even if not as a foster parent. I thought more about Little Tommy and what his future held. Work had been pretty rough, as we were working on a difficult case, and the opposing team of attorneys were bulldogs and would not back down. When we finished up with another settlement negotiation proposal, I ran out the door. Starting the day off by losing Layla and then having a rough day at work had me looking forward to the get-together even more than usual.

Hearing Nora tell us about Kyle was hard to hear. I hated for anybody to split up, but part of me was relieved. I knew that Nora had her heart set on Andrew, and it made me feel a little bit better to know that Kyle had bonded with somebody, even if it was just on a friendly level. I still felt sorry for the guy. Alexis filled us in on Dean, and I was shocked to hear her say that she loved him. That was foreign territory for Alexis, but I was ecstatic for her. But the Chloe and Brett thing took the cake for most shocking story of the evening.

Chloe ended up spending the night with Alexis and we all left when she started slurring her words. She rambled off what a dick Brett had been, and how she'd take him for everything he was worth. I didn't doubt that part. Family law isn't my forte, but I knew enough about it from law school to know that she would be getting a large chunk of change.

When I got home that evening, everybody was already asleep. I woke Leon up to tell him about Brett. Leon had known Brett for years through all of us. He said that he wasn't as surprised as he should be. He had always gotten a smarmy vibe from him, but he never thought he'd have an affair. He wouldn't have been shocked to hear that he grabbed someone's ass or something, but that was about it.

I kissed him and told him how much I appreciated him. Everything with Nora and Kyle and now Chloe and Brett made me even more grateful for how good we had it. He pulled me close and told me he would never cheat, and he would never leave. We made love, and afterward, as he spooned me, I couldn't help but think about poor Chloe.

STEPH

Saturday morning, I woke up wondering how Chloe felt. I couldn't believe she hadn't told us about it the first time Brett had cheated. I can't even imagine holding something like that inside. And I wondered what she had said to Brett. When I left Alexis's, Brett still didn't know that Chloe knew about the affair yet. I decided to text Alexis instead of Chloe.

"Hey! How is Chloe today? Did she confront the asshole?" I sent.

"Morning, sunshine! Wild night, huh? I'm gonna start a group text so Chloe can tell it herself," she replied. I hoped that it didn't sound like I was trying to talk behind Chloe's back.

"Morning, lovies! That was a wild night! I hope everyone is feeling okay today. I love each one of you!" Alexis texted us all.

"Good morning! Chloe, how are you? Ziah, how are you and Leon doing without Layla?" I replied.

"We are fine. Nora, you good, too?" Ziah asked.

"All good here. But really want to know how Chloe is,"

Nora responded.

"Hey, girls. I ended up getting black out drunk. (Major headache today, by the way! Need some placenta!) I got Heather's phone number from Johnathan and texted her before I confronted Brett. I basically told her that she's a bitch and a home wrecker, and that I hoped it was worth it. Oh, and that I hoped she enjoyed loud snoring that'll keep her awake at night!"

I waited for her to type more. I knew there must be more coming.

"Brett called me almost instantly after I sent her the text. I know she forwarded it to him. He said he wanted to talk about it in person, and I told him to go fuck himself. I went on and on about what a great catch I am (lol) and told him that he better get all his shit out of the house by Sunday evening. He begged me to talk to him in person, and I refused. I said the next time we see each other in person will be when we tell the boys. And that will be Sunday evening. I'm staying at Alexis's all weekend, and the boys are staying with Johnathan and Blake," she finished.

"Yikes. So you're sure it's over?" I asked.

"Abso-fucking-lutely," she sent back quickly.

"I'm so sorry, Chloe. I know you've worked so hard for your sweet family. On the outside you're picture perfect," Nora said. "But boy do I know that things aren't always as they seem."

"I'm so sorry, Chlo. Let us know if we can do anything," Ziah said.

"Thank you. In a way I feel completely defeated, but on the other hand, I feel free. For twenty-two years, he's all I've known. But for twenty-two years, I'm not all that he's known.

I can't trust him. And for him to flaunt Heather in front of Dean pisses me off even more."

"Wow. I'm just still so shocked at it all," I replied.

"Any chance y'all want to go to Mark's show tonight to get our minds off of everything? They're playing at Adair's Saloon. I know he'd like it if we could all come, but no pressure," I added.

"Oooh! I'll ask Leon if he wants to come!" Ziah said.

"Count Dean, Chloe, and me in! Sorry, Chlo! But we're going out tonight!" Alexis said.

"LOL, fine by me!" she responded.

"Would it be too weird if I brought Andrew?" Nora asked. She sent a blushing emoji. "I know he'd love to see everyone."

Everyone agreed that it would be fine for Andrew to join us. Chloe was the only one I was worried about when Nora asked, but it seemed Chloe had bigger issues of her own to focus on than those of Nora's.

I was excited for Mark's show. He was opening for a Texas artist named Courtney Patton, whom I loved. I think it hurt Mark's feelings that I never went to his shows unless he was opening for somebody I really liked. But the truth is, music venues make me nervous about my anxiety. If somebody who had no clue about anxiety asked me to explain it to them, I'd say that it's impossible to manage. There are triggers, and then sometimes there aren't. Sometimes the triggers set it off, and other times it sneaks up out of nowhere when everything is perfectly fine. It feels like a wave consuming your body, physically and mentally. But if you haven't experienced it, then any type of explanation makes it sound much less than it truly is. Adair's was a small venue, but it tended to get loud. So I was a bit nervous. I decided that I'd go ahead and take a pill ahead of time and not drink at all.

As the evening got closer, I texted the girls and told them that I took one of my anxiety pills. I wanted them to have a heads up so that I wouldn't be pressured to drink. I wanted to enjoy the evening with them, and I could do so without drinking.

I rode with Mark and we arrived a little bit early. That was very unusual for me, but I knew I better be ready on time when it came to his gigs. The rest of the band arrived right after us, and I sat at a table and waited for the girls. I was nervous to see Andrew. I hadn't seen him in years, and I wasn't sure how I would react to him in person. I was happy for Nora, but I still felt badly for Kyle. Just as I was thinking about them, they walked in.

NORA

I was really excited to get to be with Andrew in public. I knew he wanted to see the girls so badly, but he was also nervous about it. He knew that even though they didn't necessarily love Kyle, they had respect for him. When we pulled up to Adair's, I gave him a reassuring kiss before he got out and opened my door. It was natural for me to grab his hand, and when we entered the bar, I realized that it might come as a shock to the girls. Steph looked like a deer in the headlights as she watched us enter. I didn't want to let go of Andrew's hand, because I felt like he needed some reassurance. I knew that he was more nervous than I was. I squeezed his hand as I smiled at Steph. She must have realized she was staring blankly, and she broke into a smile.

She stood up when we got to the table and gave Andrew a hug. He told her how good it was to see her again, and she mouthed, "Oh, my God!" to me over his shoulder. I knew she was referring to how good he looked. And that he did. As handsome as he had been when we were younger, he had only gotten better with age. His dimple was prominent as he smiled, asking her how she had been. She couldn't help but smile while she was talking to him. She told him all about Ava, Logan, and Benjamin. He was engaged in the conversation, and I was happy that they were hitting it off after all these years. I went to the bar and ordered us both a beer. When the bartender handed them to me, I turned around to see Alexis, Dean, and Chloe at the table. I had no idea how Chloe would treat Andrew. It was the biggest concern I had for the evening. She stood behind Dean and Alexis as Alexis introduced Dean to Andrew. They gave each other a genuine handshake and I could tell that they were going to get along. When I got to the table, I hugged all three of them. Then I broke the ice, saying, "Chloe, you remember Andrew."

"Of course. It's nice to see you again, Andrew. How have you been?" she asked.

"I've had some ups and downs since we last saw each other, but right now I'm doing really well. I've missed you, Chloe. It's really, really good to see you," he said.

Chloe smiled. She knew as well as I did that he was telling the truth. He really had missed all of them. "It's good to see you, too, Andrew."

"Can I get you ladies anything from the bar?" Dean asked Steph, Chloe, and Alexis.

"I'm not drinking tonight, but thank you," Steph replied.

"I respect that," Dean replied. "What about you two lovely dates of mine?" He smiled at Alexis and Chloe.

"Why don't we just get a pitcher of beer?" Alexis suggested.

"Hey, can we go in on the next one and we can all just share?" I asked.

"Perfect," Chloe responded.

Ziah and Leon walked in looking like a power couple. Leon and Andrew had never met. Everyone at the table stood to greet them, and Ziah immediately gave Andrew a hug. I was relieved to see her smile at him. It seemed like everybody was accepting him as I had wished. I suspected that when they were face to face with him, they might cut him a little more slack, because he's extremely friendly and an all around wonderful person. Plus, his dimple can get him out of almost anything. Leon was very welcoming towards him.

Mark's band started playing, and Steph zoned in on watching him while we continued to visit. We threw back several beers and laughed like old times. Andrew had his hand on my leg under the table, and it made me feel comfortable. Eventually, as everyone got a bit tipsier, he put his arm around me. When Mark's band finished their set, he joined us at our table, and he and Andrew were happy to see each other. Andrew told him what a great job he had done and how good the band sounded. It was all going perfectly. We toasted to Mark and his band, and Steph raised her glass of water.

Shortly after Mark joined us, Courtney Patton took the stage. I loved her voice and her music. Anytime that Steph went to Mark's shows, I usually went with her, because it was my kind of music. I cuddled into Andrew's shoulder and leaned on him while she started. Everybody at our table was enjoying it, and I thought Steph was a little irritated that we hadn't paid as much attention to Mark's band as we did to Courtney. She can be a little too sensitive at times, but she was still enjoying herself. I knew it was hard for her not to drink when everybody else was, but I was proud of her.

Courtney introduced a song as one that had been written by two of her friends, and I listened intently. I was buzzed, and I was so happy to be with my best friends in the world and the love of my life. I couldn't believe it. I'd say that I felt like I needed to pinch myself, but Chloe used to say that, and we saw where that mentality had gotten her. As Courtney sang the first words of the song, I looked at Andrew who was looking at me and smiling. The song was *so* us. It was so coincidental. It was the reassurance I needed that I was in the exact place in my life that I needed to be. I was truly happy. I closed my eyes and listened to her sing. The song was about two lovers who drifted apart, but found each other again later in life. I loved it.

I opened my eyes and looked at Andrew. He squeezed my leg and leaned down and kissed me on my lips. I knew that he was thinking the same thing I was. The song was incredible, and Courtney sang it beautifully. I looked at the rest of our crew and they were smiling at us. For the first time, I felt like I had all their approval. Even Chloe, who winked at me, and mouthed, "I love you."

PART 4

CHLOE

Summer ended and I was excited to throw myself back into work and start a new chapter. Brett moved out right after I found out about his affair. The boys split their time between our house and Brett's high-end apartment downtown. As mad as I was at Brett, I never wanted to keep the boys from him. Telling them that we were separating was the hardest part of the entire situation. Just as everybody else had thought, they were under the impression that we'd had a perfect marriage. I didn't want to smear his name to his own children, so as far as they knew, we had just grown apart. I knew the truth would come out eventually, but I wasn't going to be responsible for causing them animosity between them and their father.

I was looking forward to putting the summer behind me and meeting my new students. My job always had a way of making me happy, even on my bad days. I had one advantage over Brett when it came to the kids, and that was that I got to see them every day at school. I looked forward to getting to see them on the days that they'd be staying with Brett, and I knew

I was blessed to have that privilege. Our divorce was imminent, but the lawyers were still hashing things out. I wanted the house. Brett wanted his car. I wanted half of the money. Brett wanted almost all of it. Just typical divorce nightmare stuff that you hear about but never think you'll have to go through. The house felt odd when I didn't have the boys. It was too big for just me. But I loved it so much. I knew it would take time to adjust to the new normal, but that was the case with the entire situation. I asked Alexis if she'd completely redecorate the house for me so that I wouldn't have to be reminded of Brett every time I turned a corner. She jumped at the opportunity. She had an excellent eye for interior design, and we were both looking forward to it.

Nora had given me the name of her therapist, and I started seeing her every other week. It was nice to get to talk to somebody about everything. A huge weight was lifted off my shoulders as I talked in detail about my feelings in the aftermath of the first affair and then now. Brett had asked if I was interested in couples' counseling, but I wasn't. I had completely given up on us, and I made that clear to him. Johnathan had told me that he was pretty sure that he was still seeing Heather anyway, but since Johnathan had quit working, he didn't have the inside scoop he used to have. Johnathan and Blake had taken my side, and Brett had written them off. I was happy to get to keep them. Brett didn't deserve them. Occasionally I'd get lost in a memory, but the therapist assured me that those feelings were normal and would come and go. To pull myself out of those moments, all I usually had to do was picture Heather. And when I really got caught up, I'd just remind myself that Brett had called Alexis a bitch. Nobody talked like that to my GBs.

I felt that with the changing of the season, good things were in store for me. For twenty-two years I had been living what I thought was a dream. But it turned out to be a series of dreams. Some were good, and others were nightmares. The most recent strain were nightmares, and I just knew that good dreams were coming my way soon.

ZIAH

The *O Magazine* piece turned out perfectly. My voice came across exactly how I had wanted it to, and the photos were absolutely stunning. Penny did a wonderful job putting it all together into one cohesive piece. I knew it would reach an audience who would otherwise not have known the numerous ways they could help in the foster care community. The issue came out in September, and Steph decided to throw me a celebration. She invited all of us over to her and Mark's house. It was a really delightful surprise, because usually I felt that Steph resented my achievements. But she was over the moon with excitement about this. She kept telling me that she had a surprise for me, and she'd give it to me at the end of the night. I was anxious to find out what it was, but I soaked up every moment of the evening.

Mark had his PA system hooked up and beautiful songs from the Sinatra era played while we all visited under the lights out back. I knew Steph had purchased the string lights just for this occasion. She and Mark didn't usually have all of us over, but Steph was enjoying playing hostess. She put a lot of thought into the details, and it didn't go unnoticed. There were several copies of the *O Magazine* issue out on display. She had gotten a hold of the photographs by contacting Penny and had them blown up on canvases for us. Steph had hung them up everywhere we turned, and we got to keep them when the night was over.

The entire evening was amazing. Alexis and Dean were there. Andrew and Nora were there. Chloe was there. Leon and me, and Johnathan and Blake. We didn't bring our kids, but there was one exception to that rule: Johnathan and Blake had brought their new baby. Leon and I were so happy to see Tommy, and to see how great Johnathan and Blake were with him. It was a match made in heaven. When we realized that Tommy would go to the state, we talked to Sherry about allowing Johnathan and Blake to form a relationship with him, so that when the time came, they would be a good candidate for adoption. It all went smoother than we could have hoped, and Little Tommy couldn't be in better hands. He would get all the love and protection that he needed from those two, and Leon and I were so thrilled for all three of them. Johnathan and Blake were so deserving of a family, and Little Tommy deserved to be loved unconditionally.

Tommy's collarbone had healed, so we all passed him around. Blake was most comfortable wearing him in the sling, so we didn't get to hold him too much. Johnathan had quit his job and was a full-time stay-at-home dad. It worked out well because Johnathan couldn't stomach seeing Brett each day. He got a chunk of money on the last several deals they had in the works and then signed off. Blake had an excellent job, and he could support them. Johnathan planned to keep his real estate license active, so if he needed to go sell a house and make a little cash, he could.

Cyrus was back with Lizzie and would spend weekends and Wednesdays with us. Our house would always be open to more children, but with the one I was currently growing in my womb, we decided to take a break from fostering for a little bit. I hadn't felt my best, and it wasn't fair to Leon or the children who came to us for me to be sick the entire time.

Dean and Andrew and Mark and Leon were talking about football, and the girls and I had a moment alone while Johnathan and Blake took Tommy inside for a diaper change.

"Listen, girls. I want you to know how much your support has meant to me recently. It's always been important to me. But to know that you have my back when the going gets tough and that I can call on you for anything has reassured me that what we have is so much more special than most friendships." Chloe teared up as she spoke.

"I second that," Nora added. "This has been a crazy time, and knowing that you guys back me up, even when you don't necessarily agree with me, has helped me more than you'll ever know."

We shared a group hug, and Steph said, "Now, hold on! Don't everybody go crying yet! I need to give Ziah her gift!" And she ran inside and returned with an envelope. I opened it to find a key.

"I don't understand," I looked at her.

"It's the key to Z's Place," she excitedly said as she did a little jump. "It's a shelter for young men aging out of the system. We'll provide meals and beds and a gathering area and more. I can't wait to show you!"

I was stunned. Steph had taken what I'd told her about the kids aging out of the system to heart and had really done something about it. Not only had she done something about it, but she'd done something *huge*.

"This is incredible, Steph. I ... I don't know what to say." I could only get out a few words.

"Just say you're available to come see it tomorrow!" she exclaimed.

"You bet your ass I am!" I said as we high-fived. "Let me know what I need to do to get it up and running, and you know I'll dive in!"

"Well, thanks to every single person here, we have everything we need. I'm sure we'll need to recruit some more volunteers down the road, but for now, we are ready to be fully functioning in a couple of weeks." Everything she said continued to amaze me. Steph and I had gotten so out of sync at times, and here she was throwing herself into a shelter for teenage boys in the system and dedicating it to me.

"I can't thank you enough, Steph. This is all amazing. I can't wait to see it! And seriously, you just tell me what I can do and when, and you know I'll be there," I assured her.

"Right now, you need to focus on growing this sweet little person and let us focus on Z's place. And when we meet him or her, you can come volunteer all you want! While I hold the baby, that is." She rubbed my belly, and I had never felt closer to her.

STEPH

I worked hard for several weeks to get Z's Place going. Mark was so supportive, and when I pitched the idea to him, he was all about it. Even though it meant we'd need to pull some of our savings, he was incredibly supportive. We knew that our friends would contribute, as well. Mark was only concerned that throwing myself into something like that might heighten my anxiety, but I think it had the opposite effect. And it made me feel good to contribute to something. I knew that I had always contributed to my home and family, but this was different. I was truly helping others.

I was so proud of Ziah for all her hard work, and I wanted to repay her somehow. This was the best idea for a gift that would keep on giving. Mark and I had already designated different tasks to our friends, and when we had the get-together to celebrate Ziah's magazine article, everything was ready to go. Ziah's reaction was perfect. I couldn't wait to dive into my new work at Z's Place. Between all the GBs, we had enough connections to keep it running 24/7 for young men who had nowhere else to go. After I gave Ziah her gift and the party died down, I hugged Mark tightly.

"You really are the best, you know that?" I said to him.

"I love you, Steph. We're the lucky ones, aren't we?"

And we truly were.

ALEXIS

By the end of summer, Dean had all but moved in with me, though he was still paying rent on his place. I still hadn't found any real flaws in him. I was convinced that he was too good to be true, but he was true. Plus, Gibbs loved him just as much as I did. I felt that our summer had been quite eventful for the GBs. Everybody had undergone a major change in their life. Chloe was divorcing Brett (thank God). Nora and Kyle were divorcing, and Nora was back with Andrew. Ziah was pregnant. I was in love. And Steph had come out of left field with a grand idea to open a shelter for foster boys aging out of the system. It was a big summer for us. Never had there been that much change before that I could recall. Every curve that came our way made us even better. We were stronger as a group for what we had gone through together, as well as what we had gone through apart. We all realized that if we were honest with each other, then we'd always have each other's back. That's what we were to each other. We were comfortable, supportive, we lifted each other up, and we made each other seem better than we were. We were good bras. And nothing would ever change that.

NORA

I was the happiest I had been in years. I had rediscovered myself with the help of Andrew and my therapist. I'd faced the issue of my miscarriage head-on in my therapy sessions, and I finally felt at peace with it all. She'd told me that part of the reason I never healed was because not only did I move on as if it had never happened, but I'd gone right back to work delivering babies. I don't know why I never put that together, but somehow, I missed it. I told her that I wasn't interested in changing jobs, so she helped me work my way through it. Talking about it certainly helped heal the wounds that I hadn't realized were so deep.

The split so many years ago with Andrew had taken a similar toll on me. I had never talked about the loss I'd felt when he moved away. My therapist helped me sort through that, too. Kyle and I moved forward with the divorce. He had started dating Danielle, and we knew that it was inevitable that we'd divorce, so neither of us wanted to hold the other back. Andrew was very patient with me. As much as I wanted to move in with him, play house together, get married, and have his babies, I needed to work on me first. He respected that, and I think it made us even closer than ever, which is hard to even comprehend.

Andrew's divorce from Claire was final, and he was happy to close that chapter. We started going on dates instead of just holing up at each other's houses and making out all the time. Since we no longer had to hide from public places, he started courting me. It felt so good to be with each other carefree. Andrew had always been a gentleman. He had never let me open a car door on my own in all our history together. But now that we were dating again, he brought me flowers all the time, he surprised me with spa days, and he cooked dinner. It was lovely. Even though I was working on myself, and we were taking things slower, I was still head-over-heels in love with him. And he had told me a million times before that he would wait on me forever. And I knew that he would if he had to. But I was in a really good place, and I knew that forever wasn't that far away.

EPILOGUE

DEAN

Christmas was my favorite time of year, and I was so happy to get to spend it with Alexis. Our life together was so great. I wished that it would snow occasionally in Texas, but that would be asking too much.

Brett couldn't get me fired after the whole cheating fiasco. I was luckily able to keep my job at the course after the asshole did everything in his power to get me fired. When he realized he couldn't do that, he slandered the club all over the place. Ziah represented us against him as we sued him for defamation. He settled out of court, which is what Ziah told us would happen.

After some strong encouragement from me, Alexis started doing some interior design on the side. She didn't take on too many clients at once, but she got to spend her days doing something that really made her happy. Her first gig was Chloe's house, and her second was Z's Place. She knocked both out of the park, and I was so incredibly proud of her.

I loved that Alexis loved Christmastime just as much as I did. We agreed on only one gift for each other, and we set a low-price limit. I didn't want her to spend much on me. And being with her and Gibbs was really all I needed, anyway.

On Christmas morning, I hooked her gift up to Gibbs's collar. We went through our candy-filled stockings and gave Gibbs his treats and toys out of his, and then moved to the tree where she had wrapped one gift for me.

"Alright, wise guy. Where's mine?" she asked.

"Look on Gibbs's collar," I said. "Go ahead, reach for it, Alexis," I urged.

She reached for his collar as she gave me a suspicious glance and grabbed the gift connected to it. She turned back around to me, as I had just the right amount of time to kneel. Her jaw hit the floor as I told her to open the package. There was a box inside. I reached for the box and opened it for her. She started crying as I said, "You make me the happiest I have ever been in my entire life. I can't imagine my life without you, and I don't want to. You and Gibbs *are* my life. I love everything about you, from your foul mouth, to your exquisite taste in music, to the way you wrinkle your nose when something embarrasses you, to the way your voice gets even louder as you get to the best part when telling a story, to the way you love me completely. I want to spend the rest of my Christmases with you. Please make me the happiest man in the world and say you'll marry me, Alexis."

She cried harder and put her hands to her face. Gibbs picked up on her tears and instinctively walked towards her, leaning on her.

"Yes!" she shouted through her sobs.

We both stood up, and I hugged her and lifted her up, as we twirled around in a circle. We pulled Gibbs into our hug.

"I love you, Dean. Merry Christmas," she said.

"Wait. What about my gift?" I laughed as I asked her.

"Oh, this will come in perfectly handy later," she said as she handed it to me.

I opened a box with very risqué lingerie inside.

"That's my girl," I smiled. "Merry Christmas, baby."

Shortly after our gift exchange, she got her phone out. I knew she was immediately group-texting her Good Bra girls. I saw her take a photo of her hand with her ring on it, and then she took a selfie with me while holding her ring up. I loved watching her light up as she talked to them.

"Babe, they are probably spending time with their families," I said.

"Dean. They've waited *years* for this moment. I promise you. They'll put Christmas on hold for this."

And just then, I heard a million texts come through. She winked at me and poured me a glass of eggnog while she continued to text them.

"Come here, Mrs. Claus," I said.

She came and sat on my lap, and I told her again how much I loved her.

The End

ACKNOWLEDGEMENTS

Thank you first and foremost to my children and my husband for allowing me to sit at my computer day in and day out and type away while the words came to me. Thank you to Kellogg for inventing Pop-Tarts, which my children lived off of while words flew from my brain through my fingertips, not allowing me the proper time to cook anything.

To Anna, Faith, Kayla, and Shanna, thank you for believing in me and always laughing at my writing and my stories. Thank you for allowing me to build characters out of our sacred times spent with one another. Anna, thank you for your passion for foster care and for making each of us better for knowing you. Faith, thank you for your humor and ability to laugh at yourself. Kayla, thank you for allowing me into your protective shell for the past twenty-plus years. Shanna, thank you for being a bright light of bubbles in this dim world. I have happy hands for each of you, and I can't believe we did it. We actually did it, y'all. I love each of you more than you'll ever know.

To Jeff Cocanour, thank you for not only creating the most beautiful cover design, but for being my publishing coach and cheerleader along the way. Thirty years of friendship and we created something lovely together.

To my brother, Eddie, thank you for being you. Without your hilarity, I wouldn't be who I am, and wouldn't have been able to do this.

And to my parents, I love you dearly. Thank you for always telling me and showing me my worth.

To Ashley Strosnider, Avalon Radys, and Renee Naude, thank you for helping me and holding my hand along the way. Your expertise is appreciated greatly.

Finally, to all of you reading this, thank YOU.